MW01051707

DOG TAGS:

A Love Story

Alexandra Landon

authorHOUSE®

AuthorHouse™
1663 Liberty Drive
Bloomington, IN 47403
www.authorhouse.com
Phone: 1-800-839-8640

First published by AuthorHouse 4/20/2011

ISBN: 978-1-4567-4795-4 (sc)
ISBN: 978-1-4567-4796-1 (e)
ISBN: 978-1-4567-4797-8 (dj)

Library of Congress Control Number: 2011904079

Printed in the United States of America

Any people depicted in stock imagery provided by Thinkstock are models, and such images are being used for illustrative purposes only. Certain stock imagery © Thinkstock.

This book is printed on acid-free paper.

Acknowledgements

To America's military men and women.
To the families who love and support them.

To the loves of my life: Dwayne, Chase and Ryann.

To my dad and mom for encouraging
me to take risks without ridicule.

Special Thank you to my sister, Chris Benson,
for making my vision for the cover a reality.

A special acknowledgement to Mark and Molly and their
two children who bravely fought their own battle. Thank
you for showing us the preciousness of life, family and faith.

Contents

Chapter 1:

Not Just an Ordinary Day

As Sarah Ryan Benton exits the gym, she enjoys the warmth of the late afternoon sun beating down on her moist skin. Sweat streams down her face, and beads of perspiration cover her body, making her skin glisten under the rays of sunlight. Still rocking to Def Leopard on her iPod, she briskly walks to her 2004 BMW 530i while balancing her navy blue business suit, which is slipping to one side of the hanger, her navy pumps, and her gym bag. Clenching the hanger between her teeth, Sarah digs through her gym bag for her keys.

"Come on. Where are you?" she says between clenched teeth.

She feels the key chain buried beneath her deodorant, soap, shampoo, and lotion. She grabs it and pulls the keys from the bottom of the bag. With the click of the remote, the trunk of the car pops open, and the doors unlock simultaneously. She continues to listen to her favorite tunes while she places her bag and pumps in the trunk and hangs her suit on the hook in the backseat. With a pat of her gym towel, she blots the beads of sweat from her flushed, rosy face.

1

She barely hears the sounds around her, and the honk of a horn behind her startles her. She turns to look at the driver with a puzzled glance. When she realizes it is her close friend and vice president of ViaStem Biotechnology and Genetics Corporation—the company at which she has made a career as a successful sales consultant—Sarah smiles. Removing her earphones, she walks toward Calvin Giovanni's pristine metallic gray 2011 Range Rover, her ears still buzzing from the screaming music.

Calvin Giovanni is one of the up-and-coming young businessmen in the field of medicine. He was recently featured in *Forbes* as the right-hand man of Mr. Harold Stevens, the founder and CEO of ViaStem. Not only does Calvin have a keen business sense, but he is also handsome with jet black hair, brown eyes, a tall stature at six feet three, and a slender yet very fit build. He is well spoken and well dressed, achieving the optimal corporate image.

With a smile on his face, Calvin gestures to Sarah's iPod. "Rocking out a bit?"

"Very funny. You startled me!" Sarah scolds him in a teasing manner. "It's flipping hot in there. The AC is broken again, but I had a great workout," she boasts with a big smile across her face and shows off with a bicep curl.

"Check that out. Very impressive." Calvin smiles.

"So how are you doing with all this media chaos surrounding the final FDA approval of the HESC G42 procedure?" Sarah inquires, referring to the human embryonic stem cell cloning procedure ViaStem has spent years developing.

"It's chaotic and wonderful at the same time. Mr. Stevens is flying out tomorrow morning to meet with the FDA and the President for approval. I just wanted to say hello since I only saw you for a few minutes at the national sales meeting in Orlando."

"I can't wait until patients can actually receive treatments," Sarah replies. "It's all so exciting, Calvin. Besides, it helps me pass the time when Stephen is deployed, which is way too often lately! Have you heard any news on the Food and Drug Administration's final approval time frame?

Smiling, Calvin nods. "It won't be long, Sarah. I bet within the week. The government is eager to have this project completed and launched. After all, for the past four years they have funded all the research and development because of the depletion of research and development dollars. The NIH wants this procedure accelerated. If President Cannon is involved, it's a big deal. He arranged for a thousand subjects for the safety trials." Calvin looks uncomfortable with that information, but he quickly pushes the conversation forward. "Remember, Harold Stevens started this company as a dream because of his son's terminal illness, but the government sees it as a multi-trillion-dollar return on their investment. So I am quite confident it will be sooner rather than later."

"How's Stephen?" he then asks. "I haven't seen him in a while. I think it was when we played golf—or should I say when he kicked my ass a few weeks ago?" Calvin jokingly laughs. "Ya know what? He always puts me to shame." He smiles. "Can you let him know that it is time? Time for him to go down!"

Sarah can't help but smile and laugh slightly. "I don't know, Calvin. Stephen hates to lose—the endless fighter. He gets back from a two-week training exercise in a week. I'll have him give you a call."

"Not that I like losing, but I owe him a beer ... or two," Calvin says, checking his watch. "Okay, I gotta get going into the sauna—I mean the gym." He cocks his head toward the building. "I know Stephen is gone a lot, so don't hesitate to call if you need anything. Call my cell or the office … until you and Kat patch things up," Calvin says, opening a door to a more serious conversation.

"Calvin, I thought she was my best friend, but I was mistaken," Sarah says. "Sometimes friendships just dissolve. I just can't get past her spreading the 'affair' rumors about you and me and the 'psych ward' crap during Stephen's last deployment. She told everyone, Calvin. Everyone! Do you know how awful and embarrassing that was? Shit—and still is? She invented an affair between us, and she doesn't even know why I had to stay in the hospital. She didn't even care to ask."

"I understand it hurt you tremendously, but you are back now and healthy. Be proud of that, Sarah. Until you are comfortable, please call me if you need me. I really couldn't give a shit what people think." Calvin glances at the digital clock on his dashboard, which illuminates 6:30 p.m. "I better get into the gym before I lose my momentum." With that remark, he smiles and offers a wave as he begins to pull his vehicle forward. "Take care."

"Take care, and thank you, Calvin." Sarah badly wants to share news of the miscarriage that would explain her breakdown, but she keeps mum.

She gets into her pearl white BMW, starts it, and heads for home, which is only a few blocks away. As she drives, she takes time to enjoy her surroundings in the mountain community of San Diego Country Estates, located about thirty to forty minutes northeast of beautiful downtown San Diego.

On her route home, she recalls the excitement shared between newlyweds Mr. and Mrs. Stephen Lance Benton when they purchased their first home in the family-friendly neighborhood in the rugged, mountainous setting tucked in a small valley just outside the hustle and bustle of the city. The couple's new home was a modest Tudor fixer-upper at the end of a cul-de-sac in the picturesque setting. Sarah immediately fell in love with the open floor plan with the foyer leading into the sunken living room. There was a small formal dining area off to the left with sliders and French doors lining the back of the home and overlooking the sprawling backyard. Sarah knew the single-level home would be functional and beautiful with fireplaces in the master bedroom to the right of the foyer and in the TV room to the left, just off the large kitchen. Down the hallway from the master was the office, laundry room, and two extra bedrooms for a growing family ... someday. Homes in the neighborhood had been custom designed on one- to two-acre lots that could accommodate horses if desired. Trails are carved throughout the mountainsides for riding enjoyment while meandering through serene scenic views. Otherwise, the large yards of lush green grass are ideal for children to play.

Stephen and Sarah had immediately noticed the opportunities for children and families; the neighborhood would give them access to private schools, parks, pools, a country club, and horse stables in a clean, safe environment. The neighborhood also offered child-friendly amenities such as swim lessons, little league baseball, soccer, tennis, riding lessons, and junior golf programs. It had made it easy for Stephen and Sarah to decide that Country Estates was the ideal community in which to raise the family they had planned to start as soon as they were settled.

Funny how a terrorist attack changes everything, Sarah thinks sadly to herself.

Turning right onto Scarbery Drive from Arena, she spots her friend and hairdresser, Laura Martin, watering the gorgeous, multi-colored flowerbeds that line the entire front of her house. Sarah pulls over and opens the passenger side window. "Hey, can you come make my flowers as beautiful as yours?" she shouts.

Laura turns to greet Sarah, offering a welcoming smile. "Do you have flowers?" she teases, knowing Sarah is challenged in the flora department.

Giggling, Sarah responds, "Ha-ha. Well actually, no flowers. None. That is why I have giant Junipers, sego palms, and tons of shrubs that are more difficult to kill. Very low maintenance."

Laura shuts the water off, lays down the hose, and wipes her wet hands on her cutoff jean shorts. Then she walks toward Sarah's car. The two women met at the gym almost immediately after Sarah and Stephen moved to the neighborhood in December 1996. Laura is a petite blonde with a short Halle Berry haircut that perfectly matches her bubbly personality, her zest for life, and her love for her two young sons, Mark and Mason. Sarah hopes to someday emulate that kind of love when she and Stephen have children.

Laura squats down and leans against Sarah's open window with her elbows up and her chin resting on her hands. "How are you? Looks like you had a tough workout."

"I did, and I'm still sweating like a pig!" Sarah says as she wipes her forehead. "So how are you and the boys?"

"We're great. Busy, as usual, with sports and school just starting a couple weeks ago. How's work going? What are you selling again? I can't remember. I just know it sounded complicated the last time you tried to explain it to me. Way over my head." Laura swipes her hand over her head and makes a whistling sound.

"Well … it's an accelerated cloning procedure called HESC G42—human embryonic stem cell cloning. Normally any type of cloning can take years, but many of the patients who will be candidates … well, they don't have years. This procedure is going to help people with spinal cord injuries and illnesses like Parkinson's disease have a better quality of life. That's kind of it in a nutshell."

"It stills sounds exciting … and still very complicated," Laura says and then switches subjects. "Oh, I just saw Stephen jog by not fifteen minutes ago with Cooper. I called to him several times, but he was obviously in his own world. Cooper heard me, though. He tried to stop, but Stephen just scooped him up. He glanced briefly at me and kept moving. I guess he was listening to his iPod and didn't hear me. He must have a lot on his mind, huh?"

Instantly Sarah has a sinking feeling in the pit of her stomach. Her thoughts stray for a few seconds. She has noticed that with each deployment Stephen has been growing more distant from her. She prays he will not have to return to war on a fifth deployment; she fears their marriage won't survive it. She still tortures herself about the miscarriage and the nervous breakdown she suffered during his last deployment. *I should have been stronger; maybe he is angry and blames me,* Sarah thinks to herself.

During her hospital stay, she had been on a cocktail of meds, but now she only relies on one prescription drug to reduce her anxiety. Now she depends on her prescription relaxation from Clonazepam, also referred to as Klonopin. Sarah clenches her teeth, hating the "mentally unstable" label, but she refuses to give up her Klonopin, even though she knows it is highly addictive and has horrible withdrawal symptoms. She's tried to get off of it, unsuccessfully. She tries to be compliant with her prescription but sneaks an extra dose when things get tough, overriding her doctor's orders of 1 milligram three times a day.

Sarah remembers how interesting the other patients had been when she discovered, four out of the eight women in the psych ward during her stay in the hospital were Navy SEAL wives.

"Hello ... Sarah?" Laura snaps her fingers.

Coming out of her brief trance, Sarah pretends everything is normal and responds to Laura's question after only a mere skip in their conversation. "Believe me, he is under so much stress. When he runs, it's the only time he has to be completely alone ... to sort things out that he doesn't want to talk about. Not yet anyway." Sarah knows he will confide in her when it is the right time for him. "Well, my dear, I better get going so I can be home when my hubby returns. I can't wait to see him! This is a first—for him to come home four days early from a two-week training exercise. How thoughtful of the navy. Maybe this means no more deployments. Wouldn't that be a dream come true?" Sarah puts her car into drive. "Take care, Laura."

"You too. Thanks for stopping. Oh, Sarah! I found the perfect hairstyle for you if you ever feel like a change," Laura yells to Sarah as she pulls away and waves good-bye.

"I'm way too chicken! You know that, but I appreciate the thought!" Sarah yells in return.

She drives to the end of the block, turns into her half-moon driveway, and shuts off her car's engine. Grabbing her gym bag and clothes, she energetically jumps out of her car and races into her home, only to catch a glimpse of Stephen's fully packed green canvas military duffle propped up against the corner of the wall in the foyer. A small mound of Stephen's dirty clothes is piled against the wall in the hallway. Coming to a standstill, she stares at the bag and whispers to herself, "I hate that bag! It means he is going on deployment. Again. I hate that fricking bag. I love my country, but I'm so tired of this! Please forgive me, God."

Sarah tries to ignore the feeling of anxiety that sweeps through her body when she thinks about Stephen leaving on deployment. After heading into the bedroom, she tosses her belongings onto the bed and quickly hops into the shower. After her shower, she throws on some khaki Bermuda shorts and a plain white T-shirt, pulls her freshly washed, long auburn hair back into a scrunchie, and quickly brushes her teeth. Even though she dresses ultra-professional at work, at home she is casual and down to earth. She forgoes the makeup because Stephen prefers her natural beauty. Her face is flushed, accentuating her beautiful emerald eyes. Though Stephen often tells Sarah she is a naturally beautiful woman, being unpretentious and modest, she usually blushes and brushes off the compliment.

Tossing her stinky, sweaty clothes into the washer, she nearly skips with excitement to the kitchen to chill a bottle of chardonnay before Stephen gets home from his run. Talking to herself, she devises a plan to celebrate his early homecoming. He usually runs five miles, so she figures a quaint BBQ on the back porch will be relaxing. Although, if he is carrying Cooper—the lovable, scraggly mutt they adopted from a local animal shelter—he might shorten his run to one or two miles.

Still warm from her vigorous workout, Sarah opens the sliding kitchen window over the sink that overlooks their large backyard, which is covered with a blanket of velvety green grass and framed by a white vinyl three-rail fence.

"Horses someday. Kids first," Sarah encourages herself.

The air smells of freshly cut grass and sweet grain, which is common feed for her neighbor's horses, Rudy and Rio. Sarah breathes deeply, enjoying the sweet scents. "How I love that smell."

Having grown quite fond of Rudy and Rio, she is always happy to see the two horses. Sarah whistles to them through the screen, and immediately both horses—Rudy, a large chestnut Thoroughbred, and Rio, a smaller, jet black Arabian—swing their heads up and look directly at Sarah. They know she will have treats for them like she does every evening. Rudy nods his large, majestic head up and down, acknowledging Sarah's presence while Rio stares for a moment and then returns to munch on his sweet alfalfa.

Sarah calls to Rudy and Rio, "Okay, boys. I'll be out in a second, you spoiled babies." Shutting the window, she clicks the AC on and laughs to herself. "Boy, do I have them trained … Or is it the other way around?" She giggles and continues to smile.

Walking out the back door from the dining room, Sarah now has full attention of both gorgeous creatures. "Hi beautiful boys," Sarah greets them, rubbing Rudy's forehead.

Rio has come to attention, not wanting to miss out on the affection Sarah is offering. She senses they know her by her scent; they smell her between their short snorts as she leans against the metal corral that meets the corner of her fence. They start tickling her face and move to her hair, continuing to smell and snort against her body until they find the "treasures."

Sarah laughs. "Ah-ha, that was quick. Now let's play

find the carrots." Sarah reaches into her pockets, covers the baby carrots in her hands, and hides them behind her back. Bringing her hands forward, she asks Rudy and Rio, "Which one? Where are the treats?" She knows full well they will both be winners. Both horses smell and snort until each pushes against her hands. "Oh, you guys are so smart. Here you go." She opens her hands flat so the horses can gently take their treats. "I gotta go, boys." She firmly rubs each horse's muscular neck, gives them a few loving pats, and quickly retreats to her home, eager to greet Stephen.

Grabbing a package of Ritz crackers from the pantry, Sarah makes her way to the stainless steel two-sided refrigerator. After opening the right door, she removes some Brie cheese and veggies to arrange on a tray and nibble on before dinner. She then grabs a small bunch of red grapes to add to the tray.

While she gathers food from the refrigerator, Sarah's attention focuses on the *TIME* magazine cover, dated March 2012, hanging on the freezer door. It pictures an extremely close-up shot of Stephen's face with the caption, *Project Restoration: The Soldier of the Future.* The article behind the photo talks about new strategic plans to increase U.S. troop levels, integrate new high tech weaponry and tactics to help soldiers win the seemingly endless war on terrorism and prove America is still the world's superpower. Most of the article's information reflects the U.S. government's power and strength to conquer the malignant jihadist enemy. The article gives rave reviews of the superior performance of the Commander in Chief, President Jack Kennedy Cannon, in the "most difficult war ever fought," which is his quote.

Gently touching the picture, Sarah admires Stephen's chiseled, ruggedly handsome features and his piercing yet

emotionless steel hazel eyes. *Maybe it's just the way they took the picture that makes him seem emotionless, distantly empty*, she thinks to herself. The article gives a very brief synopsis about Stephen's career as a lieutenant commander leading the elite Navy SEAL Team ONE that is commissioned on top-secret, covert, and classified missions and based out of Coronado, California.

With the cool air flowing from the open refrigerator door, Sarah feels a chill. In her mind she tells herself, *It's his job that he loves, and I knew that when I married him.* She prays to God Stephen will someday be like the man she married—happy, funny, full of life, loving, and caring—and not like the person he has evolved into after so many deployments. The changes have been gradual, but Sarah has noticed. Her entire being feels bruised deep within her bones when she thinks of the many horrible things he has seen, but he refuses to open up to her. *I wish he would just talk to me.*

"Okay, now stop this!" Sarah tells herself, wiping a tear from her eye. "Bury your emotions. Be strong for Stephen. He doesn't need any more worry."

Placing the platter of *hors d'oeuvres* on the butcher block countertop next to her favorite wine glasses and the bottle of chardonnay chilling in a carafe, Sarah returns to the refrigerator to find a main course. "Salmon or hamburgers? What's my choice?" Sarah questions herself out loud. Scrunching her nose, she says, "I know how Stephen feels about fish—yuck. So I guess it's hamburgers. How romantic! Now, do we have buns?" She searches the pantry and bread basket to find no bread at all. "The freezer? Nope. I guess no buns. Whatever. It will be fine." Sarah can't wipe the smile off her face for the deep love she feels for her husband.

She takes a step backward to admire the many pieces

of artwork on the refrigerator door, given to them by the neighborhood kids. She adores the Crayola crayon caricatures of mainly Stephen and Cooper. Cooper is drawn as a stick figure with big circles for his head and body, straight lines for his legs, half circles for his unusually big paws for a twelve-pound dog, and tons of squiggles for his curly fur, especially on the top of his little head. Sarah smiles lovingly at the many comical drawings of Stephen with bulging muscles in a navy blue uniform weighted down with an overabundance of medals and accented with an enormous sword, maybe from the *Sword and the Stone, Aladdin,* or *Sinbad,* and always with the American flag as a backdrop. Sarah often teases Stephen about his superhero status with the neighborhood kids, and he teases her for being the stick figure with red hair and a briefcase. Sarah cannot wipe the smile from her face, knowing the love of her life will be walking through the door any minute.

Entranced by her romantic thoughts, Sarah barely hears the front door open. Cooper tears around the corner and leaps against Sarah's legs until she picks him up. He gives her little wet kisses on her chin. "Hello, Cooper. How's my boy?" Sarah says excitedly. "Stephen? How's my baby?" she then asks as she walks toward the front door, holding Cooper to her chest with one arm. Stephen doesn't answer until he sees her walking toward him.

"Hey, sweetie. Wasn't sure if you were talking to me or Cooper. I missed you." Stephen holds her face with both hands and kisses her warmly. She treasures every moment with him. In the next second, Stephen pulls away and says, "I need a shower."

Sarah stands in wonderment at the growing distance between them. "Oh, okay. All right then. I have some snacks and hamburgers to grill after you get cleaned up, and I have a bottle of wine chilling if you would like a glass."

"No thanks. I'm not hungry." Stephen remarks.

"O-okay," Sarah returns, a bit of a stunned by his abruptness.

He quickly heads through the bedroom and locks their bathroom door. Sarah follows him and stops in her tracks, not believing he just locked the door. *He has never locked the door ...*

With the door shut in her face, Sarah returns to the kitchen, uncorks the wine, and pours herself three quarters of a glass to help settle her nerves. In her mind she realizes just how odd his behavior is. *Maybe he is having an affair. Maybe he is really depressed and won't admit it. Maybe I'm expecting too much from him and putting too much thought into all of this? Shit, I don't know.* She takes a long sip from her wine glass. The smoothness of each sip of chardonnay helps take the edge off of her anxiety, especially mixed with her afternoon dose of Klonopin. By the time Stephen comes into the kitchen, Sarah is finishing her second glass of wine.

"I'm sorry for snapping at you, babe. I'm just a bit tense. I've got a lot on my mind right now." Stephen leans close and kisses Sarah gently on her lips. "I think I will join you in a glass," he says as he pours the remaining wine into the second glass on the counter. He helps himself to a slice of brie and cracker, followed by a smooth sip of wine. "Finally home." He turns, walks into the TV room, and sits on the L-shaped leather sectional. Normally, he flips up the enclosed recliner for further relaxation, but not this time. Sarah notices he is anxious and restless.

"Honey, is everything all right?" she asks.

"Yes, Sarah," he said. "No ... no, Sarah. It's not."

"Stephen … are we okay?" Sarah dares to ask.

Taking a sip of wine, Stephen lets out a long sigh. Time seems to drag as Sarah waits to hear the worst news—that Stephen is in love with someone else.

"Of course we're okay! Oh, Sarah, we may be overwhelmed, but you are the love of my life and always will be. Come here and sit with me. I need to talk to you about something … Something strange is going on at work." Stephen places his hand next to him while setting his glass on the coffee table.

"What is it?"

Stephen searches for words. "This is going to sound weird, but I don't think I'm imagining that something is just not right at work. It hasn't been for a very long time, but I can't seem to be able to figure it out."

Sarah slides her hands over his hands, securely and lovingly. "It's okay to talk to me Stephen … Please let me in."

"Prior to the last two deployments, my men were required to undergo numerous tests such as blood, urine, feces—you name it. The men are required to take several pills—pills we've never had to take before in my entire career."

"It's all right. Maybe I can help."

"Sarah, the doctor conducting the testing is Dr. Hammond."

"Dr. Hammond from ViaStem?"

"Yes, I'm sure of it. I've met him several times. At the Stevenses' barbeques and the ViaStem Christmas parties. I know it's him, but his white coat doesn't have his name, and he never says a word to me. He just gives me an odd look. Actually, none of the 'white coats' have names. They're like robot scientists going through the motions."

"I can't believe he would be moonlighting. I'm sure ViaStem pays him well. Wouldn't you think?"

"Wait, it gets stranger. On this exercise ... well, there was no exercise. It was all testing. It started out normal, with our typical immunizations, but then came numerous physical and psychological tests. There were more blood tests, tissue biopsies, fecal samples, hair samples, saliva swabs, MRI's, and PET scans to look at our mood changes when we encountered certain objects in photos. And more pills. I asked and demanded answers, but Hammond came up with some crap about the well-being of our soldiers under long-term stress, Post Traumatic Stress Disorder, and more bullshit."

"What did the other guys do? Did they go along with it? I can't believe Cummings would go along with it. What did you do, Stephen?" Sarah anxiously rattles off questions.

"All my men participated ... but ... I didn't take the pills. But I did get the shots, Sarah. We get vaccines all the time. Now I'm questioning the validity of those. I told my men they didn't have to go along with the pills, but they all did. I was shocked. It was like someone put the fear of God in them. It was impossible to back out of the additional testing. I held the pills in my mouth and then put them in my pocket when the group of scientists moved on to the next guy. I haven't ever taken any of the pills. I'm not going to be in an experiment to prevent some undiscovered war sickness. Hammond says it is to prevent another Gulf War illness.

"Is anyone acting differently, Stephen?"

"Yes, everyone but me. The men seem numb, indifferent to everything around them and extremely agitated. I'm concerned about them going into a dangerous mission, about their abilities to focus. I just go along with it not to be noticed, but I must find out what they are doing to my men. I think Dr. Hammond knows, though. It's so strange. I need to know what the hell is going on, Sarah," he says and then adds, "There's more."

"What, Stephen?"

"We are going out on deployment within a week. There won't be much notice. I need you to be strong just one more time, and this will be behind us," Stephen shares the regrettable news with Sarah, who is obviously disheartened by the news.

"But, Stephen, you just got home two months ago. I don't understand. Why so soon?" Sarah's voice cracks with anguish. Tears pool in her eyes. She grips Stephen's hand tightly as if to not let him go.

"Honey, I need you to keep your eyes and ears open at work. See if you can find anything on Hammond. I want some answers. These are my men. Can you do that for me, babe?"

"Of course I will," Sarah says with determination. "Stephen … do you have the pills?"

"Yes, I have them in a bottle hidden in my gear. Let me get them for you." Stephen immediately goes to his large duffle and digs for the sample bottle. "This is the last time, I promise you. I've decided not to re-enlist after this deployment," he says, handing the bottle to Sarah.

"Oh, Stephen …" She hugs him closely. Knowing his love for the military, she can feel his despondence over the decision.

Stephen and Sarah embrace tightly in the need to be one.

Chapter 2:

The Journey

Running on the treadmill at a fast clip, Calvin breaks a sweat instantly in the stifling heat of the gym. "Shit. Sarah wasn't kidding when she said it was hot. Whew!"

But the heat doesn't stop Calvin's ambition to keep running. His pent-up energy from years of dedication to his work with Mr. Harold Stevens on the HESC G42 project finally coming to fruition motivates him to run faster and harder. Mr. Stevens will be flying to meet with the FDA for final approval tomorrow morning. Calvin is high on life with this success but crashing on a personal front.

How things have changed, Calvin thinks to himself about his failed marriage and his personal business success. *Talk about two extremes.*

Calvin Giovanni and Katarina Fortunata met at ViaStem in 1996 and quickly married based solely on their smoldering sexual relationship between two "beautiful people." Within a few years, the flames of the amorous foundation vanished. *We were both on the same track ... so career driven. I thought we had the same goals. What happened?* Calvin silently questions himself. *We both wanted one child. At least we did that right with Eden. Sweet Eden. She will already be five next month. I have to get her out of there*, Calvin thinks with sheer determination.

Eden is gifted with the beauty of her Italian parents, with her velvet, olive-toned skin and her long curly locks of glistening black hair that frame her large brown eyes, which accented by thick lashes. She is sweet and innocent. She is the spitting image of Kat, with the mannerisms of Calvin, which is a blessing because Calvin is considerate and kind while Kat is self-absorbed.

She said she always dreamed of being a mother, but once Eden was born, time was eliminated from her career and her enormous bonuses were also eliminated. That's when things really started changing. I saw the real Kat. I bought her the big house, nice cars, toys, horses, jewels, and wonderful vacations, but I guess that wasn't enough. She even had the freedom to spend her paychecks as she pleased. I guess beauty is truly only skin-deep, Calvin thinks to himself, growing angrier and running harder. *I guess her love for the green is more important than her daughter.*

Calvin feels sadness for his daughter, who is now being raised by their nanny, Grace. *This is my fault too. I will have to make concessions once the divorce is final, but I will fight for full custody. I don't want that bitch having any influence on my daughter!* Calvin runs harder and faster. Feeling like his head is going to explode, he switches his thoughts to the ViaStem Corporation and the ultimate success he is achieving in his career. It's something positive. Calvin slows his pace, enjoying the visions of what HESC G42 will do for terminally ill patients.

Harold Stevens's passion to develop HESC G42 had begun with the rare diagnosis of his young son, David, with the ruthlessly deteriorating disease known as Hutchinson-Gilford progeria syndrome. There are a handful of progeria patients worldwide with no treatment options, as is the case with many orphan diseases. The disease was in its discovery phase when David was diagnosed at fifteen months of age. The toddler transformed into an elderly, frail man before he reached his ninth and final birthday. Scientists considered David a success to reach the age of nine. Harold Stevens considered it a failure. His son was dead!

Harold Stevens felt it was absolutely devastating to wake each morning, pick up his young son to hug and kiss him, and notice the clumps of hair remaining on the pillow because of premature balding. David's facial features attracted glaring stares and cruel remarks from strangers, aimed at his bulging eyes, paper-thin wrinkled face, puffy cheeks, small pointed nose, and small mouth—all arranged on a larger than normal sized head. His skin was translucent and illuminated by road maps of veins. His chronological age was that of a small child, but his stature was that of a ninety-year-old man, though his heart and mind remained vivaciously adventurous like that of a child. Osteoporosis prevented many playful activities because of fractures that could result from his brittle bones. But that didn't stop David from enjoying the life he was given by God. Young David eventually perished following several myocardial infarctions (heart attacks) and strokes, which ultimately stole his fragile life, but his personality and soul live large to this day through his father's eyes and promise to his son.

Before David's death, the boy begged his daddy to continue to fight for a cure for progeria so other kids could just be kids. From that moment forward, with his inheritance from his own father, H.L. Stevens dedicated his life to fulfilling his son's dreams. And on September 11, 2012, his dream will become reality. His promise to David will help so many people with orphan diseases and aliments such as spinal cord injuries and Parkinson's disease hold great promise.

Calvin slows his pace and begins his cooldown from the strenuous run. His thoughts of going home are torn. He is excited to see his little girl and sickened by thought of being in the same house as Kat.

Chapter 3:

Undeniable

Sarah sits on the bed, watching Stephen organize his belongings for the next day of work. He removes and places his dog tags and his wedding ring on the nightstand.

"I need to do a little computer work, but it shouldn't take that long. I also need to call Warren," he tells her. Warren is Stephen's mentor from the U.S. Naval Academy and the closet man he has ever had to a father.

"All right. I will just cuddle with Cooper until you get back," she says as she gently holds Cooper and snuggles him against her chest. "I also need to review some paperwork and complete a grant application for Scripps Research Hospital."

Cuddling Cooper to her side, Sarah begins reading a document regarding the HESC G42 procedure. She glances at their wedding photo and glances down at Stephen's wedding ring on the nightstand. Her mind drifts off into a blissful memory of the first time she met him at the officer's club at the Miramar Naval Base in San Diego on August 19, 1995. He was so handsome. Stephen looked distinguished in his dress whites, standing proud and tall at six feet two

with tanned skin and sandy blond hair. His face ha
masculine features, yet his deep dimples made him at
adorable and irresistible when he smiled.

Sarah blushes as she smiles, thinking of this enchanting
memory.

His beautiful white smile captured her attention. His
shoulders were broad, and his hands were rugged and strong.
Sarah offered a shy, flirty smile as she said to her then best
friend, "Kat. Oh my God, Kat. I think I'm in love." She hung
on Kat's arm with excitement.

"Hey, you're gonna spill my drink," Kat protected her
cocktail from Sarah's swooning reaction to the handsome
young officer.

Stephen caught Sarah's flirtatious, obscure glance toward
him, but in a blushing moment she quickly turned away. Sarah
was rather shy and reserved until she got to know a person, but
her attraction to this mystery man was undeniable. She was
just the opposite of Kat, who had absolutely no boundaries.
She was carefree and wild, unlike Sarah.

Kat whipped around to check this new guy out. Turning
back toward Sarah, she gave a smile and a nod of approval.
Sarah felt someone watching her, but she continued to chat
with Kat.

Sarah remembers her heart skipping and every muscle in
her body tingling with the anticipation of a new romance.
Her best friend whispered in her ear, "You think you're in love
now ... wait until you see his ass!"

Sarah smiles as if she were back in that moment.

She remembers demanding, "Stop it Kat," but she had
been dying to look at this gorgeous guy.

Kat's eyes widened, signaling to Sarah that the oh-my-
God guy was heading her way. Sarah smiled brightly at Kat

aisle. To this day, Stephen and Sarah consider Warren part of their family.

Warren was a single bachelor who was married to the United States military and also a retired member of the prestigious Navy SEALS, serving sea, air, and land during dangerous and covert missions. Stephen had met Warren at the Naval Training Academy in Annapolis, Maryland, during Stephen's academics. Their friendship never ended following Stephen's graduation.

McNary is highly intelligent and now dedicates his retirement years to the war on terrorism, which has earned him the appointed position by the Commander in Chief as Homeland Security Czar. With his position comes great responsibility for the nation's security. McNary plays a vital role in maintaining open communications with the following departments to insure no oversights of sharing intel occur while tracking terrorists, domestic or foreign: Homeland Security, FBI, CIA, NTSB, ATF, NSA, EPA, and FDA. He appears on several reputable news programs that cover this topic for the general public and is always dressed in a mysterious black turtleneck with a black suit coat.

His slight height and baldness do not deter him from being considered a ladies' man. He is rugged and handsome, and he offers a wonderful sense of humor, often remarking, "I never have a hair out of place." Warren's bright, warm smile and sparkling blue eyes give him an air of confidence and kindness. He is dedicated to maintaining optimal health, mentally and physically, but most of all he is dedicated to his patriotic duty to his country.

Sarah laughs and giggles, looking at the memories captured in her wedding album. "Oh my gosh. That was so much fun," she says aloud.

From the office, Stephen yells, "Did you say something?"

"No, hon. I'm just looking at our wedding album and remembering how much fun we had."

Stephen takes a short break, walking back to their bedroom and sitting beside his wife. He is holding his heavy cotton-canvas camouflage uniform and tosses it on the bed. It has become second nature to Stephen to always have his combat fatigues nearby, but they send chills up Sarah's spine because she knows he might soon be gone from her again. *Back to war*, Sarah sadly thinks to herself.

"Let me show you my favorites," Stephen says to Sarah as he takes the album in his hands. He finds one of his favorites of Sarah getting ready with her girlfriends. She was wearing white, sexy panties, a bra, thigh highs, and a garter belt. "I love this one, especially with the high heels. Pretty sexy!"

Sarah leans against him, snuggling into his neck. "That one is for your eyes only."

Stephen continues to flip through the album, smiling and laughing at certain pictures that bring back special memories. "Oh, and this one." The photo shows Sarah being spanked by one of the swords as part of a tradition as she walks down the aisle. "You're blushing, my dear." Stephen teases as he leans over and gently kisses her soft, full lips.

Sarah has to agree. "Yes, I am ... I was a bit stunned and embarrassed."

"You are adorable. My beautiful bride."

Sarah feels herself becoming emotional, knowing Stephen will be leaving again, so she forces a transition in the reminiscing, "Ya know what? I'm all done with my work, and I want to spend some quality time with my husband. So you need to get back to the office and finish what you are working on. Got it, mister?"

"It is fun to look back at these memories, but you're right. Let me get my stuff done. I just need to make a couple copies. I'll be back," Stephen says in his best Arnold Schwarzeneggar impersonation.

"Hurry back."

Stephen hustles back to complete his work, and Sarah folds his uniform and neatly sets it on the bench at the end of their bed, next to his boots. From where she is sitting, she can see his large army green duffle bag that contains all his belongings while he is on deployment. Chills travel up her spine.

"Are you already packed?" Sarah asks a question she already knows the answer to.

"Unfortunately, yes. We won't have much warning, so I need to be ready," Stephen responds.

Sarah can't think of anything else to say other than a flat "oh."

She lies back against several propped-up pillows. Letting out a long, sad sigh, she stares at the ceiling, not knowing what to do with herself. She takes one last look at her calendar to make sure she is up to date with work tasks. It is shocking to her that the calendar shows September 10, 2012. Sarah has a sinking feeling in the pit of her stomach as she remembers the 9/11 attacks. "It's the eleventh anniversary tomorrow. How awful and still heartbreaking," Sarah whispers to herself.

She can still remember exactly where she was and what she was doing that fateful morning. The thought of Stephen being taken from her again leaves her with a sense of loneliness. Without a thought, she reaches across the bed, grabs her bottle of Klonopin, and pops one pill, not wanting to face the anxiety she feels, or just not wanting to feel anything.

Rolling onto her side, she can see Stephen working on his

computer in the office down the hall. She watches him quietly for a few minutes. Then she reaches for his wedding ring and rolls over onto her back, holding the ring with both hands slightly raised above her. Reflections in the four-hundred-year-old tradition of the oval silver and yellow gold of Stephen's Celtic warrior shield wedding ring beam back at her. She smiles at her grand discovery of this nontraditional Irish ring that symbolizes the strength of the warrior she believes Stephen is in his own battles. Celtic knots encompass the gold round shield centered in the oval-shaped ring, defining everlasting love of the intertwining of two souls.

Sarah stops and glances at her more traditional Irish ring of interlacing Celtic trinity knots within the perimeters of her white gold Claddagh wedding band. Two diamond eternity bands accent each outer perimeter of the band, elegant yet pure. She reads the engraving on the inside of Stephen's ring, the Irish love phrase, *Gra' mo chroio*, meaning, "Love of my heart." Sarah's band has the identical engraving.

Sitting up, she places Stephen's ring back on the nightstand and grasps his dog tags. Lying back down, she sinks into the soft downy pillows on their bed. With the tiny ball bearing chain dangling between her fingers, she holds the dog tags in one hand and gently touches the imprinted description of her husband. Guiding her finger, she touches his name, *Stephen Lance Benton;* his social security number; his blood type, which is a rare A positive; and his religious preference—Catholic.

"What are you doing with those?" Stephen asks as he walks back into the room.

"Just looking."

"Ya know what I think?" Stephen says with a devilish smile.

"What?" Sarah asks curiously

"I think it's time for a snow day."

They both laugh at the thought of a snow day when it is 85 degrees outside in beautiful Ramona, California.

Chapter 4:

Snow Day

Stephen and Sarah know a week to the military can mean an hour, day, week, or no time line at all. They desire to spend time alone with no disturbances. They no longer have an appetite for *hors d'oeuvres* but only for one another. The withered brie cheese and dried, wilted veggies are unappealing, but the young couple long for one another psychologically and physically. Their yearning for one another is sexually intense.

Stephen secures all the doors and closes all the blinds. Lowering the air conditioning to 55 degrees, he turns their lovely home into a winter wonderland. Sarah slips into her most delicate and seamlessly invisible lingerie, which accentuates her athletically sculpted body. Stephen, wearing only boxers, lights a fire that loudly pops and crackles from the dry eucalyptus wood that has baked in the summer heat.

Sarah has chilled a bottle of Tattinger champagne to add to their romantic interlude. She also lights a multitude of candles throughout their bedroom, offering a gleaming brilliance that reveals only dimly lit silhouettes of Stephen and Sarah as they enter into their heated tryst.

The air is cold, and the room is dark, dimly illuminated by the tall red and yellow flames, with hints of blue, of the fire and the flickering of candles surrounding the couple, who are caught in their own little fairytale. Stephen and Sarah snuggle beneath the downy covers, sipping champagne and giggling at the thought of it being 85 degrees outside. Their bodies simmer with lust. Stephen takes the glasses and sets them on the nightstand. He begins softly kissing Sarah's neck and mouth while tracing her curves with his strong hands. As he slides her lace slip upward, his grip becomes more firm. He pulls Sarah close to him as he cups her breast and suckles her nipple. Sarah arches her body, lost in her sensual desires, and softly moans in delight, wanting more. She grabs Stephen's hand and forces him to touch her where she is moist and warm. Stephen grasps her lacey thong and slips it down her legs and free of her body. He gently yet firmly brings her to orgasm with his touch. She gasps for air in sheer delight. Her hands trace his muscular back intricately, and then she digs her fingers into his moist, feverish skin. The air is thick with passion. She removes Stephen's boxers, pushes him over, and straddles his pelvis.

Next she throws Stephen's arms above his head and presses him against the headboard. His biceps bulge. The veins in his neck and arms are thick and reveal his strength. She leans forward, pressing her bare skin against his chest. Aggressively she kisses him deeply while pressing into his groin and rocking into his torso forcefully. Few words are spoken, just heated moans. Holding onto his biceps, Sarah kisses his neck and chest, moving to his nipples, which she suckles and tenderly bites. Stephen groans in delight. Sarah feels him become hard, and she wants him inside her to share their loving bond as husband and wife.

Sarah gyrates in sensual, rhythmic motions, which only makes him harder and makes him desire her more. Sitting upright and holding her silky auburn hair loosely behind her head, she glistens in Stephen's eyes. Offering a sexy, sultry smile and slipping forward, Sarah spreads herself, and Stephen enters her. They both moan in sexual lust. Stephen's groans become deeper and stop intermittently as he grunts for air, pulling Sarah firmly onto his torrid flesh. Sarah feels Stephen release with a flush inside of her that radiates heat throughout her body, bringing a smoldering sweat to her skin. Her moans become panting, and her tone becomes higher as she nears her pulsating climax. Simultaneously, Stephen and Sarah pant and gasp in the delight of sensually being one.

Sarah lays her head against Stephen's muscular chest and breathes a long sigh of satisfaction. Stephen breathes the same. They hold tightly to one another, enjoying the feel of their moist skin touching and the pounding of their racing hearts.

Stephen gently rolls Sarah to his side, with his left arm embracing her. He strokes her hair, which is streaked with sweat. He moves it gently away from her face, revealing her newly flushed glow. "God, you are beautiful." Stephen holds her close again, feeling her heart beat rapidly.

"I love you, Stephen. You are the love of my life."

"I love you too, Sarah.

They feel each other's heartbeat slow. Sarah props herself up on her right arm, with her left drawn across his chest as she plays with his chest hair. She smiles and says nothing.

"What?" asks Stephen, bringing a smile to his face that becomes hard to erase.

Biting her lips, she lowers her head and kisses his chest. Then she gazes at Stephen.

"What is it?" Stephen laughs.

"That was wonderful! "

Stephen smiles, fully agreeing with Sarah's account of their sexual adventure. "I absolutely love you." He kisses her forehead and continues holding her tightly.

"Stephen?"

"Yes, my dear Sarah?" he says as he softly strokes her face.

"I can't ... I can't ... swallow ..."

"Oh my God, you are such a brat." Jokingly pushing Sarah to the side, Stephen sits up and reaches for their champagne glasses. Holding hers just out of reach, he slowly sips his with pure indulgence. "Mmmm."

"Talk about brat. Come on. I'm dying here." Sarah begs jokingly.

"Not enough," jokes Stephen.

"Okay, my gosh. My dear sweet Stephen, love of my life, the sexiest man alive, may I please, please, please have a sip? Or I might die of thirst and won't be able to offer more favors," Sarah gushes.

"Here you go, you big baby." Stephen lovingly kisses her forehead, lips, and nose.

"I wish we could stay here forever, no one but us." Sarah kisses him and pulls away quickly.

"What is it now?" Stephen asks, waiting for another joke.

"What is that scratching?"

They both grow silent to listen.

Sarah perks up. "It's Coops. Poor little boy. He's probably freezing."

They both start laughing again. "Oh, how you can make me laugh, Sarah. How I miss that when I'm away from you."

Sarah hands Stephen her glass and jumps out of bed to open the bedroom door and let little Cooper in. "Oh my gosh! It's freezing out here." Sarah squeals as she tip-toes across the room to the door. *"Brrr.* I think I can see my breath."

Stephen refills their glasses as Sarah opens the door to find Cooper shivering patiently. "My poor baby." Sarah scoops him up into her arms and kisses his forehead. Tip-toeing around the bed, she hops in and throws the covers over her and Cooper. Sarah giggles as she peeks out from under the covers. *"Brrr."*

Stephen just shakes his head with a smile on his face.

Cooper makes himself comfortable at the foot of the bed under the covers, warm and cozy. He quickly returns to curl up between Stephen's and Sarah's faces.

"Isn't that sweet? He loves us, Stephen."

Sipping his champagne, Stephen laughs. "Do you remember when we went to the pound and found him? The most scraggly mutt in the bunch."

"Yeah, I remember walking through aisle after aisle, looking into each cage and into each dog's eyes, wondering how we would ever decide on which dog to choose. That part was awful. I wanted them all."

"I know. It was tough. I remember thinking, how the hell will we decide?"

"Remember when we were at the last row? We strolled by the last cage and there was this little tiny ball of fur hiding in the corner. When we were right in front of the cage, the little guy rolled over onto his back with his tummy in the air, never losing eye contact with us the whole time. He was so silly, wiggling his body and wagging his tail wildly with excitement. It was like he was saying, 'Pick me! Pick me!'"

Stephen, still smiling and laughing over the story, adds, "And remember his 'bed head' and the little smile from floppy ear to floppy ear?"

Cooper opens his eyes slightly and lifts his head as if questioning, *What's wrong with my hair?*

Stephen playfully pets Cooper's head, making the fur stand straight up like a mohawk. "Yeah, he made it pretty easy to decide. Didn't you?" he asked, looking into Cooper's trusting eyes.

"Yes, he did." Sarah leans over and gives Cooper a little kiss on the nose.

Cooper disappears under the covers to the foot of the bed once again and falls soundly asleep.

"Come here you," Stephen says to Sarah.

Sarah willingly snuggles up to her love. He hands Sarah her glass of champagne, and they toast their love for one another and whatever time they have together. Setting their glasses on the nightstand, they hold one another until they peacefully drift off to sleep.

Chapter 5:

Broken Dreams

Sarah slides her right hand slowly behind her to feel for Stephen. The feeling is familiar, soft—that of crisp cotton sheets and the empty space where Stephen should be sleeping. *He is gone!* Her fight to ward off sleep failed, as if it would have mattered. *He is deployed again. The military's week time frame shortened into less than a day.* Sadness creeps back into Sarah's soul.

In the early morning hours, she sits silently on the side of the bed, staring out the large sliding doors, only seeing through the open slits of the vertical blinds. The moonlight peers in upon her as if to tell her undesirable misfortune is coming her way. Sarah's skin feels like a spiderweb slowly being pulled away, giving her an eerie shiver. She pulls her silk robe across her shoulders to try to stop the chill and lies back down.

The pops and crackles from the fire have fizzled, and the flames from the many candles have extinguished. Her wonderful sexual interlude with Stephen has also extinguished. *I can't believe he is gone ... again.* Without a second thought,

Sarah leans over, pops 1 milligram of Klonopin, lies back down, and just stares at the moon until Cooper jumps onto the bed and kisses her. "Hi, baby. Come here, little one." Sarah pulls Cooper close for comfort.

"Sarah, baby, are you awake?" Stephen quietly asks.

Sarah flies into a sitting position, holding her hand over her heart. Cooper is just as stunned sitting beside her. "Oh my God, Stephen … I thought you were gone."

"No, babe. I was just checking e-mail. You must have been in a deep sleep."

"Yeah, I guess. That was weird."

"I have bad news though …"

"You have to go. Tonight?"

"Yes, unfortunately. I have to go now. It's about one a.m."

"Are you ready?" Because she already knows the answer, Sarah's voice grows anxious.

"Yes, I'm packed and ready. Not ready to leave you again, though. I love you, Sarah. Now take this." Stephen hands her his wedding ring, which he always leaves for safekeeping. He sits on the bed and holds Sarah tightly. "This will be the last time, Sarah. The last time."

"I'm so glad, Stephen. I want you with me always."

"Hey," he says, holding Sarah's face in his rugged hands. "I am always with you. As long as we're together, we are home, Sarah. Don't ever forget that."

"I love you very much, Stephen. So much." Sarah buries her face against his neck.

Stephen holds her tightly and gently rocks her. "I have to go now, dear. Lie down. Sarah, please see if you can find out about the pills and the tests, but keep it under the radar."

"I will, hon. And I will keep it quiet."

"Did you take your meds?" he asks, realizing her anxiety is high.

"Only one, but I'm not sure that will help right now."

Stephen walks to Sarah's side of the bed, gets one tablet of Klonopin, and has Sarah swallow it with a sip of water.

"Okay, babe. Don't hesitate to call Warren or Laura if you need anything."

Trying to be tough in front of Stephen so he won't worry, Sarah says, "Hey, I'm a strong, healthy thirty-five-year-old Irish woman. I can handle one more deployment."

Trying to lighten Sarah's anxiety, Stephen says, "Oh, and babe, please only redecorate the house one or two times while I'm gone." He smiles. "I know how stir-crazy these deployments make you."

"I think you're safe this time. I have the launch coming up, so I'm sure I will be much too busy." Sarah leans in to kiss him.

"Alas, our savings is safe." Stephen jokes. "Now lie down."

He softly rubs her forehead, brushing the hair from her face. He is amazed at her beauty, and he smiles, anticipating the rest of their lives together.

Sarah dozes off, and Stephen is gone from her life once again.

Rays of sunlight peek through the vertical blinds, waking Sarah from her sleep, which is now another nightmare to her. She tries to stop her tears from falling. Her beautiful green eyes are illuminated by the rays of the sun, revealing her true sadness. Tossing her hair away from her face, she reveals her flawless, ivory skin, perfectly kissed with freckles. Her eyes once again fill with tears as she curls into the security of the fetal position where Stephen slept. The sheets show markings of his body, but the space is empty and cold. He makes her feel safe, but now her safety is gone. Sarah holds Stephen's pillow tightly as if she will bring him back and won't have to let him go ever again. She trembles and bites her lip with angst. Her tears stream down her cheeks. She feels overwhelmed with deep sadness, once again.

She feels a sense of false security. Lovingly holding his pillow, she gently presses her face deeply into it to capture his unique scent that only she recognizes; it is as if she is lovingly embracing him for one moment longer. Sarah knows all too well that it will be what seems like an eternity before she holds him again. A sense of relief sweeps over her, knowing this will be his last deployment.

"This is the last time. I can't wait my love," Sarah speaks aloud. Cooper listens intently, cocking his head from side to side with every pitch of her voice. "Dear God, please keep Stephen safe and help me be strong through this last deployment," Sarah prays, snuggling Cooper tightly.

"It is September eleventh, two thousand twelve," she then says. Her heart feels heavy, and her stomach aches at having Stephen deployed on this repulsive anniversary. She sits silent for a moment to collect herself. Her captivating beauty is gripped with sadness and despair as she anticipates the days and months to come.

"Take each day at a time," she urges herself. "I will concentrate all of my energy on work, which is perfect timing with the launch of ViaStem's HESC G42. That will help a lot, and I have my Klonopin. Gosh, that sounds bad. Oh well. It helps take the edge off." Sarah writes a note on her bedside table to speak with her psychiatrist about possibly increasing the dosage. "That's it. I will drown myself in my work."

She straightens up and slowly stretches as if reaching for the stars. Brushing the hair from her face, she pulls it loosely into a ponytail and secures it with a scrunchie. Then she dries her tears and pops a single Klonopin just to take the edge off. Dragging herself from bed, she goes to the bathroom and stares at the mirror as if she is invisible. Right now she wishes she was. "I need to be strong for me and for Stephen. Oh, and for you too, Coops," she lightly addresses the fur ball at her feet.

Sarah continues to push herself through the morning. After splashing her face with icy cold water, she pats her face dry with a soft hand towel. Walking over to the nightstand, she stares intently down at a small square porcelain box sitting next to a vase of fresh gardenias. She feels the velvet petals, relishing their beauty. The aroma filling her bedroom is enticingly fresh and clean with a sweetness that brings a slight smile to Sarah's face. She picks up the porcelain box and carefully opens it to see Stephen's wedding ring beaming back at her. *I'm glad I have it. It's a piece of him.* Sarah holds his ring reverently as if it may disappear before her eyes, just as he had. "Please keep Stephen safe," Sarah prays to God.

As her mind wanders, she travels down a dangerous path of thoughts. Sarah is well aware of the dangers involved in Stephen's unit's top-secret missions. His position as Lt. Commander leading the elite SEAL Team ONE fills her heart with a great sense of pride and a great sense of worry.

"Stop this. Stop the negative thinking," Sarah says sternly to herself.

She sits quietly on the side of her bed, gently cuddling Cooper as he nudges his little body under her arm and camps out on her lap. "Hello, my little Coops," she says as she tussles the fur on his head. "Let's go make some coffee and get you some breakfast."

Cooper barks in agreement. As she slides her feet into her well-worn slippers, Sarah's legs feel heavy, as does her heart. She walks to the kitchen. Cooper helps lighten her spirit. Yawning, she scuffles down the hallway while holding Cooper like a little football close to her side. Rocking him upward, she gives him kisses on the scraggily fur on his head. He looks up at Sarah, almost appearing to smile at her. Her hair is mussed from a restless night's sleep. The silk robe she put on last night covers a pair of Stephen's plaid boxers, which are snapped as tightly as possible but are well oversized, paired with one of his white muscle shirts. Though impressively unsexy, wearing his clothes allows Sarah to feel a bit closer to her husband. She feels as though she is outside of her body. Her roller-coaster day is just beginning.

Still groggy, Sarah adds an extra large scoop of Arabica coffee beans into the grinder for the extra boost she will need to make it through the day. She prepares the coffee and as she waits for it to brew, she stares out the kitchen window at the steep, rugged mountains that encircle the valley. Sliding open the window, she inhales the morning air, which smells of fresh dew. The layer of fog covering the tops of the mountains gives Sarah a serene feeling within.

The aroma of freshly brewed coffee fills the kitchen. She prepares her first of many cups of java. Sitting on the L-shaped sectional in the TV room, she clicks the forty-six-inch flat screen on to watch the morning news. A kiss and a whine from Cooper alerts her that he is starving for his kibbles.

"Oh, I'm sorry, my little Coops. Let me get your breakfast right away, my little majesty." Sarah finds some lightheartedness within. Cooper hops like a bunny while she pours a small scoop of kibbles into his ceramic bowl marked *The King*. Before Sarah can set the bowl onto the tile floor, Cooper is standing tall at 12 inches, hungrily burying his face in the chewy morsels. Sarah returns to the national news after she pours herself another cup of the highly caffeinated concoction to help get her blood flowing and get rid of the emotional staleness of the morning. Sarah sits on the floor against the couch as Cooper snuggles in close. Sipping her second cup of fuel, she rhythmically pets Cooper's soft, curly white fur as she mindlessly switches from channel to channel to catch snippets of local news, Fox News, and Headline News.

She stops on a clip about ViaStem and its new procedure to help millions. "Look, Cooper. It's Mr. Stevens and Calvin." Sarah points at an old picture of the two at the ribbon-cutting ceremony. Sarah smiles at Cooper. "Just think, Mr. Stevens is on his way to Washington. He should be boarding his flight about now. How exciting!" She quickly gets up and walks back into the kitchen, still talking to Cooper, who is rolled into a little ball with his little nose resting inside one of Sarah's old slippers.

"I am so excited about this project. Thank goodness I get to go to work today. No offense, Cooper. It will keep me from thinking about Stephen being gone." Cooper's little head pops up with the sound of Stephen's name. "Anything to get me through another goddamn deployment! Sorry, God," she amends. "Now take a deep breath, girl, get off your ass, and get to work. Language, Sarah. Language." Sarah somewhat laughs as she commands herself into action.

She pours herself another cup of coffee; it becomes another mundane task, a cup of normalcy. It is the same routine she does each morning before beginning her day as the top sales consultant at ViaStem Biotechnology and Genetics

Corporation. With her undergraduate in biology from UCLA and an MBA from Pepperdine, paired with her drive for success, Sarah's pristine corporate image and her passion for the HESC G42 procedure has only led her to success. She works diligently to promote ViaStem's corporate vision of embryonic stem cell cloning and genetics engineering to conquer diseases that decimate lives. Clients are impressed by her drive to help others, and they trust her, which has made her the best. The only person not impressed is Kat, ViaStem's second ranking sales consultant.

Sarah continues preparing for her two key appointments with Scripps Research for the new genetic manipulation procedure. Her thought process is interrupted by the ringing of her phone. She gladly welcomes the distraction from her morning. Checking caller ID, Sarah cracks a smile, knowing it is Warren McNary. When Stephen goes on deployment, Sarah anticipates and is guaranteed Warren's calls of support. "He always comes through," Sarah whispers to herself. "Good morning, Warren," Sarah says in an upbeat tone.

"Good morning, Sarah. You sound good. I want to check in because I know from my end that Stephen's unit was deployed this morning. Do you have anything planned for today? Are you going to work?"

"You know me, Warren. Work, work, work. Especially when Stephen is gone. If I keep myself extra busy, I don't get so crazy, time goes a little faster … ya know." Sarah's voice drops to a whisper. In her next manic emotion, she explains to Warren that her CEO is on his way to meet with the FDA for the final approval for ViaStem's new cloning procedure.

"That's exciting, Sarah. I know it has been in the R&D stages for some time now."

"Not to mention the numerous clinical trials. I'm a bit

shocked that the approval process is here with virtually little trials on safety for humans. But it is finally here. I guess the NIH has arranged for a thousand subjects for the control trials, according to Calvin. Not quite sure how they managed that one. Warren, this will change the world," Sarah rambles.

"It is obvious you have much to do, so I won't keep you. I'm very happy for you, Sarah. I'll let you get going, but you need to let me take you to dinner soon, okay?"

"Dinner? Are you in town?"

"Yes, I came in last night. I will be conducting a Homeland Security forum at the convention center. I also have some work at the FBI command center, so I'll be in town for a couple days."

"Great. I'd like that, Warren," Sarah chimes in. "Hey, Warren …"

"Yes, Sarah?"

"Thanks for always being there for me when Stephen is gone. Your friendship and support means so much to me and Stephen," Sarah says, holding back tears.

"I wouldn't have it any other way. Now go make lots of sales."

Chapter 6:

Dark Skies

Feeling her heart getting heavy, Sarah takes the remaining cup of coffee to the back patio to feel the comfort of the warm California sun. "Come on, Cooper."

Cooper scampers past Sarah, claiming victory as king of the chaise, wiggling his scrawny body.

"Oh, I don't think so, mister. You can sit there for just a minute," she calls to him as she goes to greet Rudy and Rio. She gives each horse a carrot. "Good morning, boys. No hide and seek. Just not a great morning. Maybe this afternoon." She pats each horse's neck and turns to relax in her favorite chaise for a few minutes.

"Okay, Mr. Coops, time to move over."

Cooper hops down onto the cement, looking dejected. Sarah sits back into her most comfortable chaise, and Cooper jumps onto her lap before she gets settled.

"Oh, the sun feels so nice." Sarah relaxes with her eyes closed and pets Cooper softly. "I smell smoke ... I hope it's a controlled burn."

She reaches down for her coffee but accidently bumps her

cup, spilling most of it onto the cement. "Good gosh, Sarah." When she opens her eyes, she sees that the smoke she smells is most definitely not from a controlled burn. "Wow. That doesn't look good." She sits up and stares toward downtown.

Thick, black smoke plumes from the downtown harbor area of the city. The oily black smoke contrasts against the bright blue skies of San Diego. Sarah observes several helicopters, some military and some from local media stations, swarming the skies in the vicinity of the smoke.

She runs into the house and changes the channel from *Regis and Kelly* to a local news channel. Details are rather sketchy, but the station reports that two passenger airlines have collided. Sarah sits on the ceramic floor and leans against the couch in shock. Cooper sits silently alert next to her.

The phone rings, startling Sarah and Cooper. "This is awful," Sarah says aloud as she gets up to answer the phone.

"Hello?"

"Sarah, it's Calvin. Did Kat call you?"

"No … should she have?"

"Yes, I asked her to, but I should know better. I'm sure you have heard the news about the airliners colliding."

"I'm watching the news right now."

"I don't want you coming in today. It will be chaos on the freeways. Okay, Sarah?"

"I have to come in, Calvin. I can't just sit here. I'll go crazy. Stephen left on another deployment early this morning. I can't just sit here. I can help out with something."

"Okay, but it is a bit crazy here."

"I will see you soon."

While unimaginable chaos reigns in the heart of downtown San Diego, not forty miles away, an unimaginable excitement buzzes through the walls of ViaStem Biotechnology and Genetics Corporation. The air is filled with the expectation of success of the final approval of HESC G42. The company's employees, many whom are already at work and are unaware of the horror south of them, decorate the main conference room for a major celebration upon Mr. Stevens's return from Washington, D.C. While the festivities have already begun, Calvin Giovanni zealously plans an open house for the medical community following the approval and Mr. Stevens's return.

Work smart and work hard is Calvin's philosophy, emulating H.L. Stevens's beliefs. To work before sunrise and back home after sunset, Calvin dedicates his time and energy striving to be the best vice president so he can deservedly step into H.L. Stevens's shoes following his retirement in the near future. Just as Harold was unfortunately inspired by the tragic infliction of a monstrous disease of his young son, David, Calvin witnessed his father deteriorate from a vivacious dad to an empty vessel consumed by early onset Alzheimer's. The rapid succession of the disease stole his father's memories and prevented new memories with Calvin when he was a young boy. Calvin's father's soul was fully decimated, leaving only a shell of his body before the finality of his painful death.

The disease caused the unraveling of Calvin's family, alienating him from his mother, who mentally deteriorated and delved into severe depression. HESC G42 would have worked for David and for Calvin's father. Embryonic stem cell cloning might have reversed or curtailed both diseases. Honored by Mr. Stevens's confidence in him, Calvin is inspired to work harder and learn more to help Mr. Stevens's goal of the HESC G42 procedure approval, implementation, and long-term success come to fruition.

Calvin is well aware of the tragic events occurring in the normally beautiful downtown vicinity of San Diego. As he looks out the northwest window of his office, the skies are shades of bright blue. As he walks across his office and peers out the southern window, he views plumes of black, oily smoke filling the sky, erasing any shades of blues.

Difficult as it is, Calvin remains focused on his immediate work while trying to keep employees at ease. Unaware if the disaster is a terrorist attack or not, he has placed the ViaStem facility on lockdown until further notice. There is a knock at Calvin's office door, and he welcomes a break from the insanity that has just begun. "Come in."

Dave Perth, the chief financial officer of ViaStem, enters.

"Hi, Dave. What's up? You look like you've seen a ghost," Calvin half jokingly says.

"I have some very bad news, Calvin," Dave warns.

"Is it about the meeting today with Harold and the FDA?"

"I wish it was … I'm afraid that meeting is cancelled, for now anyway."

Sensing something is terribly wrong, Calvin asks, "What is it, Dave?" He rises from his chair.

"I just spoke with Ruth, and she is certain that Harold was on one of the flights that collided at Lindberg this morning. She verified the information through the airline's flight manifest," Dave sadly relays the news to Calvin.

Lowering himself back into his chair, Calvin drops his head into his hands and tries to wrap his mind around this. It seems impossible. "It can't be, Dave!" Calvin insists. "I just saw Harold this morning. Oh my God, Dave. This is just horrible." Calvin looks intensely distraught. "I didn't think to check on Ruth." Calvin stares at Dave for answers.

"Calvin, she said she left a message at your home with Kat. Didn't Kat call you?"

Silence stifles the room. There is no air to breathe.

"Dave, I need a moment … please."

"Of course. I'm going to meet with Jane in HR, and then I will be in my office if you need me."

"Dave?"

"Yes, Calvin?"

"How did Ruth sound?"

"She is very distraught, but she is trying to be strong. You know how she is. She always tries to be strong for everyone else."

Calvin dials home.

"Hello?" Kat sweetly answers the phone.

"Why didn't you let me know Ruth called?"

"Why didn't she invite me on your little yacht trip?" Kat snipes.

"Kat, grow the hell up!"

The line goes silent before Kat can spit any venom at Calvin. Calvin dials a different number.

"Hello?"

"Ruth … I'm so sorry about Harold. I'm so sorry I wasn't there for you. I just got the message. I'm so sorry. What can I do to help?"

"Calvin, it is all right. I need a little time to myself right now, but if you could come by this afternoon, I would like to see you."

"I will see you soon, Ruth."

Calvin feels emptiness. He sits in silence, trying to comprehend that the man he admires most is gone forever.

Chapter 7:

Smoke and Fire

Only forty-five minutes after speaking with Sarah, Warren McNary arrives at a scene of sheer chaos and mass confusion at Lindberg Airport. Though he is only in town for a Homeland Security conference, he realizes his stay will be extended for a much longer period of time before he can return to his home in Washington, D.C. He stands back for a moment to analyze the colossal event and prioritize the steps necessary to diffuse the situation.

He steps out onto the tarmac, displaying control and confidence that he can rectify and provide resolution to such tragedy. But McNary feels insignificant compared to the fire, debris, and death that surround him, just as he felt at Ground Zero eleven years ago. The heat from the fire swallows him, and the stench of fuel and burning flesh is overwhelming as he crosses the tarmac. He covers his nose and mouth with a handkerchief. The noise is piercing. McNary clearly sees everything around him but hears nothing except his own labored breathing as he absorbs the horrific scene.

The burned arm of what was obviously once a child lies

on the tarmac in solitude. A singed, worn-out, much-loved teddy bear is close but offers no comfort to the child now. A purse with its contents scattered nearby are unscathed by the explosion. A lipstick container from the purse shows no signs of melting. McNary kneels down and touches the lipstick tube, oddly discovering it to be warm but not hot to the touch. *One of those idiosyncratic phenomenons that occur during natural and man-made disasters*, he thinks to himself. The tube is partially open, the lipstick fully intact and only slightly melted. The bright pink color is certainly not a reflection of today's darkness. A man and woman holding one another tightly are still strapped into their seats, and the connected chairs are lying on their sides.

Still within his own silent world, McNary blocks all outside noise and hears only the loud echoes of his exhalations and inhalations. He looks as far down the runway as possible and sees remnants of innocent people, pets, luggage, shrapnel, and fuselage scattered by this heinous act. McNary lowers his head in prayer because he knows that within a short period of time, each of these once very human and personal items will become objects of evidence, losing all human characteristics. He feels sadness but quickly overcomes his emotions with an intense anger and urge to bring the criminals responsible for this atrocity to justice.

He re-enters the flow of the moment, only temporarily interrupted by the flood of extreme noise, the stench of death, and the pungent smell of jet fuel that nearly takes McNary's breath away. As the commander of Homeland Security, retired Captain Warren T. McNary maintains an air of confidence as he commands the NTSB, ATF, EOD, and FBI units summoned to the disaster site by orders from the Pentagon. All agencies continue to receive and share vital data with the other vital agencies involved in connection with the suspected terrorist attacks. The years of planning for a catastrophic event since 9/11 are paying off.

Usually a place of serenity and beauty, San Diego is now filled with death and despair. A temporary transport unit is set up by the FBI to conduct the investigation on-site. Via a direct connection to the White House, the President of the United States communicates to the agencies conducting the investigation at Lindberg Airport that the lead investigator and his team will be the Homeland Security team headed by Mr. Warren T. McNary.

McNary immediately takes control of the chaotic situation, deciphering much "chatter" from around the world that is drowning the airwaves at the Pentagon and providing key intel data. It is evident that the events of earlier that day were done by hands of terrorists.

"Another act of war against the United States on its home soil," McNary whispers to himself. He contacts the President. "Mr. President, this is Warren McNary."

"Yes, McNary. What is the situation?"

"It is a complete atrocity, sir. There is mass destruction."

"Has anyone come forward claiming this act?"

"No, sir, not at this time. However, when we examine past terrorist events, it appears to be an act of militant Islamic jihadists. We have not determined if it is a domestic cell or a foreign cell. I am organizing a command control center with satellite access at the far northern end of the tarmac. Until then, we are set up in the FedEx and UPS hangars. Mr. President, I am confident that our improved intel communications systems will expedite this investigation for quick retaliation."

"Keep me informed, Captain. I'm in the tunnel, and Vice

President Roberts is at Camp David." With that, President Cannon signs off.

"Yes, sir."

It is hot, and stress is high. McNary removes a handkerchief from his back pocket and pats his forehead. The beads of sweat disappear, only to return within seconds.

"Captain McNary?"asks an FBI agent on-site.

"Yes?"

"Agent Hanson, sir. We have just received information from a group calling themselves the Trio of Jihadists. They are claiming responsibility for these acts, as well as victory against the United States of America. Please come with me to the command center to review the intercepted chatter."

The two men begin the journey across the hot tarmac cluttered with debris. Agent Hanson trips, only to discover he has caught his foot on the leg of a body so charred it is barely recognizable. Both men catch each other's eye, only to quickly look ahead and continue their mission.

"Who is aware of this data?" McNary inquires.

"Just you, me, and two other agents. Agents Cleary and Jones."

"Hanson, what do you know about the grounded planes and the passengers on board?"

"They are all Boeing 737s. The first plane in line for takeoff is at full capacity, which includes one hundred and thirty-seven passengers and nine flight crew members. The two remaining flights are at one quarter capacity, each with six crew members."

"I want you to organize six FBI agents and all air marshals on board to scan the passenger manifests, look for any suspicious persons, and remove all cell phones and electronic devices. Anyone with compromised health issues needs to be removed immediately. Keep open communication with the remaining passengers, and let them know they will be removed within two hours and to please be calm and patient."

"Yes, sir."

"This needs to be kept highly confidential. At this point we are not certain of any inside connection. We are the lead on this investigation, and I want it to run smoothly. No mistakes. Do you understand?"

"Yes, of course."

"No chatter can be overlooked. From this moment on, every bit of information is pertinent to solving this case. Nothing can be taken lightly. The other investigative units will wrap up the evidence following the investigation on the tarmac unless otherwise summoned. Got that? Any mistakes and I'll have someone's ass."

"Of course. This way."

McNary and Hanson continue to make their way across the tarmac directly adjacent to the lead plane waiting for takeoff. In some locations, the tarmac is still so hot that the soles of their boots stick to the ground as if the two have sunk into thick glue. Each step makes a distinct ripping and sucking sound, which seems to echo raucously.

McNary lights a cigarette and takes deep drags as they briskly march the rest of the way to the command center, which has been set up complete with full intel communication capabilities. McNary turns to view the crime scene one more time before entering the center.

Keep the passengers as comfortable as possible until we devise a concrete plan, he thinks. He throws his cigarette down and forcefully smashes it with his boot before entering the makeshift facility that will be his home for the next several weeks. He realizes San Diego will be his home for several months.

"This is an absolute mess, a completely unconscionable, heinous act. Let's get these bastards," he says.

"Right behind you, sir," Hanson concurs.

Before the door shuts behind them, McNary is alerted by one of the agents that new information has become available. "Hello, agents Cleary and Jones."

"Hello, sir." Both agents nod in respect.

"What is it, Agent Cleary?"

"The Trio of Jihadists have claimed victory for Al-Qaeda and Lashkar-e-Tailbi and the Taliban from all locations around the world—even America. They claim their strength of three will end America as it is known today. There is more key information, sir. Have a listen." Agent Cleary hands McNary his headphones. "We have broken much key chatter on the airwaves recorded as of five minutes ago," Agent Cleary informs him.

McNary takes the headphones and places them over his ears in a calm and controlled manner. The agent offers him a chair, but McNary passes, choosing to stand. He listens acutely. He carefully analyzes all the information, taking notes and replaying the recording several times. He paces slowly. The look on his face is calculating, determined, and angry.

"Hanson?"

"Yes, sir. I have enhanced a splice of a comment taken from the conversation between the terrorists, intentionally or not, that two bombs remain grounded, totaling four bombs set to destruct."

McNary gestures, asking for a white board.

"Yes, I'll get it, sir." Agent Hanson exits the command

center and retrieves a white board from the trunk of his car. He sets it on a tripod at the far end of the trailer. He hands McNary various colored markers to distinguish between ideas.

"Okay, guys. Can you play that message for all of us to hear?" McNary asks. "Quiet, please."

"Of course, sir." Agent Cleary replays the tape.

Two Homeland Security agents; two NTSA agents; three CIA multilingual interpreters; FBI agents Hanson, Cleary, and Jones; and McNary listen carefully over a speaker to the message between the perpetrators. They listen a second and third time while taking decisive notes.

"Okay, team, let's do some brainstorming. Hanson, what is your take?"

"Well, sir ... We are dealing with well-known terrorists organizations that are proud to be known as radical Islamic jihadist-Americans and murderers in the name of Allah who have utilized airliners as weapons in the past, both successfully and in foiled plots since September eleventh, two thousand and one. All of these organizations have committed numerous jihadist acts around the world, such as the USS Cole and the Mumbai attacks."

"Very good."

McNary bullets each suggestion on the white board.

"How about you, Cleary?"

"Sir, the U.S. and its allies have foiled several major attacks that would have included airliners. There was long-term planning to achieve this on the anniversary of September eleventh, two thousand and one. The U.S. bringing the war to them for so many years has kept their war on their turf, restricting their jihadist movement on American soil. It has made them weak. They have lost strength as independent terrorist organizations. Sir, if there are four bombs and two have been successfully detonated, where are the remaining two?"

"Good point, Cleary," confirms McNary. "Jones?"

"So far all the destruction has taken place at this location. No other terrorist acts have been reported. What needs to be considered is if this attack is merely a distraction for an attack of a much greater magnitude, such as biologic or a nuclear dirty bomb," Agent Jones suggests.

"Excellent. Radio the Harbor Police to continue calmly evacuating the airport terminals as quickly as possible. Transport these people using airport shuttles to the convention center. The National Guard will take command of this sector. We need manpower on this. Have canines on hand to scan the detainees until they can be questioned and cleared for release. We need to investigate if this is a foreign cell or an inside job. Unfortunately, there will not be enough time to conduct a sweep. Keep communication open with these people. We do not need a panic on our hands.

"Alert hazmat teams in the area. Get them out here now. Freeways twenty-five, eight, fifteen, five, and sixty-seven needs to be closed up to seventy-eight. The Harbor Police will be responsible for Harbor Drive and vicinity. Only EMS allowed in the vicinity. Also, have the San Diego Police Department conduct a traffic blockade within a ten-mile perimeter of the airport. The sheriff's department will control the next ten-mile radius beyond, and have the Coronado police block all traffic from traveling on the Coronado Bridge. Consider it a key target. It's going to scare the hell out of people, but communicate to all local radio stations and TV stations to encourage people to stay in their homes and that sirens will be activated in the event of a biological or nuclear attack.

This will lessen traffic and keep people safer if a dirty bomb is released. Be prepared to sound air alerts if necessary.

"Also, alert the coast guard to block any watercraft from entering or exiting the harbor. I want F-eighteens on alert and one in the air, and move out these media choppers. No aircraft carriers are in-port, but I believe the *H.W. Bush* is conducting exercises off the coast of Point Loma. Admiral Williams will be in charge of all air tactics. Get him on the line.

"The aircrafts on the tarmac need to be secured by the FBI. Fifteen agents will be assigned to this task. Five agents will be assigned to each aircraft. Select three- to five-man teams. Immediately direct the agents to confiscate all cell phones, computers, and iPods—anything that can be used as a detonator," McNary demands. In deep thought, he repeats, "Tarmac ... tarmac ... *tarmac*."

"What is it, sir?"

McNary doesn't respond. He is in deep thought.

"Sir?"

"If their plan is as we suspect and all four bombs are here and two have already detonated in midair ... In the message they make a statement about being 'grounded.' That means one thing to me when referring to airlines. There is a great possibility that the remaining two bombs are in one or two of the remaining three grounded planes. They're on the tarmac. They're right here."

The agents and the commander agree that this conclusion is the best lead to run with, and the investigation begins right outside their door. The FBI teams are quickly organized to enter the remaining planes and confiscate all personal items from passengers.

"Sir, what about the passengers and the luggage?" questions Agent Hanson.

"Before discussing our plan of action, I need all FBI, ATF, and NTSB agents in attendance. Immediately! Have EOD on alert."

All investigative teams from the four remaining agencies are quickly alerted to move to the command center. The task is completed within minutes.

"Are all agents present? Team leaders identify yourselves as you are called. There will be no mistakes, understand?"

The group sounds in unison, "Yes, sir."

"Jones, you're up first. Gather your team." Jones stands with five FBI agents.

"Beginning with the first plane in line for takeoff, I want explosive detection canines to thoroughly go through every inch of those planes. Confiscate all devices. Nothing is insignificant. I want all passengers, including pilots, thoroughly checked for any suspicious devices. Any suspicious acting passengers will be taken off the planes prior to the other passengers and will be taken to a secured zone within the terminal, where each passenger will be extensively searched and questioned. Remove all passengers from the plane without any carry-on luggage, packages, purses, diaper bags, or pet carriers, including their pets. Have two of the five FBI agents calmly lead the passengers, with their hands in the air, across the tarmac and into the first entry to the terminal once that area has been deemed safe. That area will be secured for airline number one. Review the manifest for each plane and seek out any suspicious passengers. Look for any individuals who might have slipped through the cracks of the No-Fly list.

"I am not concerned with offending anyone at this time. In other words, pay close attention to specific ethnic groups. Secure them in a separate area. I will take full responsibility for all actions. I don't give a damn about political correctness at this time! The remaining three agents of each team will do another sweep of the plane and all contents on the aircraft. Once the interior cabin is clean, the luggage compartment needs to be cleared. The explosives canine unit will be sent into the cargo hold first. Two different dog teams will work each plane, one at a time."

McNary then reveals the second part of his plan. "Next, all luggage and animals are to be loaded onto transport trolleys that have also been cleared by the anti-bomb canines. Before any luggage or animal carrier is opened, all items are to be scanned. If anything looks suspicious, that particular item or items will need to be X-rayed. Once the pet carriers are cleared, they will be handed over to the local animal shelters. I have arranged for three shelters to be present. As you can see, they are located next to the airfreight terminals. At that time the animal shelters will provide care such as water and food for the detained pets. All pets will be scanned for chipping, which will aid in their quick and safe return to the correct owners. The animals from airline number one will be sent to the South Bay Animal Shelter, where their owners can claim them. The animals from airline number two will be sent to the North County Animal Shelter, and the animals from airline number three will be sent to the East County Animal Shelter. This plan will be communicated to all passengers. Let's go," McNary concludes.

The first plane is unloaded with no incidents. Five suspicious passengers—one American man, one woman, one man from Yemen, and an Iranian father and son—are removed before the other passengers. The five suspicious passengers are sent to secured areas in the terminal. From the segregated areas designated for high-risk passengers, threats and yells of mistreatment immediately begin. Some of the threats are accusations of profiling while others are verbal and physical signs of pure hatred for America. Some cheer for the catastrophic events of the day. A near riot almost breaks out.

"Death to all Americans! Praise Allah!" spews one man being held.

Many of the verbal remarks and gestures are made by the young boy, which doesn't surprise any of the agents because of the recent increase of cowardly young recruits. The unruly passengers are finally placed into soundproof rooms.

When the first plane is successfully cleared of its final passengers, the live cargo is carefully removed. It is very hot, and a few of the agents hasten the process. The entire cargo hold is finally loaded onto the third and fourth carts behind the animals.

"Mr. McNary, all seven animals from the first plane and its luggage are ready for transport to hangar number one. Animal Control will meet us there," Agent Jones informs him.

"Move out. Good job."

"Affirmative," responds Agent Jones.

Warren watches as the trolley begins its journey away from the main investigation. He feels a slight bit of relief knowing the first plane is heading to safety. Feeling confident, he turns to head back toward the command center. Suddenly, a deafening explosion rocks the tarmac, throwing him forward. While in transit to its destination, not even one hundred yards from the grounded planes, the luggage trolley erupts into a massive fireball that gouges a deep crater into the tarmac. Shrapnel, burning debris, and ashes fall from the sky. The driver, the five FBI agents, and all of the contents are destroyed. Screams from the animal shelter personnel are heard from across the tarmac. The investigative teams are stunned.

"Son of a bitch!" rages McNary. "Goddamnit!"

Various other expletives are heard from the other investigative units. All of their tedious work has literally gone up in deadly flames. Some of the agents near the command center sustain minor injuries from the blast but refuse to stop working.

"Get the President on the phone, Hanson!" McNary demands.

He urgently relays the current events to the Commander in Chief. "Mr. President, we have lost five agents and one civilian. Sir, it may be too early to draw any conclusions, but I believe we are near a resolution of the bomb plots at Lindberg airport. I will be in touch, sir."

"Good luck. Keep me informed."

"Everyone gather over here," McNary summons. "We need to review our plan. Something was overlooked. This cannot happen. Is this understood? *Is it?*" McNary nearly shouts. "I know it is hot as shit, but take absolutely no shortcuts. We are all aware that this may be a distraction to a bigger attack to come, but we need to all focus on the task we are doing right now. If we do not, someone else will get hurt or killed. I will not have another one of you jeopardized. Not on my watch. Not if I can prevent it. Let's go."

The groups of agents from all the responsible investigative units respond, "Yes, sir." They nod with respect for their commander.

"We will move forward with the second plane on the tarmac at a slower, more cautious pace for everyone's safety. Most likely the bomb was stored in a piece of luggage, but every

section of the entire plane is still suspect. Let's get to work."
Pointing to the second plane in line on the tarmac, Captain
McNary directs Agent Hanson, "This is your plane?"

"Yes, sir."

"Introduce me to your team."

"Canine team one is Agent Carson and his partner, Zeek."
Zeek is a stately Malinois. "Canine team two is Agent Davis and
her partner, Sam." Sam is a fierce-looking German Sheppard.
"The other agents on the team are agents Lauer, Sims, and
Lewis. Agent Carson and his canine partner, Zeek, are going
in first. Let's go team," Agent Hanson rallies them.

Agent Carson is an eight-year veteran of the FBI. Zeek,
the Belgian Malinois, is a veteran of the department for five
years and was raised by Agent Carson. He and Carson are
the perfect team. Both are hard-working, fiercely intelligent,
dedicated, and professional, with a keen sense of intuition.
They have received numerous awards for their bravery.

McNary diverts all other available agents to their assigned
airline and instructs them to maintain a holding pattern.
Then he approaches Agent Carson and his partner.

"Listen, son," he says. "Be on high alert, and take no
chances. No shortcuts. Be confident that the passengers
and the body of the airline have been cleared. Now it's your
turn."

"Yes, sir. Zeek and I never take shortcuts. We are the best
team."

"If you find anything suspicious, we have the EOD unit
ready. Got it?"

"Yes, sir," responds Carson with a verbal response from
Zeek. "Let's go, Zeek," he directs his partner. Zeek barks in
agreement.

The team is extremely careful and cautious as it enters the

cargo hold where the animals are contained. Agent Carson commands Zeek with hand signals to enter the plane and search for HEs (high explosives), frequently referred to as IEDs (improvised explosive devices) by the media. Built for function over form, Zeek enthusiastically begins his search into the unknown of the snug cargo hold. The dog begins intently sniffing each carrier, which causes some barking and growling from the pets within. The noise is unwanted because of the unknown nature of the possibility of an explosive device and its triggering mechanism.

Zeek runs directly to a specific area of the cargo hold. He halts at one particular carrier. The short-haired brownish-gray dog is nearly camouflaged in the shadows of the hull. He appears like a statue as he intently guards the kennel, fierce in appearance by his black mask and ears. At this signal, Zeek's partner, Agent Carson, enters the fuselage and approaches the targeted carrier. He hand signals for Zeek to back off. Zeek immediately obeys orders, moving behind his partner and sitting without movement or sound. The team evaluates the situation. Carson studies the carrier, which is medium in size. He is cautious as he approaches it to have a better vantage point. He can now clearly view its contents. It is excessively hot in the cargo hold, and sweat runs into Agent Carson's eyes. He wipes his burning eyes, thinking he is seeing things. What he witnesses astounds him.

He expects a bomb, but instead he discovers a puppy. The six- to eight-week-old puppy is motionless. Agent Carson notes the puppy exhibits early signs of rigor mortis—taut skin and the evacuation of bladder and bowels. It seems that the pup has succumbed to heat exhaustion. Agent Carson continues to move closer. Zeek remains quiet but stands from his position and then returns to a sitting position to remind his partner to remain cautious. Carson slows his pace. The puppy is lying on its right side, with its legs rigidly extended. Its distended belly is clearly visible. Carson notices the belly of the canine is red and swollen. Yellowish fluid is crusted over an X-shaped incision. It appears that the incision is fairly fresh. It is obvious to Agent Carson that the wound became infected and most likely caused the animal to die, not the heat.

Carson further examines another strange finding—an object protruding slightly from the center of the wound. The stitches have given way to an object that appears to be of a plastic material with a small metal device attached. It is evident to Agent Carson that this innocent puppy has undergone a recent surgery of some kind, possibly diabolical in nature. At this point, he backs off and returns to the exterior of the cargo hold with Zeek to review his findings with Captain McNary.

McNary immediately summons for EOD to intervene and remove the carrier containing the puppy's carcass, which is now referred to as the "package." The explosives ordinance department already at the far end of the tarmac arrives at the plane within seconds. They send in a robotic device that stands approximately twelve inches in height and twenty-four inches in width. It is equipped with great power that gives it strength and precision as it moves into the cargo hold to remove the carrier with its twenty-four-inch robotic claws extended. All its programming is done remotely. The robotic device the bomb squad calls Robby successfully removes the carrier from the cargo hold and onto the tarmac in approximately twenty minutes. It lays the carrier down at least 150 yards from the plane. Robby's mission is a success; there are no injuries and no casualties.

Cement blockades are placed in a straight row near the carrier for the agents to find safety if there is another explosion. Robby returns to its remote master. Now it is time for the EOD experts to intervene. The plan of action is to retrieve the package from the carrier. The second vital step is to remove the plastic contents from the dead canine to determine the exact composition of the material inside the plastic packet.

Two agents from the bomb squad suit up in the newest high tech gear known as the ISP MK 1 EOD suit and helmet to begin their mission. They are equipped with the highest quality gear, built of multiple layers of the Aramid. Aramid consists of water encapsulated by a PVC outer covering to protect the men against a blast, shrapnel, and the burning heat. The gear is also made of flame retardant material devised from HTA Kermel, which also adds superior strength and UV stabilization. First the agents climb into the ISP cooling suits that are worn beneath the cumbersome gear, which are necessary when working in extreme heat. Their helmets contain a built-in fan and an integrated communications system to allow for optimal teamwork.

Once in their protective gear, the two agents walk slowly toward the carrier. They work together systematically. They are a highly specialized unit, and their lives depend on their expertise and teamwork. One carefully opens the carrier without moving of the package. There is no detonation of the contents. The package is in full view. The team uses a magnification device that guarantees them the most precise view. The agents look at one another, perplexed at the sight. They converse through their headsets and come to the conclusion that the protruding contents are most likely of an explosive nature and will need to be removed from the package for further investigation of the possible explosive's anatomy.

The bomb team examines the visible contents and studies the slightly open wound containing the unknown plastic packet. "The wound has been closed with amateur stitching, and the puppy's distended belly has caused the stitches to give way. Only one stitch is holding the wound closed," one of the agents says. "Clip it."

The second agent slowly clips the remaining stitch holding the incision together. The first agent holds the skin flaps open with hemostats to allow for a wider view of the contents.

"I am confident this is an IED and not drugs. When I was in Iraq and Afghanistan, people and animals are used to encapsulate explosives frequently. They call them body bombs," the second agent relays.

The contents appear yellow in color, leading the agents to an immediate conclusion. "This is possibly a C-four plastic explosive commonly utilized by militant Islamic jihadist radicals," concludes squad leader one.

The agents are well aware of the damages the small bag of explosives could cause, so they decide to place the suspicious compound into a bomb safe. The safe is securely locked. The contents of the packet will be analyzed at the FBI lab. The EOD squad leaders approach McNary, and they shake hands.

"We got damn lucky that this one didn't ignite. At least we retrieved some evidence," reveals squad leader one.

Agents Carson and Zeek are sent back into the cargo hold to continue their sweep. All is clear. Agent Davis and her canine partner, Sam, conduct a follow-up sweep. All is clear. The animals and luggage are removed from the plane and taken to the location where the East County Animal handlers are waiting to take the animals to safety. Word of the dead puppy and possible explosives hidden in its belly spreads quickly. The animal handlers are shocked and sickened. One of the animal handlers from the North County Animal Shelter requests to speak with whoever is in charge. The FBI agent radios the request to McNary. He approves her request.

Animal handler Susan Franks is brought to the command center to speak with Captain McNary. She is shaken and nervous. They exchange introductions. He offers her something to drink and tries to comfort her a bit. She asks for some water.

"Please get her a bottled water from the cooler, Hanson."

"Yes, sir. Mr. McNary, there is a message from team three."

"Excuse me for just one second," McNary says to the Susan. "I'll be right back. Everything will be okay" he reassures her.

"Thank you," Susan answers timidly.

"Yes, go ahead with the third plane. Be careful and be thorough. There may be another device," McNary warns Hanson and Cleary.

"Yes, sir," responds Agent Cleary.

"Cleary, find out who is responsible for screening the cargo."

"Yes, sir."

McNary turns to Susan and sits across from her. "Is there anything else we can get for you?"

"No, sir. Thank you."

"You can call me Warren. What can I do for you?"

"Mr. McNary—Warren—I'm not sure if this has anything to do with all of this, but I thought you should know."

"What is it?"

"I work at the North County Animal Shelter on Tuesdays. Four days ago, four men came in to adopt some puppies, four puppies. They didn't all come in at once. Two came in the morning, and two came in the late afternoon. I remember them because it just seemed odd. They did not seem like the types to adopt. They passed our interview process, so it was difficult to turn them away. I know this is going to sound … well … not too nice, but they were all Middle Eastern except one white guy with the second pair that came in the late afternoon. The white guy had a brown mustache and brown hair, and he was wearing a ball cap. I didn't notice anything outstanding on the other guys … It was just a bad gut feeling. Like I said, I'm not sure if it has anything to do with all of this, but I thought you should know," Susan nervously reports.

"Thank you very much for coming forward with this information, Susan. It may prove extremely helpful in solving this mystery. And if not, no harm done. Agent Cleary will get all your contact information and take you back to your station. Thank you again," Warren thanks Susan. "Oh, Ms. Franks, have you discussed this with anyone else?"

"No, sir."

"I would appreciate if you only discussed this with me now that this is an investigation."

"Of course," Ms. Franks agrees.

"Thank you for coming forward, Ms. Franks."

"You're welcome, Mr. McNary," Susan says as Warren opens the door for Susan to return to her station.

McNary sits for a moment, absorbing the information he just received. He whispers to himself what the bomb squad commander had said to him: "It's not that terrorists would use puppies to destroy America; it's that they didn't use them earlier. It was a matter of time." McNary pauses and looks out at the war zone in front of him. "They blow themselves up for Christ's sake!"

He lights another cigarette and heads out of the command center to oversee the continued investigation.

Chapter 8:

The Yellow Brick Road

Calvin sits silently in the quietness of his Range Rover outside the home of Harold and Ruth Stevens. His hands grip the leather-bound steering wheel. The blood drains from each finger with his reluctance to leave his safety zone. Calvin grips at his gut tightly as a wave a nausea sweeps through his body. He feels perplexed by the unforeseen terrorist acts that occurred less than six hours earlier and stole Harold Stevens's life.

Beads of sweat build on Calvin's upper lip as he collects himself and exits his SUV. Reaching across the front seat, he gathers the colorful array of Gerber daisies he brought for Ruth because he knows they are her favorite. Various memories flash through Calvin's mind, making him feel more uneasy as he approaches the Stevens's home, which is located in the affluent Banker's Hill neighborhood.

The outside of the Stevens's home is as warm and welcoming as the inside. Calvin stops for a brief moment, recalling his cherished memories of working under the wing of the most intelligent man he has ever known. He holds his stomach tightly as another wave of nausea sweeps over him.

Standing outside the front gate, he stands looking at the lovely home in front of him. He pats beads of sweat from his upper lip and forehead with his handkerchief. Stalling for more time, he folds the handkerchief meticulously while cradling the bouquet. Then he slips the cloth into his back pocket as feelings of sadness and resentment overwhelm him. His feelings are grim, but his surroundings are majestically beautiful and serene. Vivacious colors of fuchsia, magenta, and peach bougainvillea vines and trees adorn the lush green lawn. Accents of fragrant lilies line the wrought iron fence and the front porch of the 1960s bungalow. The perimeter of the property is lined with perfectly manicured hedges that split at the entrance of the wrought iron gate.

Calvin opens the gate, which gives him entrance to the front yard. Time seems to stand still as he stands at the beginning of the brick path that leads to the front door. A false sense of tunnel vision causes the walkway to seem exceedingly long, bringing more sadness with each step. Talking to himself, he says, "One foot in front of the other. Breathe."

As he steps onto the porch, his legs feel heavy and his actions uncoordinated. Gripping the large brass handle of the front door, Calvin announces himself with each strike of brass on brass. The hand-carved mahogany door is framed by stained glass with rich tones of gold, green, and various blues, adding richness to the appearance of the home, but it has no calming effect on Calvin's nerves.

He once again removes his handkerchief and blots the moisture from his brow. His gut wrenches and twists with angst. He feels light-headed and faint. About to enter the home he has visited so many times in his life, he remembers when he first started working with Harold Stevens straight out of college. He can see Harold's smile as if he were standing in front of him. The heavy door opens, bringing him back from his daydream. He meets the eyes of Ruth, Harold's bride of forty-nine years. Ruth's eyes are red from crying as sadness and grief fill her heart, but she still greets Calvin with the warmest smile.

"Please come in, Calvin." Ruth gestures welcomingly.

Calvin gingerly enters the immaculate, cozy home. Without a word, he takes a moment to soak in the treasured memories he has built there. It is the home he never had.

"Thank you, Ruth," he says, offering her the gorgeous bouquet that he hopes will bring a smile to her face, even if only for a moment. Calvin offers a warm, supportive hug. "How are you doing, Ruth? How are you feeling?" Calvin feels Ruth's frail frame, which has been eroded by breast cancer. The disease has ravaged her body but not her soul. Calvin is not good with emotions; he is good at solving problems. Unfortunately, he knows he cannot solve this one.

"Thank you for the lovely flowers. You know they are my favorites," Ruth's voice cracks with sadness. There is an extended, uncomfortable silence. Holding a wrinkled tissue to her eyes, she dabs her tears away. "I am certain Harold misses you as much as you miss him. Now please have a seat, and I will put these in a vase and make us some tea. How does that sound?" she offers.

Knowing through experience that Ruth loves to take care of others, Calvin obliges. "That sounds nice."

Ruth offers him a caring smile as she exits the living room, leaving Calvin sitting alone in utter silence, surrounded by memories of Harold, his wife, and their late son, David.

Calvin is present in many of the pictures. The memories are so vivid he can almost hear Harold's jovial laugh.

"How he loved life," Calvin whispers to himself. He breathes in a long, slow breath, inhaling the wonderful aromas of vanilla, apples, and cinnamon. Harold's life captures Calvin's heart. Standing before a picture hanging on the wall, he admires the image of Harold holding his young son in front of a "Progeria Foundation Summer Camp" banner.

Calvin respectfully walks through the living room, touching the noble hearth of the enormous stone fireplace, sliding his hand along the edge, and admiring the numerous photos he has seen hundreds of times before. There are many photos. Each frame is as unique as the photo telling a story. Each sheet of glass covering the photos captures the reflections of the stained glass that frames the door. There is no layer of misty dust hiding the memories, only rays of gold and green and hues of blues that make the room seem magical in the midst of such grief. As Calvin studies each photo, he finds himself gravitating to specific framed memories such as Harold and Calvin with their arms around one another's shoulders while holding their big catches of trout that seemed to increase in size with each telling of the tale.

A smile appears on Calvin's face. Another treasured photo of Harold, Ruth, and Calvin makes them look like a family in front of their Christmas tree. Ruth's stature is beaten down by chemotherapy, showing her thinning hair but not wiping out her love for life, which is evident in her smile and the sparkle in her eyes. Calvin admires Harold and Ruth's wedding picture, which tells a marvelous story of love.

The center photograph on the mantle is of their only child, David, who looks so frail from battling progeria. He appears elderly, small in stature, weak and brittle, bald, and almost transparent. His paper-thin skin illuminates the bluish veins beneath it. When Calvin looks into the young boy's eyes, he sees the same love for life that he sees in Harold's and Ruth's, as well as the curious sparkle of a child.

"I will make the vision real. I promise," Calvin says to the photograph with passion in his heart. He is startled by Ruth's entrance to the living room. She is holding a tray of drinks and cookies. "Let me help you with that," he offers.

"I've got it, dear," Ruth responds, setting the tray on the living room table. "Are you looking at those photos again? You must have seen those hundreds of times before, Calvin." Ruth's soft voice is calming.

"I know, Ruth. And I could look at them a hundred more …" Calvin finds himself choking back his emotions. The memories tug deeply at his heart. With a slight crackle in his voice, he continues, "Harold was my mentor and a man I admired greatly, the man who felt like a father to me." Calvin loses his words.

"Like the son he never had, Calvin, now come and sit." She moves slowly and sits in the antique floral chair adjacent to the couch.

With one last glance back at the many photos, Calvin thinks to himself, *What a wonderful life looking back at me from within a few frames.* He walks to the couch and sits. Then, holding a glass of tea, he gets up and calmly walks across the dark pine floors that match the bold beams that run the length of the ceiling. There, two framed photos hold memories of the backyard picnic with Harold, Ruth, Kat, Eden, and Calvin during happier times, followed by another photo of a happier memory of Harold, Ruth, and Calvin making a champagne toast on the Stevens's thirty-four-foot sail boat.

Calvin picks up the photo and turns to Ruth with a smile. "Now these were some fun times. I'm sure Harold is toasting life. As he was leaving to catch his flight, he gave me a firm handshake followed by one of his bear hugs and a pat on the back." Calvin is not sure why he said that aloud and awkwardly returns to the couch. "I'm sorry. I shouldn't have mentioned this morning ..." Calvin chokes back tears. He clears his throat to swallow his sorrow so he can be strong for Ruth, but in his heart he knows it is the other way around. She is his strength. He wonders if she was also Harold's pillar of strength during their son's terminal illness. "How are you doing?" he asks. "How are you feeling?"

Without considering herself, she says, "I already miss him, Calvin. He was my best friend, but I know things ... things will be fine. They will turn out the way they should ..."

"Ruth, I ... I don't know what to say to you."

"You don't have to say anything at all because I know what is in your heart. You are a good man. Harold knows—knew that, and I know that. We love you like a son, dear." Ruth says, touching Calvin's hand reassuringly.

Calvin's gut twists in agonizing pain. Not feeling very well, he takes another drink of tea, which tastes bitter to him. Lately nothing tastes good to him. He sets his glass on the coaster and sits back against the couch cushion. He feels a wave of nausea sweep over him, climbing from his feet up to his head and leaving him chilled.

"Are you feeling all right? You look a little pale," Ruth says. "I'm sure it is from all that has happened today. It is most likely nerves, dear." Ruth pauses. "Would you like to lie down in the guest room for a bit?"

Calvin quickly replies with embarrassment in his voice, "Oh, no. I'll be all right. I'm sure you're right, just nerves.

If you don't mind, I think I will go splash some cold water on my face. I'm sure that will help." Calvin gets up slowly to adjust to the imbalance he feels hindering his equilibrium. He feels comfortable enough in the Stevens's home and hastily heads to the guest bathroom. Ruth offers a steady hand to help him balance. "Thank you. I'm sorry about this," Calvin apologizes.

"It's all right. I'll be in the back watering some flowers to give you some privacy, but if you need me, just holler all right?" Ruth asks him in a direct but caring manner, knowing Calvin doesn't like to ask for help—just like her husband.

As Calvin continues to navigate his path to the washroom, he guides himself with his hands against the hallway walls. He feels faint, and his vision is blurred. He stops and supports himself against the wall. Leaning against the wall with his lower back pressed firmly against it, he bends forward and puts his hands on his knees. A drop of sweat falls from his nose as he focuses on the various grains running through each plank of the wood floor. He manages to make it into the bathroom and lock the door behind him before slouching to the floor on his knees. He feels disoriented and confused, with a pounding headache perfectly in sync with his pounding heart.

Suddenly, he lunges for the toilet and throws up everything in his stomach, which isn't much, just the scrambled eggs and orange juice Kat had made him early this morning. Pushing the bathroom rugs aside, he lies down to feel the coolness of the ceramic floor against his flushed face. It feels soothing. He feels a persistent, agonizing, gut-wrenching pain, nothing he has ever experienced before. He throws up more gut-wrenching puke of acidic bile. Soon there is nothing else to empty, but the dry heaves feel relieving. It feels good. His stomach is now empty, but he cannot get rid of the taste of the pungent bile remaining in his mouth. The stench is strong, making him feel dizzy.

A knock on the door startles Calvin as he attempts to sit up. "Are you all right, Calvin? Can I get you anything?"

With the room is still spinning, making it difficult for him to respond. "Ah … yes, Ruth … I will be … right out," are the only words he can muster.

Embarrassment sweeps over him as the nausea subsides long enough for him to catch his breath and stand up. He leans against the sink to steady his balance, and the room comes to a stop. He reaches for a tissue to wipe his face and clean up any mess on and around the toilet. He feels so ill that all he can think about is getting out and going home, but that creates a new level of anxiety. He is certain now that he must have the flu; he has had the same symptoms over the past few days. Feeling faint again, he squats for a moment. He runs the tap. The cold water running over his hands feels icy against his hot skin. He leans over and soaks his face in pool of water he makes with both hands pressed tightly together. Beads of sweat are rinsed away, making him feel halfway decent again. He continues to bury his face in the cold remedy and wipes some of the water onto his neck. He feels relief when he peers at himself in the mirror and sees color seeping back into his ghostly white skin.

After drying his face, neck, and hands, he searches for some toothpaste or mouthwash—something to remove the awful bitter taste left in his mouth. He finds some mint-flavored Tums inside the medicine cabinet and downs several. Not paying attention to the chalkiness, he concludes that they are the best things he has tasted all day. After rinsing his mouth with cold water and taking one last look in the mirror, he appears almost back to normal.

Calvin straightens the bathroom as he found it before re-entering the hallway. Retracing his steps, he passes the kitchen and peeks in. "Thank you, Ruth, but I must be going now."

Ruth carefully sets down her water can and enters the kitchen from the back patio through the open French doors.

"Come sit just for a minute." Ruth gestures to kitchen table.

Opening an etched glass and white wood cabinet, she removes a clean glass and pours some club soda for Calvin. "I need to say something before you leave," she says in a more urgent voice and hands him the glass of club soda. "This will help settle your stomach."

Shyly, Calvin responds, "I am feeling much better, just a bit embarrassed, that's all."

Ruth is quick to respond, "Now Calvin, no worries. You are family. Harold and I want you to consider what I am about to share with you, and we hope you will accept the offer," Ruth suggests as if Harold was alive and standing beside her. "If you are up to it?"

"I'm feeling much better now. Thank you, Ruth."

Ruth folds a hand towel, lays it on the countertop, and invites Calvin to sit at the large, dark wood picnic-style table. Calvin sits while Ruth retrieves a white legal-size envelope from a kitchen drawer.

"Calvin, you know I've been ill for some time now. With the unfortunate circumstances of today, taking my Harold away from me—us, I believe this is an appropriate time and a necessary time to do this." She walks slowly across the kitchen toward Calvin and hands him the envelope with a smile that she wasn't expecting to have on a day like today. Calvin holds the envelope, dumbfounded.

"I stopped my chemo over a month ago. I'm not responding to the treatments anymore. I don't have much longer—maybe six months, maybe less. Who knows? Maybe more." Ruth reveals and her tone shifts to encouragement in her last comment.

"I had no idea it was so bad …" Calvin is shocked, but Ruth holds her hand up, signaling to Calvin that she needs to finish what she wants to say to him.

Calvin flips the envelope around. His name is on the front. The envelope is sealed. He gently slides his hand across the heavily typed, imprinted letters of his full name and deeply examines each character, shooting a curious glance toward Ruth almost as if seeking her approval to open the envelope.

"Well, open it, Calvin." She feels Harold is with her as she feels enthusiastic about the news yet hides her emotions beneath her calm demeanor. Ruth nods, speaking no words, just sending him an encouraging smile.

Calvin turns the envelope around and cautiously stares at the sealed flap screaming to be opened. He peels the corner of the flap, slides his finger across the inside of the envelope, and thoroughly reviews the enclosed documents. Minutes tick by. Calvin sits motionless in silence. He is stunned. The silence seems like an eternity. All he can do is questionably look at Ruth. Ruth sits patiently beside him.

Calvin attempts to speak, but his words come out scrambled. "Ruth, I can't … I don't … are you sure?" He chokes on his words but is saved by Ruth.

"Yes, Calvin, you can, and hopefully you will. Harold and I discussed this long before today, before this awful, awful tragedy. Harold wanted you and only you, and I fully agree with his decision. We trust you. We love you like a son, and we know you share our passion for the fruition of our dream … Harold's dream … David's dream—HESC G42. We have no other family, so please say yes, Calvin."

"I am so very honored, Ruth."

"The only thing we ask is that your beneficiary, God forbid, is the Progeria Research Foundation."

"Of course. Absolutely."

With great confidence, Calvin stands. "I promise I will see Harold's and your dream for David come true."

A wonderfully calm, satisfying silence falls over the room.

"Ruth, you know I would do this without transferring ownership of the company …" Calvin said.

"We know that, Calvin, but we want it this way. We want you to have ViaStem. You know ViaStem, the industry, the scientists, the people who need help, our son's history, and the HESC G42 procedure as well as Harold. Please say yes, Calvin," Ruth urges.

"Yes."

Chapter 9:

Disclosure

The devastating news of Mr. Stevens's heinous and untimely death sweeps through ViaStem like a wildfire. Calvin immediately reschedules the meeting, as he promised Ruth Stevens. Within weeks, with much influence from the President of the United States, the Food and Drug Administration gives special consideration for the early approval to market ViaStem's HESC G42 procedure because its clinical trials included so many orphan diseases like the progeria. One additional step is being studied to accelerate the procedure to offer this revolutionary option to people with no time left. This additional step is required before the procedure will be available for market release. However, the NIH will be in full control of this safety protocol and provide one thousand subjects for the control group.

Calvin Giovanni fills Mr. Stevens's position as chief executive officer of ViaStem Corporation with utmost integrity. Calvin's mission and focus is to follow Mr. Stevens's corporate vision and mission, as he promised when he accepted ownership of ViaStem. His dedication to his new position places great demands on his professional life as well as his personal life. His new position as CEO absorbs most of his days, allowing only a sliver of his time left for his family. Kat seems quite content with his balance of time between ViaStem and her, following the exciting news that the Stephenses granted ownership of ViaStem to Calvin.

Soon after Calvin Giovanni is named CEO of ViaStem, his adverse health issues begin subtly. Calvin attributes the headaches, rashes, and GI upsets to his long work hours and the enormous stress in learning about and managing such a prestigious company. In addition, the undue amount of stress remains unresolved in the murder of his mentor and dear friend, Harold. Calvin is as deeply troubled by the events of September 11, 2012, as he was by the terrorist plots in 2001.

Sarah keeps in contact with Calvin following Stephen's deployment, as she always does during his absences. He offers support and friendship. With all that Calvin is experiencing, Sarah feels she is offering much-needed support to him as well. Ironically, this time it goes both ways.

Calvin sits in his high back leather chair with his back to the door, staring intently at the plaque on the wall that states the company's mission statement. He reads each word and each phrase with care and compassion, just as Mr. Stevens would have: *To be the number one biotechnology corporation. To ethically discover treatments through human embryonic stem cell cloning. To cure or curtail life-threatening diseases afflicting children, women, and men of all ages, ethnicities, and financial backgrounds.*

Calvin is startled by a knock on his office door, which pulls him from his fixation on ViaStem's vision and mission. Spinning his executive chair to face the entrance to his office, he acknowledges the knock. "Come in."

Peeking in, Sarah greets him. "Hello, Calvin. May I come in?"

"Absolutely. It is nice to see you, Sarah." Calvin gets up, walks over to her, and gives her a kiss on the cheek.

"Do you have a second? I need to talk to you."

"Sure, come on in and have a seat." Calvin gestures toward the chair in front of his large granite-top desk, which is filled with neat files of paper.

Sarah quickly scans his office and realizes just how busy he is, so she gets right to the point. "Calvin, I have a favor to ask."

"Anything. How can I help, Sarah?"

"I know this is not exactly a good time to ask this, but I need some time off. If I can work from home for a while, that would be ideal. Once again, the affair rumors are running rampant. That combined with Stephen's fifth deployment and all of these medical tests his unit has been required to take and the horrible terrorist attacks … well, I just cannot concentrate here. I will come right back once the final approval for the launch is given. I promise, Calvin. I just need some time."

"Sarah, I completely understand. I don't mean to pry, but I have to ask. What medical tests are being done to Stephen's unit?"

Sarah smiles, relieved he didn't flatly turn down her request to work from home. "This needs to be confidential, Calvin. Stephen was very insistent about that."

"Absolutely, Sarah."

"Before Stephen left on this last deployment, he said his unit has been undergoing numerous tests, getting numerous vaccines, and taking an array of oral meds they have never been required to take except for the past three deployments.

Stephen is a pretty brave guy, but there was fear in his voice. He said Dr. Hammond was in control of the testing."

"Our Dr. Hammond?" Calvin asks in a surprised tone.

"I asked the same thing."

"Did Stephen take the pills? Did he go along with these experiments?"

"No. He put the pills in his mouth and then removed them when the physician went go to the next man. He did receive the vaccines because he didn't think much of that. After all, they get vaccines all the time going overseas. Stephen did say his men are behaving differently since taking the drugs. He said they are distracted and highly agitated. He is really concerned, Calvin, for their safety and his."

"Do you have any of the pills?"

"Yes, I have them with me. I didn't know who to ask for help, but I guess I have my answer." Sarah digs through her purse and removes the bottle of pills and hands them to Calvin. "Can you have them analyzed here?"

Calvin hesitates for a moment. "Will you trust me on this, Sarah?"

"Of course, Calvin. What is it? Is something wrong?"

"I want to involve Dave—Dave Perth. He's trustworthy, and he knows several researchers at UCLA Medical Center. I don't want these analyzed here. It is much too dangerous if there is something going on."

"Oh … okay. I trust you, Calvin. I need to know if Stephen and his men are in danger."

"Do you mind if I call Dave in now?"

"No, not at all. The sooner I have an answer, the better I will feel about all of this."

Calvin phones Dave's office and asks him if he can come

by immediately."He'll be right here. Sarah, I promise I will be direct and honest with you on anything we find."

"You know something, don't you? Please tell me, Calvin. Please," Sarah begs.

"Sarah, it is nothing but a thought ... not backed by evidence."

"But you thought of something right away. Just tell me, Calvin. Please tell me. We're talking about Stephen for God's sake."

A knock on the door sidelines their conversation.

"Come in."

Tension fills the room as Calvin and Sarah realize it is not Dave Perth.

The door opens, and Kat saunters in with an "I'm a smug bitch" expression written all over her face. "Well, well, well. I haven't seen you forever, Sarah. I understand Stephen is on deployment again. So sorry. Come to think of it, this is the last time I saw you—right here in my husband's office," Kat snipes.

"That's enough, Kat. This is a private conversation, and you need to leave ... *now*." Calvin gets up from his chair, grabs Kat's arm, and escorts her out of the office.

Sarah is stunned by the nasty behavior between Calvin and Kat. It keeps her speechless. Before Kat leaves, she intensely stares at Sarah, who is looking straight ahead but can feel Kat's burning glare.

"I apologize for her behavior, Sarah. It's pretty obvious that things are bad between us. You didn't deserve that." Calvin returns to his black leather executive chair.

"I guess I should prepare for some more rumors about us, huh?" Sarah tries to lighten the mood.

"This is pretty serious, Sarah. I'm sorry you had to witness that. You and I have been friends for a long time, and you have known Kat for longer, but she has changed. I don't know her anymore," Calvin reveals his family secret.

"I don't know if I'm out of line, so just let me know. I noticed a change in her long ago. We used to be such good friends, but she was beyond cruel during Stephen's last deployment. You know all about that … or at least most of it. I had to sever the friendship. I had no other choice, Calvin." Sarah's voice withers.

"I know she spread some vicious rumors, which is bad enough, but what more is there?"

"I can't believe I'm going to share this with you. I-it's so personal." Sarah ponders her decision. "The reason I was admitted to the hospital—the psych hospital—is because I had a nervous breakdown after I suffered a miscarriage. The baby was five months along." Sarah nearly breaks into tears.

"Sarah, I'm so sorry. I knew Kat had been cruel, but I had no idea it was this bad. Did she know?"

"Yes. She never bothered to talk to me about it. She just used it in her favor. I shouldn't be talking about Kat …"

"Don't be sorry, Sarah. We are going through divorce proceedings, or at least we were until I gained ownership of ViaStem. Once she heard that news, everything came to an abrupt stop," Calvin says with concern in his voice.

"Inherited ViaStem?"

"The news has not been made public yet, but the Stevenses have given me full ownership of ViaStem. I met with Ruth Stevens the day of the terrorist attacks. She has decided to end her treatments, so they have given her about six or seven months to live. I met with her team of attorneys, and she and Harold signed the company over to me to continue the dream. Now Kat doesn't want to go anywhere. I have never seen her act like the perfect little wife ever in our marriage. Sarah, it makes me sick. All she wants is power and money. She doesn't even pay attention to Eden anymore. It's all about her now. She's only sticking around for the prestige and hopefully some cash. I don't know what to do. I'm speaking with some very good attorneys, though. I will not subject Eden to this!"

"Calvin, I'm so sorry you are going through this. I'm so sad to hear about Ruth. She is such a sweet lady. This should be such an exciting time for you. How honorable that the Stevens chose you. Congratulations. They chose the perfect person."

"Thanks, but I have a bad feeling, Sarah. A very bad feeling with nothing to back it but a bitch for a wife."

A second knock at the door distracts the two from the eerie conversation.

"Who is it?" Calvin checks before allowing the person to enter.

"It's Dave, Calvin."

"Come on in, Dave."

Dave enters with a puzzled look on his face. "What was that about?"

"Kat just busted in, and it wasn't pretty."

"I understand." Dave averts his attention to Sarah. "Hello, Sarah. How are you? I hear we can expect great things from you with the HESC project. Of course, you always work hard. That's why you're number one."

"Thank you, Dave." Sarah blushes.

"So what's up?"

"This has to be confidential, Dave." Calvin insists.

"Okay. Of course."

"Sarah's husband, Stephen, was sent on his fifth deployment this week. Before he left, he told Sarah that his unit was forced to undergo numerous medical tests, take vaccines, and ingest pills they have never taken before. Well, Stephen hid the pills in his mouth, and Sarah brought them to me to see if we could analyze them. Dr. Hammond was in charge of the testing, Dave."

"What the hell is Hammond doing testing military personnel?"

"I don't know, but I don't like it. He represents ViaStem. I want to know what is going on, and I want to know what these pills are. Can you have one of your buddies at UCLA analyze them as soon as possible?" Calvin hands the bottle to Dave.

"Sure. I don't see a problem. Why not here?"

"I have my suspicions, Dave. Hopefully I'm just being hypersensitive to everything that has happened. I would feel more comfortable having these analyzed off the property."

"I'll get right on it. I will deliver them tonight after work. I'll let you know what I find."

"And, Dave ... I need you to review all financials to see if there is any money allocated for military research and who is providing the funds."

"Got it."

In unison, Calvin and Sarah thank Dave as he exits the office.

"Until we have something to go on, Sarah, it will be business as usual. And you, my dear, will work from home for as long as you need to. I will approve the paperwork for an extended leave of absence."

"Thank you, Calvin. I truly appreciate everything you are doing for me and Stephen. Please let me know if I can help with your situation with Kat. I'm a pretty good listener. I'm so sorry you have to go through this. I really am. Before I go, I have to follow up on something you said earlier."

"About what, Sarah?"

"You said you were suspicious of something and you had a very bad feeling about it. What did you mean?"

Calvin leans forward on his desk with his head in his hands and forcefully rubs his head before sitting up and looking Sarah in the eyes.

"Are you all right?" she asks.

"That's one of the problems. I've been noticing some strange things. I have rashes all the time and the headaches are excruciating. I feel nauseous all the time, Sarah. I keep attributing the symptoms to stress, but I'm not sure anymore."

"What do you mean you're not sure anymore?"

"I-I'm … I'm becoming suspicious of Kat."

"Do you think Kat is making you purposely sick? Do you believe she would make you sick so you will fail as CEO? That wouldn't make sense if she is enjoying the spotlight so much."

"I know it sounds crazy, but yes. I suspect she is making me ill because she thinks she will get everything."

"Oh my God, Calvin. Get out. Get the hell away from her if you think that. That is a pretty serious accusation, but you need to listen to your gut."

"I'm preparing to leave soon. I need to be able to take Eden with me. I can't leave without her, and I can't draw negative attention to ViaStem by being accused of ripping my child from her home."

"Oh, Calvin … this is serious stuff. What can I do to help?"

"Promise me something, Sarah."

"Anything … anything."

"If something happens to me, look at Kat."

"Don't say that, Calvin. Just get the hell away from her."

Calvin checks his watch and lets Sarah know he has a meeting and must go.

Sarah is unsettled by what Calvin has just confided in her, but she listens to him and goes on with business as usual.

Chapter 10:

Be Careful What You Wish

Following the initial headaches, rashes, and nausea, weight loss is another apparent symptom of Calvin's "illness." It becomes more noticeable as his tailored suits begin to hang on his normally tall, athletic stature. Calvin falsifies his symptoms to the company physician, Dr. Jack Hammond, to prevent any leaks of his ailing health to the outside business world, which could prove disastrous for ViaStem. A hostile takeover would be inevitable. In the weeks to follow, Calvin's condition worsens with signs of further weight loss caused by extreme nausea and vomiting, which causes severe dehydration. His rigorous work schedule rapidly disintegrates because of his extreme fatigue. As his health deteriorates further, his symptoms escalate with debilitating headaches and mild sporadic seizures. Dr. Hammond urges Kat to get Calvin to a hospital immediately for proper care rather than attempting to treat him at home. Kat exhibits great love and concern for her husband but lets Dr. Hammond know that Calvin refuses to let his illness go public.

Dr. Hammond takes the initiative and hires a full-time

home health care nurse to help care for Calvin. Kat is livid with Dr. Hammond's decision and vows to take care of her husband secretly at home as Calvin wishes. Calvin's health begins to improve once he has nursing care twenty-four hours per day by someone other than Kat.

To maintain the stability of ViaStem in the fragile state of launching HESC G42, CEO responsibilities are assigned to Dave Perth, corporate financial officer of ViaStem, who fills Calvin's position in secrecy. Excuses are made that Calvin is on continuous business trips to further the advancement of HESC G42. Dave Perth presents outstanding performances for investors, the FDA, the NIH and, the government of the United States.

Even though Calvin is now under continuous medical care and his health seems to be improving, Kat insists on taking time off of work to care for her gravely ill husband. She demands to the home health nurse that she at least prepare his dinners so they can spend some quality time together. The nurse follows Kat's sentimental instructions. Kat grows agitated with having a stranger live in her home and having Eden see her father so ill. Therefore she arranges to transfer Calvin to their luxurious cabin located in Big Bear, California, the following week. Kat's next set of instructions to the current nurse is, "You're fired." That gives Kat less than a week to care for him by herself.

A new full-time nurse will reside at the cabin while Kat returns to work to squash rumors of Calvin's declining health. Kat believes the cabin will be an environment that will bring comfort and relaxation to Calvin without the stress of ViaStem hanging over him. Calvin disagrees now that he is beginning to feel better. His gut-wrenching stomachaches and excruciating headaches have significantly subsided. But when Kat wants something her way, she gets it. Eventually Calvin agrees to go for a short period of relaxation toward recovery. In his mind, he feels safer away from his wife.

Within three days of the decision to transfer Calvin to the cabin and the firing of the home health nurse, Calvin's health declines again. He is now covered with skin manifestations and is also experiencing blinding headaches. The severe gastrointestinal illnesses have also returned, causing severe and frequent vomiting and diarrhea, which leads Calvin into a state faltering between semi-consciousness and unconsciousness caused by dehydration. Kat prepares her car to transport Calvin to his new and temporary home at their mountainous retreat to heal and recover from his aliments. Their journey begins at dusk to prevent anyone from seeing Calvin in his state of decay. The drive to the cabin is supposed to last approximately two to three hours, depending on traffic. Dr. Hammond insists on arranging for an ambulance to transport Calvin, but Kat vehemently insists otherwise. As usual, she gets her way.

Calvin's last wish to Dr. Hammond is to not let this go public, no matter what. He warns that the news would be devastating to ViaStem's longevity and the end of Harold Stevens's dream.

As dusk arrives, Kat assists Calvin into her 2012 Lexus with the help of the new nurse, who will be residing at the cabin and caring for Calvin. She will arrive later in the evening so that she can have her own transportation. Dr. Hammond sees the couple off and gives Kat a warm hug as she weeps with concern for her husband. He has an uneasy feeling in his gut.

After losing contact with Calvin once he grew ill, Sarah continues to try to reach Kat via phone to follow up on

Calvin's health, but her calls go unanswered. Sarah reaches out to Dr. Hammond, but he insists Calvin is recovering well. With no return phone calls, Sarah is deeply concerned about Calvin's health and safety after he disclosed to her Kat's odd behavior surrounding his health. Sarah finally goes to their home and finds it dark and empty. Her fear for Calvin's life mounts.

When the couple drives off, once they are out of sight, Kat's demeanor toward Calvin turns abusive. Calvin is in a semi-state of consciousness as he tries to balance a hefty bag of frothy mucous between his legs while he can barely hold up his head.

"Goddamnit, Cal. Can you close that bag? It fucking stinks in here. Or put your window down," Kat demands. She covers her mouth and nose with a cloth in pure disgust of her husband. Calvin continues vomiting and having bouts of dry heaving. He is also exhibiting an obvious fever with extreme chills. Kat refuses to close the windows to provide some warmth for him, stating the vulgar smell may cause her to pass out.

"That fucking stench will kill me, so the windows stay open," Kat rants cruelly.

They finally arrive at the cabin to the great relief to Calvin and to the selfish relief of Kat.

"That was the worst, most painfully disgusting drive of my life. Let me get rid of your vomit bag so it doesn't spill in my car. The stench is overpowering." Kat exits the car, exaggerating near suffocation by deeply inhaling and exhaling while bent over with her hands on her knees. "Fuck. That was absolutely disgusting. I'm so glad to be rid of him. I just couldn't do this at home any longer," she says to herself.

As quickly as she can, she hustles around the Lexus to

retrieve the trash bag of vomit and discards it in the garbage container. "One piece of trash gone. And now for the other," Kat spouts aloud to herself and in reach of Calvin's ears, if he were coherent.

Once inside the cabin, Kat's behavior changes to a caring, loving wife as Calvin becomes more alert. It is difficult for her to portray the loving wife much longer. Her nasty, evil personality bleeds through the pretty cover.

"Let me help you, honey," she coos as she leads him to the bed, which is set up by the fireplace with a fire already ablaze. "Look, honey, a nice warm fire for you to rest by." She helps him into a hospital bed.

She then goes to the refrigerator to retrieve a bottle of Gatorade and pours it in a glass over ice. She inserts a straw to make it easier for Calvin to drink. "Here you go, honey. Now I want you to drink this. You need your fluids," she says as she holds the straw to Calvin's mouth for him to sip. He coughs after swallowing the liquid and complains of a severe burning in his throat. Then he fades off to sleep.

Kat grabs her purse, locks the door behind her, and stirs rocks up behind her Lexus as she speeds home. "Thank God it's over!" Kat smiles.

Within the week, Calvin is dead.

As promised, Sarah alerts Warren of the oddities surrounding the mysterious illness and sudden death of Calvin Giovanni, the replacement for H.L. Stevens and the new CEO of ViaStem. Sarah informs Warren that Dave Perth, the corporate financial officer for ViaStem is next in line as CEO and somehow Kat is, unimaginably, the new CEO of ViaStem Biotechnology and Genetics Corporation. She asks Warren for his help in finding the truth.

Warren confers with the company physician about the

symptoms that led to Calvin's death. Poisoning is discussed because of the current facts. Both suspect arsenic when looking at his illness in hindsight. Dr. Hammond, filled with guilt for not acting on his instincts, informs Warren that arsenic is metabolized by the liver into a natural compound, which makes it untraceable. However, traces do remain in the hair, urine, and nails. "If we can get a sample, that could be evidence," he says.

With Kat citing religious beliefs, Calvin's body is immediately cremated per request of his loving wife. No burial, just a short service for the opportunity to announce his replacement. There is no autopsy or questions asked and certainly no questions answered. Kat plunges into the corporate world as the new CEO of ViaStem while Dave Perth is relieved of his duties. Questions are asked, but none are answered.

Warren portrays himself as an assistant to the San Diego medical examiner in order to conduct a follow-up interview with Katarina Fortunata-Giovanni. She will only agree to meet him in front of her home, which she now has up for sale.

"Hello, Mrs. Giovanni," greets Walter McClery as he flashes his identification.

"My name is Katarina Fortunata," she cordially greets him. "Please call me Kat. I don't have much time, Mr. McClery. I must get back to work. I'm the new CEO of ViaStem Biotechnology and Genetics Corporation, and there is much work to do," she boasts.

"I guess congratulations for you are in order, and I will keep it brief. I just have a few questions," Warren insists. "Wasn't your husband, Calvin Giovanni, CEO prior to his death?" he questions. He already knows the answer, but he is profiling her behavior.

"Yes, but I worked closely with him and Mr. Stevens; therefore I am the best person for the job now," Kat arrogantly boasts again.

"According to Dr. Hammond at ViaStem, upon your insistence, Calvin refused to go to a hospital for care that it may raise public concern. Is this true?"

"Well, actually, I tried many times to get Calvin to seek proper care, but he insisted his illness remain in the strictest of confidence, Mr. McClery, for investors and the company's public image."

"I see, Mrs. Giovanni."

"Excuse me," Kat abruptly interrupts. "It is Ms. Fortunata, not Giovanni."

"Oh, pardon me, ma'am. Mrs. Fortunata, when did your husband's illness begin, and what were his initial symptoms?"

"It's Ms., sir. Calvin started getting stomachaches and headaches almost immediately following his acceptance of the position of CEO of ViaStem, and he just got sicker from that point on with really no recovery, obviously," Kat rants, obviously irritated by his mispronunciations of her name.

"What were his symptoms, Ms. Fortunata?" McClery interrogates her, knowing something suspicious is going on. He notices Kat begins to fidget.

"He had, like I already said, stomachaches, headaches, vomiting, diarrhea, and rashes," Kat callously responds, getting very impatient.

Observing Kat's nervous behaviors, Warren slows the interrogation. "How did you take care of him if he didn't go to a hospital?"

"I waited on him hand and foot, prepared mainly soups, and he mostly drank tea and Gatorade to increase his electrolytes," Kat says in a very frustrated voice.

"So let's review this once more …" McClery continues but gets cut off by Kat.

"Look, Calvin got very sick, and he wanted to go to our cabin in Big Bear to try to recover from whatever it is that he had. I did the best I could. I'm not a doctor, and he didn't want one, and if you are one of the several people who do not believe I should be in his position as CEO, well you are wrong. I have gone to great lengths to earn this position, more than you will ever know. Now I must go. Good-bye, Mr. McClery," Kat growls defensively. She gets into a rental car and squeals away.

Warren immediately calls Sarah to arrange a meeting. They meet in a parking lot at a local shopping mall and sit in Warren's car.

"What did you find out? Did she act strange?"

"Yes, she was acting very nervous and strange, offering way too much information for someone as smart as she is supposed to be," Warren states. "She now goes by Ms. Katarina Fortunata. She got extremely defensive when I asked about her husband's illness and death and drove away in a rental car."

"Did she sound at all caring about Calvin's illness and death?"

"Not one bit, Sarah," Warren replies. "We need more information, but from what she divulged, I would suspect he was poisoned. I met with Dr. Hammond as well, and there are so many clues in hindsight."

"Oh my God … This is horrible. Oh my God. Poor Calvin,"

Sarah expresses sadly. "Do you think she did this? Did she kill him?"

"I'm definitely suspicious and expect she is involved, but I think there is more to this ..."

"Like what? Who? Why?"

"I have several questions I need answers to. For instance, I would like a sample of the Gatorade she said she frequently fed him. It is often used as a cover for ethylene glycol poisoning. Gatorade is sweet and sugary and covers the taste, something he might not question in his state. Ideally I would like to get a good look at their home as well as the cabin, as they are possible crime scenes. I would like a sample of his vomit and stool for testing, especially if there is any blood in his stool. Unfortunately, the cremation took care of most of the concrete evidence that would have led us directly to the cause of death. I want to know what the plan was ... Why did he slowly get sick, then improve, and then get sick again? Then why did they go off to the cabin? To be finished off? I'm going back to the cabin; maybe they haven't thoroughly cleaned it, although that is highly unlikely. I might find some trace evidence. I'll then try to get into their home."

"I want to go," Sarah says.

"Absolutely not. There is something malevolent going on, and I suspect it possibly involves more than just Kat. I don't want you in any danger. Do you understand, Sarah?" scolds Warren.

"Danger, schmanger. I want to go!"

"No, and that's final, Sarah! This is not a game. I want you here to keep your ears and eyes open. I need you as an informant. I need you here," Warren says, playing to Sarah's need for involvement. "And, Sarah, don't do anything on your own. This could be extremely dangerous," he adds to try to put a little fear in Sarah.

"Warren, I didn't mean to get you involved in something like this …," she states, knowing she has involved Warren in a very precarious situation.

"I know that, Sarah, but I am now involved. I will let you know what I find."

Sarah kisses him on the cheek, exits his car, and offers a wave as she pulls away in her own vehicle.

Warren immediately drives to Big Bear and only has to ask a few people for directions to the Giovanni cabin. Big Bear is a small, mountainous community where everyone knows everyone. Warren reaches the cabin with some daylight left. He parks clear from view of the cabin and conducts a stakeout for about one hour. It is desolate. Driving to the entrance of the driveway, Warren parks. He puts on a pair of latex surgical gloves to pick up any evidence and avoid leaving any fingerprints. He also carries a small flashlight and a few bags to hold evidence, which he prays he finds.

As Warren exits his car and walks up the driveway, he passes the garbage cans and catches the stench of something foul. He opens the first can and finds one large green trash bag releasing the pungent odor of bile. It smells of vomit. He takes the bag. He walks the evidence down to his car and places it into a large cooler in his trunk before returning to the cabin.

All the doors and windows are locked, and everything is dark. He goes to the rear of the cabin and picks the lock allowing entry into the cabin. Upon opening the door, he is overcome with the smell of bleach. Warren is now discouraged about finding any viable evidence. With his flashlight on, he scans the premises. Most of the rooms have been cleaned, so he doesn't expect to find much. The cabin is neat and orderly, with a stack of firewood still arranged by the enormous stone fireplace. While standing by the fireplace, Warren smells an odd odor, but it is one he can't quite place. He gets a salty taste in his mouth, and his throat begins to burn. He immediately concentrates on the wood.

He takes a scraping of ashes from inside the flue of the fireplace and then takes some bark from the area of the woodpile outside, where he discovers several dead rats. He looks into the refrigerator but discovers nothing. It is spotlessly clean and has been disinfected. He investigates the bathroom, which is nearly spotless except for a single pubic hair wedged tightly under the toilet bowl. *I hope this is his,* Warren thinks.

He returns to the open area where Calvin's bed was possibly located and sprays luminal as he backs out the cabin's rear door. When he turns off his flashlight, he sees a spotlessly clean floor. He flashes his light around the cabin once more. To the lay person, one would never know someone had just died here.

Warren walks back to his car, where he is met by a stranger. "Hello," greets Warren, on high alert.

"Hi. I live just over there and saw you putting your trash into your car, and I just want to let you know that pickup is tomorrow morning. Because of the strike, they're a couple days late," offers the neighbor.

"Thanks, but my wife and I were visiting with Kat and Calvin last week and she lost a good set of earrings. I promised I would find them, considering I think I accidently threw them away. I want to get out of the doghouse, if you know what I mean," Warren explains humorously.

"That's a shame about Calvin. He was a good guy," responds the neighbor.

"Yes, he was. He will be missed," says Warren. "Did you know them very well?"

"No. Everyone is pretty private up here. Although in the past week there have been many visitors and much activity. I guess people are paying their respects," the neighbor replies as he turns to return home. "Well, you have a good night."

"Hey, thanks," Warren closes the conversation and heads home.

Before going home, he delivers all the evidence to a good friend from his navy days, Dr. Joe Morrow, who is now the director of the forensics department for the FBI in San Diego. Joe agrees to work all night if need be to return the results to McNary as soon as possible.

The next day, Joe comes through with the results, and they are astonishing. They reveal to Warren a possible conspiracy in progress. Mr. Stevens was killed in the terrorist attacks, and now Calvin has been murdered and his "loving" wife is CEO of a major biotech company that just launched a world-class cloning procedure to cure the incurable, which is already worth trillions, according to investors.

In private, Joe reveals his findings to Warren. "The cause of Calvin's death is poisoning, and the weapon is ingested arsenic and CCA pressure-treated wood, which has incredibly high concentrations of arsenic. The incineration of such wood is illegal, and it is impossible to purchase. Unless, of course, you are the government."

According to Dr. Morrow, the wood delivered to the cabin had to be CCA to account for Calvin's exposure to such high levels of arsenic. Dr. Morrow informs Warren that further research using X-ray fluorescence spectrometry can verify these conclusions.

"Sadly, this man died a painfully horrible death that was initially slow through ingestion and then for some reason was sped up to hasten his death with the inhalation of the arsenic in the wood. There is no way she did this on her own."

At this point, Warren has all the evidence he needs from the cabin. Now he needs to find a way to get into Ms. Fortunata's home.

Chapter 11:

Without A Trace

Within days of breaking and entering into the Giovanni's cabin, Warren McNary receives a highly classified call about Lieutenant Commander Stephen Benton and SEAL Team ONE from a source within the Pentagon.

"No names. Calling from outside the walls. Not much time. Listen carefully," relays the Pentagon source.

"Understood," confirms McNary.

"Information about your request."

"Yes, go ahead."

"Afghanistan. Four bodies and five Dog Tags. Burned. Three confirmed by DNA. One unconfirmed. Too badly burned. One missing. No identification of key subject other than tag recovered at site."

"Status?"

"Presumed KIA. Possible cover-up."

"Go on," affirms McNary.

"Actual date of discovery nine-twenty-twelve. Public knowledge eleven-two-twelve. New tags issued. No remains. Highly Classified."

"Notification?"

"Tomorrow."

"Watch your back," the caller signs off.

"What the hell is going on?" Warren asks aloud while sitting in his car. "Shit, I need to figure this out quickly. Most of SEAL Team ONE was burned, but Stephen is unconfirmed. One missing. Listed as KIA. Mission dates changed. All so sketchy. Why the cover-up? Who's behind it? Were they killed by an enemy within? I can't have Sarah receive this news from strangers."

Chapter 12:

False Hope

Because of the terrorist acts occurring the same day of Stephen's deployment, now more than three months ago, Warren is keenly aware of Sarah's sadness and loneliness. He calls almost daily to check on her. She is always grateful to hear his voice, knowing he has a busy schedule investigating the latest attacks on American soil. It offers her some solace knowing Warren is still in San Diego.

One day he calls Sarah to ask if he can come by to visit with her.

"I would love that, Warren. I miss you," Sarah responds happily.

"I'll see you soon," replies Warren.

Sarah senses something alarming in his normally calm voice. Within the hour there is a knock at her front door. She knows it is Warren and excitedly hops up from the couch to answer it, with Cooper yapping closely behind her. To her surprise, a military chaplain and Stephen's commander are standing in the doorway, with a military vehicle as their backdrop. Sarah's heart sinks. She is fully aware what this means to a military spouse. Stephen is dead. Stephen has been killed in action. Stephen is missing. Stephen is never coming home to her. There seems to be endless silence between the men and Sarah. She doesn't want to hear them speak. She doesn't want to face their dreadful news. She wants to scream but cannot find her voice.

Warren pulls up directly behind the white car and quickly exits his vehicle, knowing he has missed his opportunity to comfort Sarah as she hears the worst news of her life from strangers. Sarah pushes past the two officers and runs into Warren's outstretched arms. Warren holds Sarah tightly as she falls to her knees, screaming, "No no no! Not Stephen! Not my Stephen! It was his last time!" Sarah cries violently as she gasps for air, deeply shaken by the implications. Her body shakes with fear, and her mind is clouded with disbelief.

Letting Sarah just weep, Warren continues to hold her tightly and tries to comfort and sooth her. With one hand, he waves the officers away. When she calms, Warren helps her up and leads her into the house. He has a flashback of walking behind the newly married couple as Stephen carried Sarah over the threshold, laughing and kissing her. He forces himself to try to remain focused on the present situation. After helping Sarah to the couch, he gets her a glass of water. He wishes he had something much stronger for himself before telling Sarah the worst news possible.

"Sarah, Stephen is missing. Some of his men's remains have been identified," Warren sadly and regrettably informs her.

"No, Warren. It can't be. Oh my God, not my dear Stephen. He always comes home to me … always. I don't know how to live without him, Warren." Sarah weeps as she holds on tightly to Warren's shirt. Taking a deep breath, she regains her composure and looks deeply into Warren's eyes for answers, guidance ... something—anything. But she finds nothing. With inner strength, she asks for the entire truth from Warren.

Now Warren needs to take a deep breath. He knows this is going to be difficult, but he knows he cannot tell her much because it will endanger her after the phone call he received yesterday.

"Sarah ... this is going to be very difficult to hear. Are you sure you want to do this right now?"

"Yes, Warren. It won't bring Stephen back, but I need to know ... I need to know," Sarah chokes to get her words out.

Warren responds with as much compassion as he can muster. In a shaky voice, he says, "Sarah, Stephen and his unit disappeared the first week of their deployment."

Sarah covers her mouth in dismay.

"I will not be able to elaborate because much of this is classified and is still under investigation. Only three of five bodies were identified. They were badly burned, Sarah. They could not identify all of Stephen's men. There are no remains."

Sarah weeps at the thought of her husband being burned to death. She will never be able to put him to rest with a proper burial. Her tears seem endless. "Where, Warren? Where were they found?"

"In a cave in Afghanistan."

Sarah leans forward in pain. "He must have been so alone. Oh my God. He was burned to death. No. My poor Stephen and his men. Oh my God, no ... Stephen burned ... No, I can't believe that." Sarah lowers her head and holds her hands over her ears, trying not to hear this horror.

Knowing he is about to commit the biggest lie he's ever told, he says, "Sarah. Sarah, stop." He can't bear her sadness and grief.

Sarah calms herself and searches Warren's eyes for answers once again.

"Sarah, Stephen's toe tag was found but not him. One man is not accounted for. So there is hope." *How can I give her such false hope?* Warren shamefully thinks to himself.

"Hope … So he may be alive? Maybe he got away and is hiding? I will hold on to that, Warren. Can I please get it back, Warren? Stephen's tag … please?"

Removing Stephen's lone dog tag from an envelope, Warren hands it to Sarah and prays he won't have to answer any questions about Stephen's body, knowing there isn't one.

Sarah holds Stephen's charred tag ever so gently. She breaks down crying and pulls the tag close to her heart, rocking back and forth as she feels her heart shatter into a million pieces. As she stares at the only remaining piece of her husband, a single tear falls onto the blackened tag, causing a light gray stream of sadness. Warren sets the envelope on the table and sits with Sarah, comforting her as much as possible during this devastating period in both their lives.

Barely able to speak, Sarah weeps, "I want my Stephen back, Warren …"

"I know, sweetie. I know," Warren responds sadly, knowing these are just words that mean nothing to Sarah at this moment in her life. She is truly overcome with disbelief and pain.

"Until I know for certain, I will consider Stephen alive. I must." Sarah whimpers, barely able to speak.

"I hope and pray Stephen comes home to you, Sarah. He will come home, just not yet," Warren says—another lie he should not tell but does just to offer brief comfort. He knows Stephen may never come home to her. He had just gambled with Sarah's heart—the biggest gamble of his life.

Chapter 13:

The Abyss

Sadness overwhelms Sarah, but she struggles to find some joys such as hiking the mountains alone or walking in her neighborhood with Cooper, watching children play happily without a care in the world. She spends time with Rudy and Rio because they have an uncanny calming effect on her psyche. These activities offer a small bit of comfort during this dismal time in her life. Sarah desperately misses Warren, who is back in Washington, D.C., for a while before he will return to continue the terrorism investigation.

Sarah's patriotic beliefs allow her to be happy and proud that her husband fought for America's freedom, but another part of her desperately aches with sadness of the cruel reminder that she will never have Stephen home again. She will never have a family with him. She is truly alone.

Sarah waves at her neighbors' young children playing in their front yard as she pulls her 530i over to retrieve her mail. She feels exhausted, and every muscle in her body feels heavy, especially her heart. She sluggishly gets out of her car and walks to the community mailbox. It's within walking distance to her home, but these days she drives everywhere to avoid contact with people. She cannot bear having to talk about this with anyone, not even her mom. She isolates herself.

Operating like a robot, she inserts her key and opens the four-by-four inch box to discover only junk mail. Alone in her world, she slowly removes the mail and stares at the ads, but she doesn't see any words. She doesn't care. As she turns to return to her car, the two young boys who were playing in the nearby front yard look up at her with adorable smiles of missing teeth. She cannot help but smile back at their sweet, innocent faces.

"Hi, Mrs. Sarah. I made a drawing for you to hang on your frigerator," Sammy gleefully greets her as he jumps up and down on his tiptoes.

Before Sarah can say anything his twin brother, Stevie, chimes in, "I made you one too! *See!* It's Cooper," he exclaims, proudly displaying his work of art.

Competitively, Sammy chimes in, "Oh, oh! Mine is Mr. Stephen. See! He is in his uniform, with lots of medals. He is a hero," he says as he holds up his drawing with outstretched arms so Sarah can see. Some of Stephen's body parts are stick figures, and some take on the appearance of sausages.

Sarah bites her lip to avoid melting down in front of the two four-year-old boys. She kneels down to their level and gives them each a warm hug, not wanting to let go. She gratefully takes their beautiful drawings and knows she will treasure them forever.

"Thank you so very much, boys. I will place them next to all of your other wonderful drawings. I just love them. They are wonderful," she says with tears in her eyes.

Within a second, the two little boys skip off to play again.

Sarah stands admiring the drawings that have brought a rare smile to her face.

"Excuse me? Hello?" a deep British accent startles Sarah back to reality.

"Oh, excuse me. I'm so sorry. I guess I'm blocking your mailbox," Sarah says with embarrassment. She and the man both try to move by each other only to move in the same direction. They laugh a bit.

"Hello. I am your new neighbor, Cole Blackman. I moved into the house across the street from you, the one that was for rent," the man introduced himself, extending his hand to Sarah.

Sarah hesitates but then shakes his hand. She has become withdrawn since the news of Stephen's presumed death. The military has yet to offer any explanations or the return of his body.

Shyly Sarah introduces herself. "Hi, I'm Sarah Benton. Welcome to the neighborhood. You will like it here. It's a nice place to live." She pauses, looking down at the drawings just given to her and feeling weak and lightheaded, "I must go. Nice meeting you, Mr. Blackman."

"You too, and please call me Cole," he says as he smiles warmly at her and gently releases her hand.

Sarah nervously turns and walks back to her car. Her heart races wildly. She feels her heartbeat in her throat. Sarah dares to look back to find Cole Blackman still watching her with a smile on his face. She returns a shy smile, gets into her car, and drives home. After pulling into the garage, she automatically closes the door. She is alone.

Months go by. Sarah slips into an abyss of depression, and she is desperate to escape its grasp. Her loneliness is torturing.

She tries fighting her sadness by forcing herself to walk Cooper to get the mail. Some mornings, forcing herself to get out of bed is the most difficult event of her day. Robotically, Sarah walks to the mailboxes with Cooper and opens her four-by-four inch slot. Today she pulls out a few sympathy cards and a thick stack of bills and junk mail. She realizes it has been a several days since she last collected her mail, which means another week of her life has gone by and she wasn't aware of the time. She reacts with tears before she can even remove all the wasted paper from the box. Trying not to cry outside her home, she hears a voice from behind her.

"Hello, Sarah Benton," greets Cole.

Sarah quickly collects herself, wiping her tears while slowly turning to face him. She notices he has his hand extended once again to shake hers. She hesitates, feeling a bit uncomfortable. She is out of the safety of the walls of her house. She becomes embarrassed and feels more tears coming as blood rushes to her face, making her flushed. Reaching her hand out, Sarah shyly says, "Hello, Mr. Blackman—I mean Cole. I apologize for being such a bad neighbor … I should have brought you some cookies or someth—"

Cole senses that Sarah is uncomfortable about something, but he isn't sure what, so he gently takes her hand and returns the hello in an attempt to steady her quivering fear. "Stop, Sarah. I'm not trying to make you feel guilty. I just never see you around."

Sarah quickly looks down. Fighting tears, she responds in a wavering voice, "Um … I-I have so much going on right now. I'm not very good company …" Pulling away, she continues, "I have to go now. I hope you are getting settled in, Cole." Sarah quickly turns and walks briskly back toward her home. "Come on, Cooper."

"I will take that as a good sign," responds Cole.

"What? Excuse me?" Puzzled, Sarah turns to look back at Cole, who is still standing by the mailboxes.

Smiling warmly, he says, "You called me Cole instead of Mr. Blackman."

Not really knowing how to respond to his remark, Sarah shyly says, "Well, okay. You are easy to please. I guess I owe you some cookies. Okay?"

As he starts to walk toward his house, he smiles and waves. "No pressure, but I love chocolate chip."

Sarah feels distracted as a rare smile comes across her face. "Good-bye, Mr. Blackman."

Shaking his head and laughing, he waves again. "Good-bye, Ms. Benton … for now."

Sarah smiles nervously and walks toward her house. She continues to walk forward but dares to look back. Cole stands still, watching her and smiling. Sarah snags the curb with the toe of her shoe and nearly trips but quickly catches herself. "Cooper!" she exclaims, trying to blame him. Completely embarrassed, she quickly walks forward again, shaking her head and laughing at herself.

It feels good to laugh, even if it is just at herself. Before entering through the garage door, Sarah dares herself to look back once again. Cole is slowly making his way toward his house but watches and smiles warmly at her. She enters her house, filled with distant sensations. It has been so long since she has felt anything, so it feels good to laugh and feel warm inside.

Sarah hates baking, but it is the first thing she does upon entering her home. It helps occupy her mind instead of the sad thoughts that have embedded themselves in her mind and soul since Steven's disappearance. Digging through her nearly bare cupboards, she finds a box of chocolate chip cookie mix. *Thank goodness it only requires one egg, a quarter cup of oil, and water*, she thinks, because that is all she has in her refrigerator besides two apples, half a gallon of OJ, some cottage cheese, and one small can of V8.

Before delivering the fresh cookies to her new neighbor, Sarah freshens up, wiping cookie dough from her chin and taking a Klonopin before leaving her house. She feels her stomach rumble. "Butterflies."

Carrying freshly baked chocolate chip cookies, she walks slowly across the street, trying to be a bit more graceful than her walk home earlier today. Without Sarah having to knock, the door opens.

"Hello, Ms. Benton," Cole greets Sarah with a welcoming smile.

Sarah hands Cole the cookies, purposely flashing him her Irish trinity knot wedding band. "Hi, Cole. Welcome officially to the neighborhood," she adds, handing him the treats.

He holds the door open for Sarah and says, "Please, come in."

Sarah notices that Cole is wearing an Irish Claddagh ring with the crown reaching away from his heart, meaning he belongs to someone special. For some odd reason, this gives her comfort. "Oh I can't. I have to—"

"No, no. Not this time," he objects. "Please join me for dinner. It's simple, just a barbeque. I have too much food for just me. Come on, just for a short time?"

Sarah has no plans to eat dinner, but she hesitates before accepting his rather innocent invitation. She believes she should pull away from Cole, but instead she agrees. "All right, but just for a little while."

She cautiously enters Cole's house and slows down to look at several framed photographs he has laid out on the counter in the kitchen. "Is this your family, Cole?"

"Yes, that is my family. My wife and daughter were killed by a drunk driver five years ago. She was Irish like you," he said, pointing to Sarah's wedding band. "She gave me this as a gift, and I can't seem to take it off," he adds, referring to his own ring.

"Cole, I am so very sorry."

To change the subject, Cole says, "Hey, let's go sit outside on the back patio. It's a lovely evening." He shows Sarah the way. "Why don't you make yourself comfortable and I'll get you a glass of wine or a beer?"

Relaxing a bit, Sarah says, "I would love a glass of chardonnay if you have any ... or a beer?"

"Coming right up."

As Sarah sits by the fire pit and enjoys the warmth of the flames, she cannot stop a loop of memories of Stephen from running through her mind. She reminisces about their many barbeques together on their patio and how they would giggle and laugh with each other like it was their first date. She smiles as she remembers how Stephen would insist on wearing the full apron and chef's hat covered in red chili peppers, which always made her laugh. Now it brings tears to her eyes. Cole enters the patio area carrying two glasses of wine, one chardonnay and one merlot.

As he hands Sarah her glass of wine, he notices tears welling in her eyes. "What's wrong?"

"I'm sorry. This is embarrassing. I thought I was ready to be out in public, but I guess not. There are so many things that bring back memories of Stephen, my husband." Sarah gestures to the barbeque, the fire pit, the wine, and the entire backyard. "He has been missing in Afghanistan for five months now. They have determined him killed in action, but I have no body to bury. He was a Navy SEAL." Sarah lowers her head in sadness and possibly guilt. "I shouldn't be here. I have to go. I'm sorry."

"Stop. Please sit. I am truly sorry for your loss, but I do understand many of the feelings you are going through, Sarah, and it is okay to be here," Cole responds compassionately.

Sarah takes the glass of wine with a trembling hand. She holds the glass with both hands to steady it. She takes a few sips and tries to relax. She wipes her tears away with a tissue Cole gives to her. "Thank you Cole. I'm sorry."

"Please don't apologize."

"Cole … I …" Sarah breaks into tears. "I better go. I'm so sorry."

Cole sits next to Sarah, takes her glass of wine, and places it on the patio table. Then he takes her hands in his. "Sarah, it is okay to cry and be sad. You have suffered an incredible loss. Look at me, Sarah. I want to be your friend."

Sarah can only nod as she tries to lock every tear inside. He takes Sarah in his arms and just holds her and lets her cry. She wants to resist, but she cannot.

Over the next few weeks Sarah and Cole build a trusting friendship with no pressures and no strings. Sarah finds it difficult to deal with the guilt she feels at having a close friendship with Cole, but she also feels safe for the first time in months. It feels good to laugh and smile. He is a great escape. They spend their time together talking about their careers, more hers than his, and life and laughing and sharing their happy and sad feelings about their families that they never dare talk about with others, not even Warren. They spend time barbequing, walking Copper, watching movies, and playing tennis. Their newest event is golf.

Sarah reminisces in silence about the many times she and Stephen spent playing golf and how much fun they had, but instead of burying her feelings, she now shares them with Cole.

Laughing whimsically, she teases, "Oh my goodness. Please spare me the drama, Cole. I'm glad you have a day job, because your golf game leaves little to be desired. Let's see you sink this putt, Mr. Blackman," she challenges. "I'll bet you five bucks. Are you up for it?"

"Why of course, my lovely Sarah, but only five?"

"My lovely, huh?" she says, teasing Cole about the most overly used word in his vocabulary, which she absolutely adores. "I up the bet to ten dollars and dinner. How about that?" Sarah giggles as she takes a drink of beer. She is sitting in the golf cart with her legs propped up on the dash. "Oh … wait. I need to up the bet. I could use a new golf outfit." She puts on a big smile and poses.

"Here we go again. It's always about the clothes, isn't it, Sarah?" Cole laughs.

"Well, you know I only like the game for the clothes. Have you learned nothing about me, Cole?" Sarah toys with him.

"What? The clothes and not my delightful company?" Cole sounds crushed.

"Oh please. Forgive me, but of course your company is the priority."

"But of course, my dear. You are so full of shit." He laughs.

They both sit in the golf cart, drinking their beers and laughing. Cole gets out of the cart and sinks the putt with a very cocky, proud look on his face. He turns and bows to Sarah. "You owe me dinner and ten bucks, my love."

Following their comically competitive game of golf, Cole and Sarah stop by the local market and head directly to the butcher to select their steaks. Cole then heads to the liquor section to choose a nice bottle of Merlot, and Sarah heads to the vegetable section to select fresh toppings for a healthy salad. The two friends pull into Sarah's driveway and have a fun barbeque.

The only stress Sarah has is the stress she continues to place on herself. In everything she has done in the days following Stephen's disappearance, she interjects some guilt into the picture. She questions herself on whether or not she should be enjoying her new friendship with Cole. Should she have Cole in their home? Sarah finds comfort in talking with Cole about Stephen's life and death without feeling threatened by any infringements on her personal space. For the first time in months she feels calm and safe again. She feels happiness again. As harmless as their friendship is, Sarah questions herself, *Should I still be mourning Stephen in solitude?*

Chapter 14:

Girls' Day Out

It has now been more than seven months since Sarah learned of Stephen's disappearance. Still reeling from the lack of answers surrounding Stephen and his unit of men, she remains in disbelief that he is dead. She is now conducting her own investigation without Warren's knowledge. She is obsessed with finding the answers behind her husband's disappearance.

During their weekly calls, she and Warren talk about anything and most everything except for Cole and her aching need for answers. Sensing this before the end of each call, Warren reminds Sarah how important it is to keep him updated on any key information she discovers and insists she is not to get involved because of the danger.

Stephen's only charred dog tag returned to her by Warren on the awful day that still seems like just yesterday, Calvin's strange death and accusations regarding Kat's possible involvement, and finally President Cannon awarding the Purple Heart to Stephen posthumously weigh heavily on her.

"Why did this take so long after his disappearance?" she asks herself. "They considered him dead a long time ago. The other men received awards long ago. So many questions. So much red tape! So much bullshit!" Sarah says angrily.

She truly believes she has no other options other than to get fully entrenched in this mystery and seek her own answers. "I've been living in the dark for much too long, and I need to find peace in order to move forward in my life."

Feeling stronger and healthier every day from spending time with Warren, Cole, and her friend, Laura, helps her not to dwell in her sadness and makes Sarah feel confident in her personal covert mission to find the truth.

Her dining room table now resembles a giant jigsaw puzzle of time lines—from the time Stephen left on deployment on Sept. 11, 2012 to present-day, March 2013. Included are the many additionally suspicious events that occurred during that time frame. Standing at the edge of the table, reviewing the numerous pieces of evidence, Sarah studies specific time frames and evidence. She rearranges the data according to how she believes it was planned and implemented and then by the outcomes.

Colorful sticky notes of clues and questions written in Sarah's handwriting are scattered throughout the room, along with newspaper clippings, Warren's notes, Dr. Hammond's briefs surrounding Calvin's death, Dave Perth's brief on the pills Stephen was taking, Warren's FBI friend's report on the trace evidence she copied from Warren's briefcase during dinner one night, and mounds of other evidence of events that continue to go unsolved.

Sarah rubs her tired eyes and continues to stare at Warren's FBI friend's report. *I wish I could make sense of all of this. Shit!* Sarah vents her frustrations.

The only evidence that Stephen is alive is one dog tag, which Sarah learned from Warren is a toe tag that was discovered in a cave in Afghanistan. The badly burned tag gives Sarah hope that Stephen is still alive and surviving in the harsh elements of the violent country. The ambiguity of the circumstances of events ignites her drive for more answers. She has difficulty saying the word *death*. The thought of Stephen being gone from her life is incomprehensible.

Sarah allows no one, especially Warren, into the dining area, which she can—thankfully—hide behind pocket doors. She dares not reveal the obsession she has hidden in the room between the kitchen and the formal living room. The blinds are closed, and the house is dark. All the doors are bolted. "I am on my own," she says.

Engrossed by the enormity of events in front of her, she notices something new, something unfamiliar in her collection—a picture of Mr. H.L. Stevens and Calvin at the ribbon-cutting ceremony of ViaStem. The hairs on the back of Sarah's neck stand upright. Goose bumps spread like a firestorm over her body. The air feels stale and thick, making it difficult for her to breathe. She has to sit to stop the room from spinning.

She forcefully rubs between her eyes to prevent the migraine that is certain to follow. She is stunned, frozen in the moment. Her mind races, but she cannot remember putting the photo in her collection. "I have never seen this photo before ... ever." She is certain of that.

She leans forward with her elbows on her knees and rests her head in her hands. She examines the floor around the table and thinks about when she and Stephen put in that flooring . She can see him in her mind. It was a tough yet fun project that they did as a team. They argued about this and that, but they mostly laughed and shared precious memories together. She recalls how they kept the room barren for a couple weeks before replacing the furniture so they could share romantic dances and indoor picnics that always led to romantic lovemaking on several scattered oversized pillows. Sarah now realizes how precious her time with Stephen was. She is so very grateful for the memories. They bring a rare smile to her face while pulling at her heart.

She stares into nothing but air, but she sees and hears Stephen talking and laughing as he walks through the dining room and outside to hang out on the patio and share the stories of their days while drinking a couple of ice-cold Fat Tire beers. Sarah gets up from the chair and retraces his same steps. She opens the sliding door and steps out onto the patio. The sun is bright, forcing Sarah to blink to adjust her eyes to the light. It makes her aware of what a recluse she has become. Admiring the backdrop of rugged mountainous terrain, she breaths a deep, relaxing breath.

Her skin is warm from the sun, and her head isn't spinning anymore, so Sarah is ready to get back to work investigating her new clue. As she walks back toward the door, her keen eye catches the shadow of a faint partial outline of a large shoe print leading up to her back door. The fear that just left her now sweeps back through her with a fury. Judging by the footprint's length and width, it's obvious to Sarah it belongs to a man, but she places her foot inside the outline of the print anyway before re-entering the dining room.

The fear she feels brings her back to last week when she found the garage door unlocked though she was certain she locked it. She had also found the bathroom blinds raised one half inch. She now believes these instances were not only in her imagination. She scans her memory for other oddities but cannot recall any. Even though she feels fear, she doesn't want to run from it any longer.

"I can't keep running, not any longer. I need to face it and fight it. I can't be afraid all the time." Sarah exits the formal dining room into the sunken living room, closing the pocket doors behind her as she always does. But this time she is smiling at her strength and perseverance.

Continuing to ponder the photo, the shoeprint, and the other oddities that caused an enormity of self-doubt makes her realize that her worries of going crazy are only illusions. She almost feels a great sense of relief. "I'm not going crazy. Even though the thought of someone sneaking into my home has now put me on full guard, I must be vigilant," Sarah encourages herself.

She thinks back to things she didn't pay much attention to, too lost in her world of despair to notice. Now alert that someone might be tracking her movements, she is forced into the present. Quickly moving through the house, she checks the locks on all the windows and doors and makes a mental note to change the locks. She takes a couple tablets of Klonopin to help steady her nerves and two extra-strength Excedrin and then lies on the couch, trying to comprehend all of this. Her mind reverts back to the intriguing photo that mystically appeared. She cannot just let it go. It is now part of her obsession. Trying to relax, Sarah closes her eyes, but her mind won't shut off.

Normally, Sarah would run to Warren for help ... or Cole, but she doesn't this time. She goes into the bedroom, removes a gun case from under the bed, and enters the combination to allow her access to Stephen's Browning Hi-Power 9mm. His unit had switched to carrying Sig Sauer P226s, so he left the 9mm for her protection when he was deployed. The gun is big and heavy, but it's all she has, and she wants to fight back. She wants to be strong and brave. She no longer has the love of her life. She is alone.

The phone rings, interrupting her thoughts. Sarah takes a welcomed break to get away from her endlessly dark thoughts.

"Hello?" she asks.

"Hello, Sarah. It's Kat," Kat coolly introduces herself as if they have spoken everyday for the past seven months, fifteen days, ten hours, forty-five minutes, and seven seconds since Stephen's disappearance.

Sarah, reeling with feral confidence, demands, "Why are you calling me? I tried to reach you after Calvin passed, and you never return my calls. *Never!*" Sarah raises her voice, releasing her anger and frustrations. She quickly pulls the receiver away from her mouth as she nearly hyperventilates. *Be calm. You need her. She is part of this sick puzzle. She can help you. Use her!* Sarah silently reinforces her mission.

Changing her demeanor, Sarah softens her tone. "Kat, forgive me. I'm so sorry for unloading on you like that. I'm stressed, and I shouldn't take it out on you." Sarah grovels in disgust but not in disgrace. "I'm very sorry about Calvin. I hope you know that. I didn't really have a chance to speak with you at his service."

"I know, Sarah. Please don't worry about it. I understand," Kat remarks without emotion.

Not even an apology for blowing our friendship off … nothing. Sarah grits her teeth. *Who the hell is this person? She's not the friend I used to know. But I need her … I need her.* Sarah says silently to herself.

"I've been so busy with Calvin passing and filling in as CEO … well, I guess time just slipped away," Kat offers a half-assed apology. Sarah cringes but knows she needs vital information from Kat, no matter how degrading her behavior makes her feel.

Kat continues speaking, "I understand you have taken a leave of absence from work. I saw Calvin's signature on the form. So I gather you personally discussed this matter with him and not HR."

Bitch! Sarah screams within.

"Do you know how much longer you will need to take off? We were delayed on the launch, so your absence was not really noticed. However, now that the FDA is giving final approval, I will need you back as soon as possible."

Sarah offers no response, just silence.

"I know you, Sarah. Are you wallowing in your sadness and loneliness? You know that won't help Stephen come home any sooner."

Sarah almost comes unglued. "Kat, Stephen is missing and possibly dead. That's how things are going," Sarah abruptly responds, shocked that she said the word—*dead*. She feels sad and hurt, almost as if she betrayed Stephen by using him to get what she needs. "What do you want, Kat?"

"Oh my God, Sarah. I am sorry, so sorry. I had no idea. When did you find out, honey?" Kat asks sweetly in the most concerned voice she can manage. She fails miserably.

In a salty tone, Sarah responds, "It's been more than seven months now since I last saw my husband. I can't believe it's been that long ..." Sarah's voice drops as she faces Stephen's profound absence from her life. How quickly her strength and confidence fades.

"Well that answers why I haven't seen you at work, but I've been incredibly busy wrapping up Calvin's—"

"Kat, excuse me, but what do you want?"

"I want to take you to lunch tomorrow. It will be good for both of us to get out, don't you think? Can you meet me tomorrow at the Sea Café in Del Mar?"

Sarah is dumbfounded. Struggling with the thought of not only having to leave her fortress and listening as Kat goes on and on about herself nearly kills Sarah, but she knows she must do this. She realizes this will be the perfect opportunity to inconspicuously interrogate Kat. *She is the main suspect in Calvin's death. I must do this for Calvin … I promised him,* Sarah thinks to herself.

"Well, sure," she obliges in a flat voice. "That will be nice. I haven't been out of the house for months. Since my leave of absence, I have no idea what is going on outside my walls," she continues, not elaborating on her newfound friendship with Cole. "What time?" Sarah feels devious but intent on her motives.

So this is what it feels like to be Kat, Sarah thinks, grinning confidently. *I will learn from the best.*

"Let's meet at twelve-fifteen. Park in the underground parking. You know how crowded it can get on the street level."

"Oh yes, thank you. I'll see you tomorrow."

"It will be fun to catch up, like old times. I'm really looking forward to seeing you, Sarah," Kat gushes pretentiously.

"I'll see you then," Sarah says suspiciously, feeling like she is going to throw up.

She wants to slam down the receiver and crush all of Kat's bullshit, but instead Sarah calmly hangs up the receiver, watching in slow motion as it connects with the body of the phone. Her mind races in sheer disbelief of the conversation that just took place. She had been certain she would never speak with Kat again. Sarah is amazed at the impeccable timing.

"My investigation is officially underway."

As she drives to Del Mar, California, the next day, Sarah realizes her love for life has been chiseled down to a shattered heart that reminisces about romantic dinners with Stephen followed by long walks through the lovely quaint seaside village. They cherished going for lunch at one of the many sidewalk cafés, window shopping at the extravagantly expensive boutiques, or just walking on the cobblestone walkways and watching people. They would sit at their favorite coffee shop, observing people and trying to guess who was a native or a tourist without looking to see if the men wore black socks with sandals. It was usually pretty obvious, but it was just pure fun and interesting to watch all the different cultures.

"Oh, and the designer boutiques are to die for," Sarah would say to Stephen.

And of course Stephen's classic response was to shake his head in a negative motion and ask, "What did you buy that we can't afford?" He did it all the while smiling.

Del Mar is a grand location filled with exquisite restaurants and the most upscale night spots. Sarah dined there many times with her key clients, joined by the lovely company of her husband. Kat often dined with her clients in the same establishments, but Calvin had always been absent.

Del Mar is also famous for its exciting horseracing. It also has a wonderful climate for schmoozing with customers and closing deals. However, since the recent terrorist attacks, the town is now quiet and moving at a sluggish pace. To an outsider, the atmosphere might appear normal, but to natives it is obvious that the quaint little village of Del Mar is still gorgeous and grand but wounded and healing.

Traffic is still thick but nothing like the hustle and bustle months ago. Sarah looks ahead for the turnoff to the underground parking for the multiplex of shops, nightclubs, and restaurants that includes the Sea Café. Her heart races; she is nervous out of the safety zone provided by the walls of her home. The anticipation of seeing Kat for the first time since her sniping remarks in Calvin's office months ago, Mr. Stevens's death, Calvin's death, Stephen's dea—disappearance, and Kat's very questionable promotion as CEO of ViaStem nearly causes Sarah to choke.

After finding a rare parking space, Sarah sits quietly meditating in her car. She thinks of the mystery photo of Calvin and Mr. Stevens that just showed up in her dining room. She calms herself and allows the pace of her heartbeat to slow. "Be calm, Sarah. You have to be calm," she says aloud.

After applying a new sheen of lipstick and doing a quick check of her face and hair in the rearview mirror, she reaches for a bit of courage—Klonopin. She takes one with a sip of Dasani water and a deep calming breath. She is now ready for the challenge. "I can do this. I have to."

Locking her BMW, she walks across the parking lot, her high heels clicking loudly against the cement, causing an obvious echo and making Sarah feel conspicuous. Relief overcomes her when she reaches the elevator, which she rides to the second level. As the doors open, the restaurant is directly ahead of her. She spots Kat sitting at a center table on the Plexiglas-enclosed patio. *Directly in the warm California sun, of course. Always the center of attention,* Sarah thinks to herself.

As she exits the elevator, she walks confidently toward Kat. Dressed in a crisp white linen suit, she tucks her clutch tucked under her arm. Her long, auburn hair flows freely in the cool breeze lightly fanning off the Pacific Ocean. Unpretentious, Sarah doesn't notice the attention of many fellow diners. However, Kat jealously does.

"Hello, my old friend." Kat hugs Sarah and kisses her on both cheeks. "Look at you. So very thin and pretty as usual. I hope this table is okay with you. I thought the sunshine would feel comforting and maybe we could catch a few rays. Hopefully the excess noise from the other tables won't be too distracting." Kat gestures with her flirty eyes toward some gentlemen sitting adjacent to her.

Her flirting has already started, Sarah thinks.

"This is fine, and yes the sun does feel wonderful," Sarah agrees. "Kat … not to get to personal so quickly, but how are you doing since Calvin's passing? How's Eden?" Sarah inquires with genuine sincerity.

"Well, Sarah, it all happened so fast. I'm not sure I have really dealt with it yet. I just haven't had any time. I'm not sure if I'm ready … I took him to our cabin in Big Bear toward the end to try to let him rest comfortably, and before the end of the week, he was gone," Kat says flatly with no emotion. She briefly glances toward the table of businessmen. "Oh, and Eden is doing fine. She spends a great deal of quality time with Grace. That woman is a godsend."

Sarah disapproves of Kat's obvious indiscretions but overlooks them because she promised herself that this could lead her to the answer of Calvin's demise, to something … clues … evidence—anything.

Just to say something, Sarah restarts the conversation after an awkward silence. "How is it being CEO of ViaStem? I guess congratulations are in order." Sarah almost chokes on her words. "What is the status of the HESC project?"

"The promotion was a delightful surprise that I worked so very hard for. It is a demanding workload, but I wouldn't trade it for the world. Unfortunately, the approval and launch of the HESC procedure is a bit delayed but should be finalized quite soon. Sarah, it will be very lucrative. And, of course, it will help so many ill people. It is such an exciting time in our lives! Get ready to increase your bank account, Sarah. Tremendously! If you ever get back to work, that is. I will … *we* will be rich," Kat exudes loudly, trying to impress those around her.

"Just think how Mr. Stevens and Calvin would have loved to see this day," Sarah comments.

"At least we get to see it. You know, for them," covers Kat. "I want to share some very exciting news. As you know, Mrs. Stevens is very ill and may pass any day now. The Stevens willed ViaStem to Calvin, and I'm obviously his beneficiary. Isn't that an honor?"

As Sarah thinks about the details, she tries to absorb them all but has difficulty digesting them. *Honor? What a load of crap, Kat. It's all about the dollar to you. I can't believe the Stevenses would allow Kat's greed close to their company, their dream.* Sarah just sits, stunned with no words.

"I have the house up for sale, and I am purchasing a ten-thousand-square-foot home in the very exclusive Rancho Santa Fe," Kat boasts.

Sarah sees an opportunity to investigate further. "When do you move in?"

"I only have to wait another two weeks, and I'll be out of that—" Kat changes the subject, realizing that Sarah lives in that "godforsaken place," which is beautiful and not godforsaken in the slightest. "Next week I have the Salvation Army coming to take everything but Bob and Frank—you remember my kitties—and what's in my personal safe. It's a new start for me. I have already sold the horses and the cars. They were really Calvin's, not mine.

Liar, Sarah thinks to herself.

"I'm renting a lovely beach house until we move. It's just down that street. It's just lovely." Kat points in the direction of her new place mainly for the table of men to know where she lives.

Sarah takes a mental note that if she wants to search Kat's house for clues, she will have to do it soon, within the next day or so. Sarah smiles and gives a slight laugh, really wanting to vomit.

"What's that laugh for?"

"Is that the personal safe you could never remember the combination to? Didn't you used to hide the combo in a box of Lucky Charms?" Sarah takes the opportunity to dig for further evidence. Excitement and nerves shoot through her body. *Be calm … don't get overzealous,* Sarah tells herself.

Without taking a breath, Kat continues with a laugh, "Oh yes. Now I have the combination hidden in the laundry soap of all places. Me, do laundry?" Kat then lowers her voice to a whisper, partially covering her mouth as if everyone is paying attention to only her. "The safe at my new place will have a manual and key security system. Absolutely no worries of anyone stealing my most precious jewels."

I don't care, Sarah thinks.

Then Kat says, "Oh, exciting news. I ordered a new CLS 2013 Series Mercedes. It was close to one hundred thousand dollars, but I have always wanted one, and now I can have whatever I want! It is top of the line, Sarah. Midnight metallic black, black on black wheels, cream leather seats—it's loaded," Kat boasts for the second time in less than twenty minutes.

She is already spending the Stevenses' fortune! Sarah feverishly loathes Kat as she silently thinks to herself but wants to scream out loud. She is white knuckled from her firm grasp on the arms of her chair, which cause her hands to cramp. Thoroughly disgusted by Kat's greed and cattiness, she says, "Oh my God, Kat, how can you think about something like that with all that has happened? I mean, Calvin's death alone for God's sake. Never mind all the other horrible events."

"Come on, Sarah. All I did for months is wait hand and foot on poor, sick Calvin, cleaning up his puke and shit."

Wow. Tell me how you really feel, Sarah thinks to herself sarcastically.

"You know how men are when they get sick. It's all about them. It gets pretty old pretty quick! To be quite frank, Sarah, I was glad to leave him at our cabin with the nurse, for his sake and mine. I mean, it was no secret our marriage was pretty much over. Thank goodness for home health agencies! It is just time to move on, Sarah. It's time!" Kat expresses with sheer discernment.

Sarah is completely stunned at what she is hearing. *Such callousness. Such wickedness spewing from someone I used to consider a dear friend.* Sarah takes a sip of her ice water just to help her swallow the disturbing conversation. She expected this lunch with Kat would be difficult, but this is absurd.

A pretty blonde collegiate waitress wearing a white blouse, skinny black pants, and a black apron double-tied around her waist approaches the table, which allows Sarah a few more seconds to assimilate what she has just witnessed. She is confident Kat is involved in Calvin's death, and she is determined to get as much information as possible because after this, she never intends on seeing Kat again.

"Hi, ladies. Can I get you a beverage? Some flavored tea, wine, or a cocktail perhaps?" the waitress encourages.

"I'll have a glass—no a bottle—of Dom please. I am celebrating. And what would you like, Sarah?" Kat laughs. "At a hundred and eighty-three dollars a bottle, I want it all for myself. Just kidding. I'll share."

"I'll just have a Pellegrino with a lemon, please," Sarah politely responds to the waitress.

"Oh, what a party-pooper, Sarah. You should be celebrating," Kat says loudly while sneaking a peek at one of the handsome gentleman at the neighboring table.

Sarah thinks to herself, *Is this for real? Celebrate what? My husband's—*

Kat's cell phone rings, offering a welcomed interruption for Sarah. Her mind swirls with the clues she has just heard, and she makes note of them so she can plan her next move—searching Kat's house. *I have to get into Kat's house, but I must talk to Ruth Stevens to seek out the truth regarding the will of ViaStem.* Sarah organizes her next plans while Kat is busy on her phone.

"Hello? Oh, hello. How are you? Is my baby ready? Why not?" Kat scrunches her nose and pouts while stomping her feet like a spoiled child. "Were you able to get me all the amenities I want?" she says, talking in baby talk. "Fabulous! Chow, darling." She closes her cell phone and sets it on the table.

Sarah's skin is crawling by this point. It takes great effort for her to just sit still and not get up and run or reach across the table and strangle Kat. The waitress arrives with the champagne, Sarah's slender green bottle of Pellegrino, and a glass of ice with a lemon wedge fitted on the edge just in time. She opens the classic bottle of Dom and pours Kat her first glass before proceeding. Kat gulps down the first glass, and the waitress pours her another. "Are you ready to order?" questions the waitress.

Classy, Sarah observes silently.

"Can we have a second?" Kat rudely interrupts her, taking a second phone call. Before answering the phone, she glances at the gentleman she has chosen at the adjacent table, raises her glass, and takes a sip. Then she turns and answers her call. "Hello? Kat's voice immediately changes to a nervous, uncomfortable tone. "Yes. I know. I understand. This is not the best time. Can we speak later? Okay then. I will be expecting your call tonight," Kat's voice pitch is almost a whisper as she closes the call. "Um … where were we?" she poignantly asks Sarah.

Sarah is highly suspicious but too furious to investigate any further. She only wishes she could have heard the voice on the other end.

"Ladies, are you ready to order now?" asks the California sun-kissed waitress, who is also annoyed with Kat but is groveling for a big tip, especially if she can get Kat to drink the whole bottle of Dom.

Kat rudely jumps in front of Sarah, claiming her alpha-dog position, "Yes, I'll have the Santa Fe Chicken Salad with roasted yellow peppers on the side and honey mustard dressing on the side as well." No please. No thank-you. No manners.

Looking toward Sarah, the pretty young waitress softly asks, "And what can I get for you?"

"I'm going to pass. Thank you though," Sarah politely responds.

Sickened by Kat's behavior at this point, Sarah slowly and

gracefully gets up from the table, gently folding her napkin and placing it on her place setting. She removes twenty dollars from her purse and places it under the effervescent bottle of Pellegrino. Pushing in her chair, she leans into it, both hands gripping the back to give her a moment to collect herself. She looks up intensely into Kat's greedy, brown, devilish eyes as she snobbishly sips her Dom.

Placing her clutch under her left arm, Sarah slowly and calmly walks around the table, stops directly in front of Kat, and leans in very closely. In an extremely calm and distinctly firm tone, she says, "You have changed, Kat. I don't know you anymore, and I don't want to either. I don't know what you are up to, but it doesn't sound or feel right. But that really doesn't surprise me at all. You've been changing for a while now, and that is not a compliment. I will not see you again, and I will not miss you for one second. I cannot believe this selfish, greedy little bitch sitting in front of me. I don't know what the hell you are up to, but I will find out. The truth will come out, Kat! And if it's not too late, please remember one thing—your daughter, Eden. Good-bye, Kat. Oh, and one more thing. I quit!" Sarah sternly and confidently whispers into Kat's ear before exiting the restaurant. She enters the elevator and smiles, watching Kat disappear as the doors close.

Kat is stunned, embarrassed, and concerned that the guy she wants at the next table heard the harsh conversation. But within seconds, she is back on her cell phone, sipping champagne.

Chapter 15:

Flying High

Sarah exits the elevator and boldly walks the path back to her car with a fully confident smile. She feels a high radiating through her body that she hasn't felt for months. *I did it. Oh my God, I did it. That arrogant bitch.* Sarah can't erase the smile from her face, nor does she want to.

Automatically unlocking her BMW, Sarah plugs in her iPod to the auxiliary adapter on her dashboard and searches for Bon Jovi. She wants to rock. She cranks Bon Jovi's "Have a Nice Day" as her victory song as she squeals out of her parking space. She draws attention, but this time she doesn't care. Zipping toward the exit, she only slows to pay the parking fee and lessen the bump near the spikes and bold warning sign—*Do Not Back Up*—that momentarily slows her path. Taking a right, Sarah purposely drives by the Sea Café and throws one last triumphant glance through her sunroof at Kat. Kat avoids Sarah's glance with a rare sheepish look on her face. *She's so guilty. Now I have to bust her,* Sarah thinks.

Reaching Freeway 5, she decides to take the back roads home to Ramona. Taking speeds much higher than the limits set by law, she corners turns like a professional race car driver. Or so she thinks. Whipping the car into fifth gear, she explodes with exhilaration! Sarah loves the momentum of the day. She sings as loudly as the music will cover her novice voice. She laughs, knowing she sounds like one of the *American Idol* contestants Simon used to throw under the bus, but she continues to belt out the songs as she races toward home. The sun beaming through the sunroof makes her feel even higher. She drives faster on winding roads leading through the back mountains on Route 67.

Sarah playfully remembers she and Stephen playing rock star in his F150 truck with the dark, tinted windows tightly shut to conceal the many times they creatively mouthed the words incorrectly, creating new lyrics to fill in the blanks to one of their favorite songs—Neil Diamond's "Sweet Car-o-line." *Dun, dun, dun.* How they would laugh and laugh, always continuing their rock star status. "Sweet Car-o-line," they'd sing. "So sweet, so sweet, so sweet." They had cheered loudly and laughed hysterically.

"Gosh, we had fun! How I miss you, Stephen," Sarah says to herself with a smile on her face.

No more nagging Warren for answers. She used to dread him leaving on business trips because of her insecurities. Now he'd been gone for three weeks, and she only feels empowered that she will find her own answers. She is now in control of her destiny.

"Tonight is the night. It's time to get some dirt on Kat."

Chapter 16:

No Worries

Sarah makes a failed attempt to reach Ruth Stevens.

"I must find out if what Kat said about the Stevenses leaving ViaStem to Calvin and Kat is true," she told herself. "I can see Calvin, but Kat? No way. Ruth was not shy about her dislike for Kat. I also know that Ruth must be in her final days and possibly desperate to ensure ViaStem is left in the best hands."

Sarah tries one more time to reach Dave Perth at ViaStem. "He will know what is going on," she tells herself.

"Good morning, ViaStem Biotechnology and Genetics Corporation. This is Teresa. How may I help you?"

"Ah, a familiar voice," Sarah says. "Good morning, Teresa this is Sarah Benton—"

"Oh hi, Sarah. How are you? We sure do miss you around here. I hope you come back soon. Oh my gosh, I completely interrupted you. I apologize, Sarah."

"No problem, Teresa. I hope you and everyone are doing well. I'm trying to reach Dave, Dave Perth. Is he in?"

"Yes, I believe he is. Let me check if he is in a meeting. I'm sure he would love to speak with you." Within seconds, Teresa returns to the line. "I will put you right through, Sarah. It was so nice to hear your voice. Take care, and I hope to see you back soon."

"You too, Teresa. Take care."

Sarah only has to listen to a short composition of elevator music until Dave answers the call. "Good morning, Sarah. How are you?"

"I'm … good, Dave."

"We are launching the HESC G42 procedure next week. We could use a sales whip like you. When will you be coming back?"

Skipping over his last question, Sarah says, "That is so exciting, Dave. I can't wait to hear the success stories for those patients who need this procedure. How are things since Calvin … since Calvin died?"

With grave concern in his voice, Dave says, "Well as you probably have heard that Kat is the new CEO, which blows my mind. This is probably being recorded, but I don't give a damn. Mr. Stevens and Calvin worked so hard to complete this project, and it is just chaos around here now. Nearly every day Kat meets with a small group of consultants, including a couple government officials and a couple of our lead researchers. It doesn't seem like they're very productive. The launch was anticipated months ago, but the scientists said one step of the procedure needed further research. I don't know, Sarah. It would be nice if we could turn back time, huh?"

"Oh, Dave, I think that all the time. Every second." Sarah gets lost for a second in a thought of Stephen.

"Sarah …"

"Oh gosh, Dave. Tangent. Sorry about that. Just thinking

of Stephen. He is missing in Afghanistan … not sure if you knew that."

"Oh, Sarah, I am so sorry. I did hear that. Bad things are happening all around us. I'm so very sorry."

"What do you mean, Dave?"

"Dr. Hammond suffered a massive coronary a week ago. He is dead," Dave reluctantly passes along the news.

"That is just awful. Can I ask you a question about Dr. Hammond?"

"Hold on, Sarah. Let me call you back on my cell phone. It might be more secure."

"All right. Call me on my Blackberry."

"Okay, I'll call in a second."

Sarah waits in anticipation of any news Dave might have regarding Dr. Hammond's involvement in the testing of Stephen's unit. She feels her Blackberry vibrate in her hand and immediately touches the green telephone button. "Hello, Dave?"

"Yes, Sarah. I am out of the building, so I can be more relaxed about our conversation. So what did you want to know?"

Sarah is suspicious of nearly everyone, but she needs information on what Dr. Hammond's involvement with Stephen's unit was. "Was Dr. Hammond involved in testing with the military? Especially Stephen's unit?"

"I apologize for not following up with you, Sarah, but I'm concerned I'm being watched. Since Hammond's death, I have been able to dig a little deeper, though. He and a group of scientists were conducting some pretty extensive testing on several military units, but they're coded, so I can't tell if Stephen's was part of the experiments. All I know is this type of testing is excessive for pre-deployment and post-deployment analysis, which is what the report claims is the purpose of these tests."

"Can you draw any conclusions, Dave? Anything?"

"Yes, I can, but I don't have any real proof, and I'm afraid I might disappear, Sarah. I'm suspicious of a cover-up. I do know that the initial team of researchers is gone."

"Disappear? What do you mean gone?"

"Dr. Hammond is now deceased. So are five other scientists, and another five have not been heard from. They just moved on. To where, I don't know. No one knows."

"Why do you think there is a cover-up?

"No investigation, no discussions—nothing. Just like Calvin's death. Everything is hush-hush around here since Kat came into her undeserved position. Sorry. I get so damn angry when I think about the whole mess. And the pills, Sarah. Those are one step in the cloning process. Many of the shots were not vaccines. They are another part of the cloning process. You received the report, right?"

"Yes, I did. Thank you. It's being researched. Don't worry, though. Everything is confidential. I apologize for not calling, but things have not been much better on this end. I just had lunch with Kat, and I wanted to reach across the table and strangle her, so don't apologize."

"Another thing that makes this whole thing more confusing and suspicious is that the scientific team before Hammond that was working on this project with the military is all gone."

"No investigation?"

"No investigation, no records, no answers."

"Dave, do you know if there are any other ViaStem scientific research teams working with the military at this time?"

"Not right now. Hammond's team was the last, and they ended their research approximately seven months ago. Though I just got a requisition for new funds for future work with the military beginning in January 2014. The request is for research, but nothing significant is explained. I don't get to see privileged information anymore."

"Does it sound like something is amiss …?"

"Absolutely. I don't trust anyone around here anymore. I was going to leave, but I need to know what is going on. Something bad is going on."

"Please be careful. Please let me know if you come across anything else. Stephen told me Dr. Hammond conducted in-depth testing on his men, and now I don't have Stephen, his unit is gone, and I have no answers."

"Be careful, Sarah."

"I called for another reason too."

"Anything, Sarah."

"Kat and I had lunch yesterday, and I quit. God, I hope she doesn't bury ViaStem. There is no way she knows what the hell she is doing, Dave. No way."

"I don't blame you for leaving, and I agree about Kat, but to be honest with you, I don't think she is really in control. Government agents are here all the time. They are supposed to be ensuring that the procedure approval is accelerated for the public. I think that's bullshit."

"I don't know what to say, Dave. You know, you should be CEO. You know that, don't you?"

"Yes, but I'm not. I've actually been demoted to assistant financial analyst. 'They' don't want me near the financials of the company."

"This just gets more convoluted."

"What's even worse is that Harold and Ruth Stevens

transferred ownership of ViaStem to Calvin, and you know what that means. Now that Calvin is dead, Kat will be the sole beneficiary once Mrs. Stevens passes. She is supposedly in full control, Sarah. Calvin was like a son to them, but in their wildest dreams, I doubt they ever thought something like this would transpire."

Silence takes over. Sarah is at a loss for words. Her mind runs wild with possible reasons for what is happening and who might be involved. *One thing is for sure. I know Kat is involved, but to what extent?* Sarah thinks to herself. "Dave, is Ruth aware of what is going on?"

"Did you know she is losing her fight against her breast cancer? Well, she is such a fighter, but she finally entered a hospice about a month ago. I know she is aware of the circumstances because I told her. You know what, though? Her reaction took me by surprise. She didn't seem concerned in the slightest that ViaStem was under Kat's control. But Harold's and Calvin's deaths nearly killed her. She's a fighter, though. That's a fact."

"I would like to go see her. Will you tell me where she is?"

"Of course. She is at the Mercy Hospice in Hillcrest. Sarah, be prepared. She is not doing well at all. She is ..." Dave's voice nearly disappears, and Sarah cannot say the word dead one more time.

"Thank you, Dave. I must go now. Take care of yourself. Be careful."

"Take care, Sarah, and be careful too," Dave warns.

Sarah immediately jumps in her car and heads down the mountain to visit Ruth Stevens. She feels guilt for not visiting the ill woman more during her devastating illness. "I can't believe I only sent flowers to her home. How selfish of me! Damn it, Sarah."

Forty-five minutes later, she arrives at the Hospice Center to visit with Mrs. Stevens. "I haven't seen her forever. I hope she will see me. I hope she remembers me," Sarah says aloud before exiting her car. Sadness feels her heart as it has for so long now, but adrenaline pumps through her body after the events of the day. "Maybe Ruth can offer some pieces to this puzzle."

Waiting in the visitor area, Sarah is anxious. She paces and waits.

"Miss? Mrs. Steven's will see you now. Please do not stay long. She is very weak," the nurse in the white uniform informs Sarah. "Her room is the last on the right." The nurse points down a hallway.

"Thank you."

Sarah begins her journey down the corridor, smelling a slight scent of disinfectant. The temperature in the hallway is cool. The bouquet of Gerber daisies she carries sweeps against her pant leg. Death surrounds her, making her feel a bit uneasy.

When she enters Ruth Stevens's room, the air feels warm. Mrs. Stevens immediately looks toward Sarah and smiles. She is covered by a homemade patchwork quilt that she made for her son, David. A couple pictures of Harold Stevens, David, and one of Calvin rest on her nightstand. The vertical blinds are slightly open, allowing the warm sun to shine in.

"Come, dear. Come sit with me," Ruth insists. Her voice is scratchy and almost a whisper.

Sarah walks over and smiles down at Ruth. *What do I say? How are you?* Sarah thinks to herself. "Hello, Ruth." She bends down to give the older woman a soft kiss on the cheek. "Thank you so much for letting me visit. I'm sorry I haven't—"

Ruth interjects, "No worries, Sarah. I understand that you have been going through your own challenges. No worries." She gently pats the back of Sarah's right hand.

Still holding the bouquet of bright colorful daisies in her left hand, Sarah is speechless and nervous.

Realizing Sarah's anxiety, Ruth chimes in, breaking the silence, "Are those beautiful flowers for me, dear? You know, Gerber daisies are my favorite, but then again I believe I received a lovely bouquet of these about every other week from you." Ruth offers a grateful smile and holds Sarah's hand.

"Yes. I know they are your favorites because Mr. Stevens was always sharing stories of the two of you and how you wanted those flowers at your fiftieth wedding anniversary, tons of them. I'm sorry Ruth. I'm sorry about Mr. Stevens," Sarah says with regret.

"That's all right, dear. I will be with him soon." Ruth smiles. "I just love them. They are just lovely. Please, sit." Ruth pats a space on the bed beside her. "I was so sad to hear about Stephen."

"We both share the feelings of loss. But I came to ask you a question, Ruth."

Ruth continues to hold Sarah's hand. "Ask me anything you want."

"Dave Perth shared with me that you transferred ownership of ViaStem to Calvin, but now he is gone and … and … Kat …" Sarah cannot find her words.

Ruth holds Sarah's hand tighter and looks directly into her eyes with a comforting expression.

A knock at the door startles both ladies, and they break

into slight smiles. "Excuse me," says the young volunteer candy striper in the traditional uniform—white blouse and skirt, with an apron adorned by a red cross. "Can I get you anything?"

"Yes, dear. Can you please put these beautiful flowers in a vase for me?" Ruth asks softly.

Sarah can see Ruth growing tired. She is frail and weak.

Still holding Sarah's hand, Ruth continues, "Now where were we? When Harold passed, I thought I would not be able to hold on. We both loved Calvin like he was our son, our only son since David was taken from us. We both knew Calvin was the best person to run ViaStem. He knew our dreams, and we knew he would make them come true. I was devastated when he became so ill … so unexpectedly. And his death was fast … so fast, Sarah." Ruth's voices withers, and she takes a long slow breath. The color in her face drains, leaving her pale.

Sarah knows she must go and let Ruth rest, but she needs to know that Ruth is comfortable with how the company is being run by Kat.

Ruth intervenes in the silence, "What did you want to ask? You may be direct, Sarah. What do you want to know?"

Sarah is doe-eyed and speechless. "Ruth, I love ViaStem, and I think the world of Mr. Stevens's dream … your dream. Kat—" she just blurts out of nowhere. Her ideas and words are scrambled. She lowers her head, trying to search for the right way to say what she came to say, but she is lost.

Ruth reaches up and tips Sarah's face to eye level with a gentle touch on her chin. "Everything is all right, Sarah. I am at peace with our decision about ViaStem. I have secured an excellent team of attorneys to control this situation, long term. Calvin was sole heir, but his beneficiary is the Progeria Foundation, not Kat. Trust me. I am at peace."

The candy striper softly knocks on the door, brings in the flowers, and sets them on the end table.

"Thank you, dear."

In a joyous moment of silence, the two women look at one another and just smile. Ruth Stevens takes another deep, long breath and closes her eyes for the last time. Sarah knows she is gone to be with her beloved husband in heaven. She leans forward and kisses Ruth on the cheek. She then holds Ruth's hand for several minutes, admiring the woman lying beside her. She sheds tears—tears of sadness, tears of joy, and tears of relief. Ruth still has a slight smile on her face, bringing one to Sarah's face. "God bless you."

Sarah gently rests Ruth's hand over her heart. Before exiting the hospice, she stops at the nurses' station and informs the staff of Ruth's condition. They rush to her room. Sarah converses with a nurse before walking through the automatic doors into the comforting sun.

Sarah smiles, knowing Ruth is at peace. She cannot help but wonder about Kat's reaction. *Why is she unaware of this?*

Sarah opens her car door, still smiling, knowing Kat is not in charge and will not be at peace when she discovers the truth. She wishes she could be a fly on the wall when Kat gets the surprise of her life.

Chapter 17:

To Catch a Thief

It is nightfall, a time Sarah normally dreads because of the invasions of horribly vivid nightmares that consume her mind, leaving her wondering if she is teetering on the edge of reality or falling into the abyss. But not tonight.

She arranges clothes on the bed, all the while conversing with Cooper, who continuously cocks his head from side to side as if watching a tennis match.

"I think you understand what I am saying, don't you, Coops?" she questions him, knowing she sounds ridiculous, but she has no worries. Her only goal tonight is to discover evidence in Kat's house.

She wears black workout tights, a tight black, long-sleeved T-shirt, and black boots. Not sure of her choices, she shrugs and gives a faint laugh, knowing she chose her clothes to imitate the televised images of illusive career criminals. She throws her hair up in a twist and secures it with a clip to keep it from hanging in her face. No distractions, full concentration—that's the plan. She checks her small black gym bag, which contains latex gloves that will prevent her from leaving any fingerprint evidence, a compact flashlight with fresh batteries, a couple small paper bags to collect the evidence she prays she finds, long forceps, a screwdriver, a wrench, a pen, and of course, her new best friend—her fully loaded 9mm—once again devised from watching too many detective shows. "Thank goodness for TV." Sarah smiles at Cooper.

Excitedly, she drives to Kat's house. She parks her BMW on the street around the corner and wishes it were a dark color rather than white. But luckily it is a particularly dark night with heavy clouds covering the moon. She sits patiently, watching the house until full darkness fills the skies.

"So far everything is going my way. Perfect for committing a class-one burglary for breaking and entering after twilight," she tells herself. It is pertinent that Sarah knows Kat, Eden, and Grace have left the premises before she initiates her plan.

Calvin's death and Kat's instant rise to corporate fame convinces Sarah she is doing the right thing. She is intent on learning the truth, no matter what the stakes. She always follows her gut instincts, and they have proven her right up to this point, so she refuses to disregard them now. As she sits one block from Kat's home, Sarah reviews her plan in her mind. Because she is obsessively organized, she has studied her plan thoroughly from the detailed written protocol she devised earlier this afternoon.

"Remember to enter through the side door where she used to hide a key under the rock to the right of the door. There is no streetlight to reveal my presence. If there is no entrance, break in through the back door. Hopefully there is still no alarm system, not in this neighborhood. This godforsaken—" Sarah gets revved up for her mission when she remembers

Kat's sarcastic remarks about Country Estates. "That bitch," she says as she recalls their lunch, bringing her blood to boil. Sarah continues rehearsing her plan. *Watch out, Kat.*

"Once inside, go directly to the laundry room to retrieve the combination hidden in the detergent as Kat eluded to during lunch earlier today. Once that is recovered, scan the pathway to Kat's bedroom closet, where her personal safe is hidden in the floor. Open the safe, recover the goods, and get the hell out."

Sarah almost laughs as she strategically reviews her plan because it emulates a thriller movie. She knows she shouldn't laugh, though, because she needs to take this seriously or else she wouldn't have a 9mm accompanying her. A car full of teenagers whizzes by, bringing Sarah back to reality. "It's time."

Preparing as much as possible before exiting the car, she puts the flashlight in the side pocket of her bag for easy access, already having tested it a thousand times before leaving her house. Then she pulls the latex gloves onto her somewhat clammy hands.

Next she stealthily walks across the side lawn leading to her intended entrance of the house. The walk seems endless. The quiet is eerie to Sarah. She can hear her own breathing and her heart pounding in her ears. *Calm down,* Sarah soundlessly encourages herself. *Pull yourself together. You can do this. You must.* Her breathing and the sounds of her footsteps crushing each blade of grass seem loudly exaggerated. When she walks over the decorative rock lining the walkway, it seems to echo with a loud grinding noise. She quickly ducks behind a large shrub as another car passes by. Finally, reaching the side door to the garage, she checks under the rock for the spare key. "Jackpot. How lucky."

Entering the garage, she quietly closes the door behind her, leaving it unlocked for a quick getaway. The garage smells of freshly cut grass mixed with the distinct smell of gasoline. Her journey hasn't seemed real until now. She's been pretending this is not that dangerous, but it is. Her fears are now real. This is real. She swallows her cowardice and continues on.

Once inside the garage, she pulls the small black flashlight from her bag. The metal feels cold. With a click, she aims the beam from the flashlight toward the floor and makes her way from the side garage door to the door leading into the house using the same key. *No problems. I'm in.* Sarah hears only her short, quick breaths. High on adrenaline, her heart pounds in her chest. She steadies herself and calms her breathing before moving on. Her hands are trembling, and she feels dizzy as she slowly closes the door behind her.

She enters the dark prison. She thinks of happier times shared with Calvin, Eden, Stephen, and Kat. *What happened to that equation?* Sarah wonders. Now there is only darkness surrounding her. Sarah can feel the wickedness in the house. The evil is thick. She moves toward the laundry room.

Unable to quash her emotions, Sarah talks in a faint whisper to herself, "She seems unshaken by Calvin's death. He disintegrated right in front of her eyes, and she was celebrating at lunch today. How can anyone be so callous? She hid him away while he rotted. She went about her daily activities as if nothing was going on … unless, of course, she needed to act like the loving, caring housewife. What a pile of crap. And her rise to CEO—that is pure bullshit. What a deceitful little skank!"

Kat's uncaring, aloof behavior following Calvin's illness had initially piqued Sarah's curiosity. When Calvin disclosed to Sarah his suspicions of Kat making him ill, Sarah had been on alert to Kat's every move. Even following Calvin's death, Sarah had nothing to go on, no solid evidence to point to Kat. She hopes all her frustrations will be resolved tonight. She must know the truth, no matter how ugly and painful it might be.

As she walks down the hallway toward the laundry room, her boots sound like a squeegee against the ceramic tile flooring. Upon reaching her destination, Sarah scans the laundry room with her light. Her hand is still trembling, so she takes an extra second to steady herself. She feels jumpy. Startled by a shadow behind her, she loses her senses. She cannot move. The muscles in her back ache from tenseness. Something presses against her leg. She forces herself to look down and with great relief sees Bob and Frank, Kat's black and calico cats, respectively.

Sarah releases a great sigh of relief. "Oh, thank you, God." Both cats rub through her legs in figure eights, vying for her attention. Sarah greets the kitties. "Hi, guys. You scared the living daylights out of me." She takes a moment to scratch the cats on their backs, resulting in high arches of pure bliss from both Bob and Frank. The boys are content, and Sarah is back to her investigation.

She spots fabric softener, a bottle of liquid detergent, and an empty laundry basket. A couple hand washables hang from a rack above the washer and dryer. A shelf runs above the rack, which holds a couple storage boxes and another box of laundry detergent—powdered. Excitement sweeps over Sarah. She knows the combination is hidden in the powdered detergent, which is her primary clue and therefore the first place she will search. *Straight from Kat's mouth.*

Setting the gym bag on the floor, she holds the flashlight in her mouth, steps onto a flimsy plastic step stool, and reaches for the box of generic soap. As she stretches upward, she is startled by Bob, who has sneaked under the stool, causing her to grab the corner of the box and pull it down onto her. As the box comes down, so does Sarah, right onto her bottom on the hard ceramic tile.

"Ouch, Bob! You little shit!" Sarah shoos Bob away. He scampers out of the room with a meow, as if laughing at her gracefulness. Once Sarah regains her footing, she looks around the room and discovers a white and blue speckled wonderland. The paper revealing the combination to the safe directly is lying in the center of the mess, covered with white dust.

Sarah smiles and flashes her light across the floor. "Oh, crap. What a mess. Thanks a lot, Bob." The culprit has long since left the scene. With no time to waste, Sarah grabs the combination and stores it in the side pocket of her bag, which is now a light shade of gray. She doesn't think twice about the mess on the floor. Her black spy clothes are a different story.

"This looks inconspicuous." She laughs sarcastically. "Not for amateurs. Don't try this at home."

She is covered from head to toe in powder. Bending over, she unclips her hair and shakes her head wildly, spewing more powder everywhere. With the sleeve of her T-shirt, she attempts to wipe off her face. Dusting off her pants and top only makes the powder smear into the cloth. It is a futile attempt.

"Now I match my bag," Sarah comments humorously. Not wanting to waste any more time trying to rid her clothes of the dusty mess, she begins her walk to Kat's room. Flashing the light behind her, she notices ghostly footprints and chuckles a bit, shaking her head in amazement that she is actually doing this. Stopping, she removes her boots and finishes her journey in her socks. "Good. No marks."

As soon as she reaches Kat's bedroom, she heads straight to the closet. Flipping the closet light on, knowing it will not be seen from the road, Sarah feels a sense of sadness sink into her heart. Not one of Calvin's belongings, not even a family photo of Calvin, remains in the room. Sarah once again feels a sense of the danger of the situation. Her sense of humor quickly leaves her, and her serious side takes over.

The closet is only filled with Kat's designer clothing, purses, and shoes. Amazed by the numerous pairs of shoes, Sarah begins lifting each shoe rack, seeking the lid to the floor safe. She finally discovers it under the fifth shoe rack. Removing the combination from her dusty gray bag, she suddenly feels a chill of nerves sweep through her. Her hands begin to tremble, and her breathing is short and rapid in anticipation of what she will discover. As frightened as she is, she hopes she finds something to condemn Kat. "Calm down. You can do this, Sarah."

Setting down her flashlight, she turns it off and lightly blows onto the piece of paper to clear the dust so she can see the numbers. Her first attempt to open the safe fails. The second attempt fails. Sarah's nerves are on edge. *What if she changed the combo?*

Beads of sweat appear on Sarah's forehead. With the back of her forearm, she wipes at the dust, smudging a white streak of sweat across her forehead. Taking a deep breath, she attempts opening the safe for the third time. It opens.

"Third time is a charm," Sarah says, relieved by the outcome, still overcome with nerves. Lifting the lid of the safe, Sarah holds her breath for an alarm to sound, knowing full well it might also be a silent alarm. "One thing I forgot to find out at lunch."

She picks up her pace just in case. Removing many precious jewels, she continues to look for something related to her investigation, some evidence that appears odd. She isn't sure what she is searching for, but she continues to dig.

Toward the bottom of the safe, she discovers an envelope with the flap unsealed and tucked in to keep its contents enclosed. The envelope feels of a heavier weight paper, and the inside is lined with a fancy satin finish. The tri-folded letter she removes from it is printed on the same weight of cream colored paper. Her hands tremble as she opens the letter. She immediately recognizes the letterhead. It is distinct. She has seen it on many of Stephen's awards and accommodations.

The seal at the top signifies the emblem of the President of the United States—the embossed gold eagle with olive branches in its talons, the symbol that reads *The White House.* Sarah feels no fear; she is just intrigued to learn why Kat would receive a letter from the President of the United States. Maybe it is for Eden in response to one of her many letters congratulating the President on his support for our troops, though they were obviously written with Grace's help; her son serves in the army.

The letter reads, *Congratulations on your new promotion as CEO of ViaStem.* Sarah thinks this is odd, but it doesn't intrigue her like the second letter. Removing the second letter from the envelope, she sees another distinct emblem—that of the CIA—which fully engrosses her attention.

Sarah reads on and discovers that the introduction is directed to Katarina Fortunata. Spiderwebs pull from Sarah's skin. Goose bumps pop up over her entire body. She shivers with the fear of what is to come. She continues on with utter despair smeared across her face. She feels nauseous, gasping for air she covers her mouth with her right hand, still gripping the envelope and feeling that there is something more inside it, something soft and pliable.

She falls back against a shoe rack, which gouges her in the back. She feels nothing. She sits shaking and stunned, not knowing whether to cry or scream but longing to do both. She continues to finish the letter, unable to control her tears. She weeps. Tears stream down her cheeks, leaving etchings in the white dust covering her face. In the midst of a breath, Sarah hears the front door open. She quickly swallows her angst and turns out the light to the closet. She quickly scoots herself to the back of the closet until she feels the wall press against her back. Even though it is pitch black, she holds onto her legs bent at the knee as tightly as she can to make herself seem insignificant. She doesn't know what to do.

Maybe no one will notice me, she prays. She continues to grip the letter in one hand and the envelope in the other. She now knows the danger from the incriminating letters discovered in the safe is significant. She has no other choice other than to face it. Her fear is true.

I know I will be caught. She wants to cry out and scream with anger, but she traps all of her emotions within the confines of her skin. Her chest is going to explode. Her head pounds. Her heart aches with such unimaginable pain of the few words she read above a lengthy encrypted message. Sarah knows she has no time to concentrate on something so perplexing.

She hears a man's voice say, "Come and get it." The faint voice sounds familiar, but Sarah is too distraught to concentrate.

She remembers her gun. She wants to move, but she doesn't

dare. Her muscles ache from the forced stillness. She feels faint from taking shallow breaths through her mouth, which is covered by her hand to silence any noise, any sound, any whimper. Sarah contemplates whether to attempt to search for her 9mm in the pitch black or to remain still.

Will he see the powdery footprints, the laundry soap? Will he find me? she wonders. Remaining a statue, Sarah barely breathes but listens intently to the voice down the hallway.

"You guys, what a mess. Goddamnit. I don't have time to clean this up. It will have to wait. And look at the footprints," discovers the mystery man.

Sarah's heart plummets. *This is it. I'm doomed. My mission is foiled. No one will ever know the truth.*

The silence seems everlasting—an eternity.

She hears footsteps. Silence. More footsteps. Sarah agonizes. She can only listen and await her fate.

The front door opens and closes, and Sarah releases a deep sigh with the click of the lock. She must hurry. *Just take everything with you. Quickly now,* Sarah demands herself to move. She is shaking uncontrollably but determined to succeed at her mission.

In complete darkness, she quickly folds the letters and slips them back into the envelope. She closes it, tucking in the flap and still feeling something thick inside it, but she will have to look later. There is no time now. She feels for her flashlight but is disoriented from moving in the dark. Crawling forward and feeling for the opening of the safe, she feels the jewels she removed. Some of the sharper pieces pierce her latex glove and dig into her skin, but she ignores the pain. She bleeds but has no time to stop it.

She grows more anxious, knowing she is possibly dripping blood onto the carpet, but she cannot see in the vast darkness.

Her mind feels scattered and confused. She knows she put her flashlight … She can't remember if it is to the left or right. More tears flow. She is dizzy with fear. Finally she locates the flashlight and clicks it on. Some of the fear disappears without the blackness or the unknown intruder.

Quickly now. Sarah takes one last view of the inner safe and then replaces the removed belongings without care of how they land. She doesn't care; she just wants out. She places the envelope and its incriminating evidence into her gym bag and zips it closed. Closing the safe, she places the shoe rack back in its original position or as closely as she can remember during this unnerving time. She looks at her hand. It is smeared with blood. With her flashlight she scans the carpet for blood but doesn't see anything obvious. She lifts the shoe rack and dares to look. Sarah spots a drop of her blood being absorbed by the carpet. Unnerved and confused as to a solution, she covers the area with the shoe rack, hoping to conceal the droplet. Quickly pulling on her boots, there is nothing she can do but run.

Grabbing her bag, she hustles down the hallway and stops in her tracks when she reaches the kitchen. She stands for an extended second and stares in amazement at the floor. It is covered with paw prints. *They covered my tracks.*

Chapter 18:

Nightmare

It's a beautiful warm day in San Diego. The skies are crystal clear and the brightest blue. Sarah is relaxing in her favorite cushioned chaise on her back patio, soaking in the comforting rays of the sun. A relaxing breeze feels soothing, sensually touching her face and body, making her feel free from any burdens life brings. Cooper lies close to her as her most loyal companion. She sips buttery chardonnay and peers through her aviator sunglasses, which illuminate the pristine picturesque mountains surrounding her home. She suddenly jolts from bliss and back to the nightmare she has plunged into.

The nightmares that invade her sleep have come to life. Last night was no dream. It is a true nightmare she is forced to live. Warren warned her numerous times not to interfere, but she did, and she believes she will pay dearly. She is now trapped in the darkness of her home, too frightened to sleep, eat, or change the filthy gray clothes she thought were so appropriate for her amateur crime spree. Her hair is caked with white powder, and her face is streaked from rivers of tears that run down her dust-covered cheeks. She feels fear like she has never experienced before.

"What was I thinking? That this was a game of some kind?" Sarah questions herself. "What have I done? What am I involved in?" She finds herself in a panic mode, which drives her to hide from the wicked people she met in the letters in Kat's home.

Sarah races through the house, frantically checking and re-checking the lock on each door and window. Her skin crawls with fear. She knows she is in real danger. "This is the President and the CIA, and I left my DNA at the scene. I know it is just a matter of time before they find me." Racing from drapes to blinds, she tightens each so no rays of sunlight can peek in and no one can see in. She is in darkness … again. Alone again.

In a state of panic, Sarah paces from room to room, feeding her neurotic fears. She paces by the envelope she stole from Kat's safe last night. She wants so badly to pretend last night was just a dream, but she cannot escape the reality of the words she witnessed, the words she needs to untangle to see the real picture. But what she currently understands is startling. The full conspiracy is confirmed by the distinct seals of the President of the United States and the Central Intelligence Agency.

Her Klonopin won't help her now. Her reliance on Klonopin will force her to make a very difficult decision of experiencing the excruciating withdrawals to stay awake or take the risk of sleep. At this time she prefers manic.

Staring at the dried blood on her hand from the tiny puncture wounds left by Kat's jewelry, she prays the droplet of blood hidden under Kat's shoes will not be discovered, but her gut tells her a different story. Her frantic fear last night had led her to a state of mind where she lost control of her senses.

"I panicked! I left my blood. They will come. Soon. The tiny drop of blood is concealed for now, but once they discover the missing documents, they will find it," Sarah fearfully says aloud. "My DNA will lead them right to me. The map of my death."

She had found incriminating evidence and had left incriminating evidence as well. Sarah makes an elementary decision to live or die. She chooses to fight to live. Now she begins developing a plan to reveal the conspiracy to the world, and she understands she has only hit the tip of the iceberg. Extrapolating more evidence from the encrypted CIA letter will be a daunting task, but it is one she is prepared to attack.

Sarah peeks out of a slit she makes with her hand in her office blinds to check if Cole is home. His house looks as lonely and deserted, as it did yesterday. She longs for his security but knows she can tell him nothing. Sharing her secret with him would put his life in danger. "I need Warren. He will know what to do." She knows he is out of the country and is difficult to reach, but she tries relentlessly to reach him to no avail. She is able to leave one message on his cell with the hope of it reaching him soon. She is bewildered by the situation she has ignorantly thrust herself into. She is unable to think clearly making irrational decisions.

Cooper senses her uneasiness and hides under the bed.

Only adding to her mania, Sarah continues drinking strong coffee to keep her awake. Sweating, pacing, and checking and re-checking her fortress, she carries her loaded 9mm close by her side.

She carefully removes the letter and the soft, pliable packet she had felt inside the envelope the night before but had no time to investigate during the chaos. She lays the letter on the counter next to the packet of powdery substance. She is hypnotized by the diabolical plot lying in front of her. She knows she must tell someone of this evil plot, but without Warren, who? She can only trust him.

Opening the letter, she forces herself to read each word that forms the conspiracy involving the CIA and ViaStem. Sarah feels dizzy and nauseous, races to the bathroom, and empties her gut. Kneeling in front of the toilet, she is covered in a cold sweat and weeps uncontrollably. She feels no relief.

As she once again attempts to absorb the contents of the letter, the phone rings, causing Sarah's heart to freeze. She sees from the caller ID that it is Warren. "Oh, thank God." With trembling hands, Sarah answers the phone only to hear silence on the other end. "Hello? Hello? Warren, is it you? Please, God," Sarah begs.

The line goes dead, and Sarah throws the phone onto the couch as if it burned her hands. Covering her mouth with both hands, she stumbles backward into a table, causing an heirloom vase displaying bright yellow sunflowers to rock, fall, and shatter on the tile floor. It doesn't faze Sarah, as her eyes remain fixed on the phone. Tears stream down her face. The phone rings again, causing Sarah to jump. She wants to jump out of her skin and run away from this fear. She slowly walks toward the echoing rings, stepping over chunks of porcelain. Once again the caller ID screen reads *Warren McNary*. Her head pounds, and her gut churns. She answers the phone and speaks hesitantly and quietly into the receiver, "He-hello? " She waits in agonizing pain.

"Sarah, it's Warren. I just picked up your message. I just

called, but the call dropped. You sound frantic. What is it? Are you all right?"

Sarah becomes hysterical.

"Sarah, please calm down and tell me what's going on."

"I didn't listen to you, Warren. I'm sorry. I had lunch with Kat yesterday, and she said so many things that … that last night I-I broke into her house, Warren, and I'm now involved in a horrible nightmare." Sarah weeps out of control.

"Sarah, you need to focus and tell me what happened. Did you find something? What are you talking about a horrible nightmare? What is it?"

"Warren … I didn't think. It is all a plan … the CIA … ViaStem … all the death," Sarah spews the incomprehensible news at Warren.

Warren is fuming at Sarah's involvement, but he doesn't unleash his fury because he knows the damage is already done. He needs to get Sarah under control in order to obtain all the information she is trying to communicate to him.

He firmly demands that Sarah calm down so he can understand what she is trying to tell him. There is an extended silence that kills him. "Sarah … are you there?"

Now somewhat under control, Sarah speaks in a shaky voice, which only cracks a few times. "I broke into Kat's house last night and found two letters. One is addressed to Kat from the CIA, and the other is from the President of the United States, congratulating Kat on her promotion as CEO of ViaStem. There is a list … a 'kill list' … Oh my God, Warren. Calvin's promotion was only punishable by an agonizing death. His murder was the only way to get Kat in control of ViaStem. It's only my theory, but it is the only way their plan would work, Warren."

Silence. Sarah tries desperately to hold back tears.

"Sarah, please continue …"

Sarah continues with fear in her voice. "Mr. Stevens and Calvin wouldn't go along with the plan, but Kat did. They killed … It was a diversion, Warren. Calvin, he was poisoned with arsenic.

"Sarah, how do you know that?"

"In the CIA letter, almost the entire page is encrypted. I've been trying to decipher it, and I think I've uncovered some clues. I found *qdthirtyeightmicrogramsas* hidden between so many other numbers and words.

"What does that mean? It just sounds like a bunch of letters, Sarah."

"I broke it down, Warren. I know *AS* is the symbol for arsenic, so I Googled that. That search came up with a slew of variations, one on how to kill with arsenic. I know qd means once a day. Thirty-eight thousand micrograms of arsenic once a day can lead to a slow death."

"That seems primitive for an encryption, Sarah."

Sarah disregards Warren's remark, consumed by the idea of a conspiracy.

Warren knows exactly what CAA and ASH3 signify— Calvin's death. Trace evidence was discovered during his investigation of the recovery of Calvin's pubic hair collected at the Bear Mountain cabin. *Hair—the keeper of trace evidence,* Warren thinks to himself

Sarah continues, "Kat followed those instructions on how to slowly poison Calvin. Calvin warned me that if anything was to happen to him to look no farther than Kat. I believe I have the remaining sample of arsenic. What I don't understand, Warren, is that Calvin was recovering. Remember? And then she convinced him to go to their cabin, and he was dead in a week. Oh God. I should have done something. See, now

Kat can work hand in hand with the government. I know there is so much more hidden in the encryption. It's difficult to concentrate, so overwhelming …" Sarah's thoughts race wildly.

"Sarah, what do you think this plan is?"

"I also found a splice of wording that spells out *project restoration*. That is "Project Restoration," the title of the *TIME* article about Stephen. It's on my refrigerator. Then I discovered the word *soldiers,* the initials *C,* and the words *test, pilot, no witnesses,* and then a bunch more letters and numbers I haven't figured it out yet. It is only a developing theory. I don't know. Something is not right." Sarah's voice fades.

Warren pieces the evidence he knows with what Sarah is telling him, and he knows this is a full-blown conspiracy. *With the President and criminals hiding under the umbrella of the CIA, nothing good will come out of this situation.* Even though he is aware from hearing Sarah's somewhat neurotic tangents, he is confident she is more than competent to understand the danger of the theorem unraveling.

Warren demands Sarah's attention, "Sarah, you need to listen to me closely. Do you understand? Do you understand, Sarah?"

"Yes, Warren."

"We need to get off the phone. *Now.* It may be dangerous. I will come back as soon as I can. We are wrapping up this project. Do not talk on this phone or your Blackberry. No e-mailing or texting. Stay off the Internet. And don't leave your house or turn on any lights. Use a flashlight if you need to see something. No electricity, Sarah. It will get hot and stuffy, but you cannot have the outside air conditioner running. Do not answer your door for anyone, not even if it's someone you know and trust. You are not home. Do you understand?" Warren demands.

"Yes, Warren. I promise," Sarah says apologetically. "I'm so sorry, Warren. I didn't listen to you." Sarah's voice grows shaky, and she begins to cry.

"It will be okay, Sarah. I promise. I will be back in a couple days. I will try to leave earlier, but I don't want to look suspicious and possibly alert someone. Be strong, Sarah. I know you can do this," Warren says with confidence but worries in silence not to alarm Sarah further.

"Please hurry, Warren. Please," she begs.

Warren silently analyzes the information Sarah has just revealed. He knows this is a conspiracy, and he is confident that Sarah's life is most certainly in danger and possibly his as well.

Sarah awakens to the darkness of her once-safe environment, which is now a prison. She can't shut off her mind. The possibility of a conspiracy loops repeatedly in her thoughts. She hides in the corner of her closet, where she feels the safest. No windows, no doors, no light. She is alone with her fear. She is filthy, still covered in detergent but too paranoid to take a shower for fear of "them" watching her or reading the water meter as it ticks away the minutes of her life. She won't waver from Warren's orders, not this time.

She holds her legs tightly to her chest to make herself seem small and insignificant, wishing she could disappear. Her gun lies to one side, and the letter and its contents sit on the other side of her body. Clicking on her flashlight, she reads the letter again and again, now obsessing over the words that deeply haunt her. She aches for Stephen. How she wishes he were here to keep her safe. How she misses him. She lays the letter down and crawls to retrieve Stephen's burned tag and wedding ring. These belongings are as close as she will ever be to him again. She crawls back to the closet in pure blackness. Her body involuntarily twitches. She is lightheaded, and her eyelids feel heavy, but she is manic.

Sharply awakened by rustling, she holds herself completely still. She stoically listens to the eerie silence. With great relief, she realizes it is Cooper walking over her shoes to be with her. Sensing evil, he retreats, distancing himself. His absence doesn't faze her. She is too preoccupied by the events.

Seconds have turned into minutes, and minutes have turned into hours of waiting in black silence. She has to leave her hiding place just long enough to use the restroom. Without her flashlight, she crawls to the hallway bathroom. The wool carpet is rough against her skin. Shamefully Cooper has no other options than to relieve himself on the carpet. Sarah is keen to his disgraced body language and cuddles him, repeating, "Good boy. It's all right. You're a good boy." Cooper relaxes his tense muscles and licks Sarah's chin.

In desperation she crawls to the hallway closet and searches for a case of bottled water, which she easily identifies by touch. Desperately ripping open the plastic cover, she opens several bottles of water, chugs a few, and then pours bottle after bottle over her head. The soapy taste doesn't deter her. The air is thick and stale, and she relishes in the coolness. Cooper licks her wet skin. Sarah pours water into her hands, making a makeshift bowl for Cooper.

Crawling to the bathroom across from the closet, she wipes the grime from her face with a hand towel. Still alert to her surroundings, she stops frequently just to listen. She is grateful for the silence. She crawls back to the closet, removes the grimy clothes she can no longer stand against her skin, and shoves them into the closet. She rinses as best she can with bottled water. The water rescues her from unbearable thirst, and how wonderful if feels flowing over her chafed skin. With the small hand towel she grabbed from the bathroom, she pats her face and body, purposely leaving a light mist of moisture on her thirsty skin. She barricades the perimeter of her bedroom with the empty bottles to give her a warning signal if someone enters the room from the front of the house, office, or rear bedrooms. Crawling back to her cave, she drags two bottles of water and tucks one in her bra. Her thinking is more rational now, at least for the time being.

With nothing but time, she clicks her flashlight on and again reviews the CIA letter and searching for more detail. She reviews and studies each detail of the encrypted message. "What is the hidden message? Keep searching," she rambles to herself and continues to question everything she holds in her hands. Her muscles ache from the enormity of the evidence she holds. *Mr. Stevens wouldn't go along with it, nor would Calvin. That's where Kat comes in. That is why she became CEO with no questions. But why ViaStem? And no questions about Calvin's sudden illness and death. And no body to bury. Are there more victims?*

Sarah takes a break from the endless questions pounding in her head. She picks up Stephen's last remains—his burned toe tag. Her mind swirls with thoughts and wanders aimlessly.

Why a toe tag? Those are for dead soldiers, for identification. Where is Stephen's body? Where is Stephen's other tag? Maybe he is alive. Maybe he was burned to death with his men. Oh dear God, I pray not. Sarah loses control of organized thought processes from the manic rollercoaster she is riding. She clenches the burned tag, holding it against her heart. Then, holding it away from her, she flashes the light on it but cannot read the scorched tag. She pours water over it, which washes away some of the dusty chunks of debris. Something isn't right. She sees something strange ... odd. Immediately she crawls to the bathroom sink, grabs her toothbrush and toothpaste, and returns to her cave.

Her wet bra and panties give her a chill, so she yanks one of Stephen's button-down shirts from a hanger and wraps herself in it to feel warm and safe, as if Stephen were holding her. Before working on cleaning the tag, she brushes her teeth several times. Heaven! Because of extreme exhaustion, her mood quickly switches from frightened to sad, weak to strong, rational to irrational, but she makes the decision to remain awake rather than chancing falling into a deep sleep if she takes Klonopin.

Without hesitation, she wets the tag again and squirts a small amount of toothpaste on it—the only cleanser she can identify by memory in the pitch black. Trying to save battery strength, she intermittently turns her flashlight on and off to check her work. Wetting the toothbrush, she begins what becomes an endless obsession to clean his last remains. With each brush, the tag reveals a little more devastating information. Most of the engravings on the tag are legible now except one important piece of information.

She continues to scrub until the morning sun peeks into her windows. Exhaustion wins over Sarah's mind, and fatigue overtakes her muscles. Her hands ache. She has been awake all night.

"I must move." Sarah crawls from her cave and lies stretched out on the bedroom floor. Stephen's shirt is wet in the shape of panties and a bra. "My back ..." Her lower back aches as she presses it against the carpet. Her legs feel numb, as does her mind. She rests her eyes only for a moment though. She dreams of Stephen. The dream makes no sense, but it is filled with him and only him, and that makes her happy.

Shaken from her peaceful dream, far from this nightmare, she knows she cannot sleep. She fights to stay awake. As she fights to conquer sleep, she crawls to the front hallway and peeks at Cole's house through the window. His car is in the driveway. How she would love to run to him, but she cannot. "I will put his life in danger."

She will never go against her promise to Warren, never again. The note she left on Cole's front door is gone. He must have read it by now. She's saddened that he hasn't called or come by.

Tired of being locked up in the dark closet, Sarah crawls back to the bedroom but not into the closet. She scoots to the blinds that look out to the backyard. Her hands and knees feel raw and sting with the scrape of each coarse fiber of carpet. She daringly peeks out from the bottom corner far from the door opening. She sees Rudy and Rio munching away on their Bermuda hay mixed with rich alfalfa. The day seems extraordinarily bright, making the mountains appear more majestic than usual. Her patio furniture is covered in dust and cobwebs. She spots a spiderweb with a white egg sack tucked against the corner of a chair.

The patio umbrella has blown over once again because of the Santa Ana winds sweeping down from the mountains. She continues studying her backyard and discovers minuet, insignificant details. A mother rabbit appears from a hole in the ground to look for food while she leaves her babies safely hidden in their burrow.

The sunlight that catches Sarah's once lovely face now reveals dark circles accenting her sad eyes, which have lost their lively sparkle. Her porcelain skin is now pale and sunken in despair. Her body appears frail and tired from unimaginable stress. She suddenly pulls away from the window and tries to catch her breath.

"It's Cole." He is on her back patio trying to peek into the dining room. "Why? Why doesn't he just knock on the front door?" Sarah questions his actions. "Be still, he cannot know I am home. Cooper. Where's Cooper? He cannot bark. Not a sound."

Sarah whispers for Cooper, who emerges from under the bed. He scampers into her arms, and she quickly crawls to the dark closet to hide. Pressed firmly against the back wall of the closet, she folds into her upright fetal position to make herself feel inconspicuous. Holding Cooper tightly, she feels the abrasions on her knees stretch with pain. She grimaces but utters no sound. She waits. She hears footsteps outside her sliding back door. Shadowy movements intermittently appear through the cracks in the vertical blinds.

Cole peers in the glass door. Sarah can see him, but she is certain she is completely covered in blackness. Her heart stops. She cannot breathe. Her chest deeply aches. She holds Cooper's snout and turns him away to avoid his barking at the shadows. Cole finally leaves.

Sarah sporadically naps during the day. She believes it is safer. She convinces herself of that, anyway. Her mania makes it difficult to gain relief from shutting her eyes. She is restless. When she wakes, the sun is saying goodnight. A dreadful feeling eats away at her gut. She hates nights. She has hated nights for what seems an eternity. Darkness means nightmares, and now she is living one.

Sarah cracks the door just enough to see the inside of her bedroom. To keep her mind occupied, she returns to cleaning Stephens's dog tag. The mystery is coming clearer with each stroke of the brush. What she discovers is another nightmare. Rinsing her eyes with clean water and drying them with the shirt she is wearing only makes the horrible discovery more vivid. She wonders if she is hallucinating. Is she bordering on the fine line of reality? With a sickening feeling, she examines his tag closely. Everything is correct: his full name—Stephen Lance Benton; his social security number; and his religious preference. Everything but his blood type. He is A positive, not A negative.

"He is A positive, not A negative," she says aloud to herself. "*Shit!*" Needles fly through Sarah's body, stinging her flesh. She holds the tag to her heart, knowing Stephen is in terrible danger.

Sarah grabs the persecuting letter to search for new clues buried under hundreds of letters and numbers. She reads it over and over and over. In an enlightening trice Sarah's mind flashes back to the clues she extrapolated from the encryption. She repeats aloud to herself, "Soldiers, CG, no witnesses." Vehemently she grabs the letter and searches for a link for those words. "Project Restoration. CG … CG …? What is that? At ViaStem our clinic trials always have a control group. Maybe that's it?"

Sarah sits in silence pondering her theory. "Project Restoration … to restore what? Soldiers." Sarah chokes with an eerie sensation traveling up her spine. "Why ViaStem? Biotech? Cloning?"

She gasps. "ViaStem … Oh my God. Cloning. No witnesses. Shit … a control group. For what? Cloning soldiers? It can't be. It's too crazy." Defeated and sitting in a slumped position, Sarah asks one more question. "What happened to Stephen?" She sleeps for what seems seconds but in actuality is hours. She loses track of time.

Sarah awakes to an excruciating headache—her first true withdrawal symptom. As she crawls to the bathroom, her body aches. Her equilibrium falters, and she steadies herself against the wall on her trip to the bathroom. Her eyes feel painfully strained, her muscles twitch, and her skin crawls. She has tried to stop the drug before, and the withdrawals were butchering. It has always been easier to keep her friend, even though her doses have reached levels of six or more grams per day, three or more grams over compliance.

Giving in, she takes half a tablet, hoping to rid her body of the uncomfortable symptoms, but it is a futile effort. She needs more just to take the edge off but dares not.

Chapter 19:

Two Plus Two

The sound of plastic bottles crunching under the weight of an intruder startles Sarah from her drug-induced coma. With her mind clouded with cobwebs, she pushes up against the back wall of what has been her safe haven for the past couple days. She has lost track of time. With little water and no food, her body is listless. With no Klonopin, she is in full withdrawal. She feels nauseous and feverish. Fear once again drives adrenaline through her veins, jolting her back to reality.

Sarah picks up her Browning Hi-Power 9mm and slowly removes the safety. Once a bullet loads into the chamber, she firmly grips the fierce cold metal and aims the gun directly at the entrance of the closet, ready to fire, ready to kill the intruder to save her own life. Beyond her pounding, throbbing headache, Sarah gains control of her weapon, holding it steady and deliberately.

Footsteps move away from her bedroom. Silence. The silence echoes within Sarah's head. How it aches. With the next crackle of plastic, Sarah is well aware of the movements of the intruder, who is now heading in her direction. With utter anguish, Sarah hears footsteps enter her bedroom. With the flick of the overhead light, Sarah squints from being in the dark cell. Cooper scurries from the closet. Sarah remains still as she fights the withdrawal. *Breathe, Sarah. Stay in control.*

She breathes calmly, relaxing her muscles so she can make the most accurate shot she may ever have to fire. A familiar voice greets Cooper, but Sarah is frozen in the moment and disoriented from the frightening circumstances of the past week.

Warren walks directly in the path of her aim, turns, and spots Sarah at the back of the closet, aiming the 9mm directly at him. Slowly raising his hands in front of him, he moves slightly to the right while talking Sarah out of her deep concentration, which could trigger a reaction that could end his life.

"Sarah … it's me, Warren. It's Warren, honey. Please put the gun down. Everything is okay now, Sarah," Warren says in a calm voice. He encourages her to relax while he moves slowly away from the target zone, even though he knows a bullet can travel through the closet door and hit him, killing him instantly.

He doesn't see Sarah even breathe. He is three days behind schedule, and it is obvious that she has hidden herself in the safety of her dark closet. Her flashlight dims as the batteries fade. Warren can see her leaning in fear against the wall.

Warren notices she is filthy, gaunt, and pale with fear. He continues to talk to her, trying to get her back to reality and get her to lower her weapon. He sees her exhale and move. She stares at him as if he is only in her imagination.

"Sarah, I'm here now. You can come out. It's okay now,

Sarah. You are safe. It's Warren," he continues to relay this message to her until she finally believes he is real.

Sarah realizes she is not dreaming. She lowers the gun and sets it on the floor. Warren slowly and carefully moves toward her. Coming to reality, she weeps and shivers uncontrollably. Warren enters the closet and picks up the gun.

"Warren …" Sarah cries, holding onto him tightly.

Warren helps her up and sits her on the bed. He just stares at her face, which reveals the horror she has lived for the past six days. Her lovely face is pale and thin. The dark circles under her eyes steal their emerald beauty. Her beautiful auburn hair is knotted with white chalk. She appears weathered and filled with sadness. Her knees are caked with dried blood, but it doesn't seem to faze Sarah. Nothing seems to faze her. She is nearly incoherent, lost in another world. Her body language is that of unequivocal defeat. Warren feels badly that he left her here three days longer than he promised.

"I'm so sorry, Sarah. I got here as fast as I could. I thought I would be three days, but there was a national emergency—"

"What? What emergency? What now?" Sarah begs for the truth.

"We don't have to talk about that now. We need to get some food and water in you. You look very weak." Warren tries to distract Sarah from another piece of bad news to avoid fracturing her fragile state.

"Goddamnit, Warren! What emergency?"

Warren is slightly stunned by Sarah's abruptness.

"Vice President Roberts was assassinated yesterday morning," Warren timidly relays the tragic news.

Sarah rocks forward, releasing a gasp of agonizing pain at all the tragedy and death that has occurred in her life in the past year. Tears well in her sad eyes, which long to regain their sparkle.

"What is happening, Warren? What the hell is happening? Everything is falling apart!" Sarah screams as tears streak her face. Looking into Warren's concerned eyes, she searches for answers, but he has none to offer. She just stares at him and slowly shakes her head in disbelief. She doesn't break down or become hysterical. Instead she lowers her head and weeps. Warren sits beside her and holds her tightly and safely.

With Warren still holding Sarah, she whispers in a scratchy voice, "Warren, I believe I have deciphered the encryption of the CIA letter. It is horrific. As far as the letter from the President to Kat, it only confirms a conspiracy."

"Sarah, we can discuss this after you get cleaned up and eat something—"

Jumping up, Sarah angrily snaps, "Goddamnit, Warren. Fuck that! Fuck this whole thing. People are being killed, experimented with. We will discuss this now—right now."

Warren is stunned by Sarah's hostile response but tries to understand. He turns toward her and reaches out to hold her hand. "All right. Tell me what you have found."

"Sorry," she says. "Remember the theory I was so convinced of? Kat killing Calvin, the CIA, Project Restoration, our soldiers …" Sarah begins the story.

"Yes. Yes, Sarah, I remember."

"I unscrambled numerous clues beyond what I had already extrapolated last time we spoke. I identified several initials identifying people of possible interest. People who have been murdered and possibly many who will be murdered to keep this project a secret." Sarah breaks off, rubbing her eyes, which feel like they're going to explode from the pressure in her head. "I found Calvin's initials first, and that piqued my interest to concentrate on finding more names. I did … many more. I found H.L. Stevens—" Sarah's voice cracks and slurs, but she clears her throat to cough up the next initials. "Stephen's, all his men … When they deployed this round, they were already dead, Warren." Sarah is shaking, trying desperately to hold it together.

"I also discovered that the charred dog tag you gave me, it's incorrect. The information is incorrect. It's wrong, Warren. Stephen's blood type is incorrect on the tag Warren. He is A positive, not A negative. That's pretty significant."

Sarah drags herself to her feet and returns to her dungeon to retrieve Stephen's tag and the envelope holding the two letters and the packet of arsenic. She places them on the white down comforter, opens each letter, and places the bag of grayish-white substance that feels heavier than a powder so Warren can have full view of the evidence. She shivers just looking down at the murder plot unfolding in front of her.

Regurgitating chunks of information without making sense, Sarah has to stop herself from speaking. She gathers every ounce of strength she has left to keep her story organized and unemotional so Warren will understand the urgency of each word. She unfolds a wrinkled piece of paper she took from one of her shoe boxes meant only to protect the shoes from any damage. The flimsy, crackled paper now contains scribbled data that won't protect the President, the CIA, Kat, and—unfortunately—ViaStem from any damage if she can tell the world about the conspiracy, which she vows to do to avenge Stephen's suspicious disappearance as well as all of the other names hidden in the letter.

Sarah directs Warren to look at each point she has written

on the lightweight chronicle. The first point introduces a rather long list that confirms Sarah's theory; it lists the President and CIA, Kat poisoning Calvin with instructions from the CIA, and the finality of Calvin's death most likely finished by the CIA burning the CCA wood.

"It probably didn't take much to finish him off. He was so weak and ill at that point. They knew he found something and needed him out of the way," Sarah continues, directing Warren down the list of proof. "Then we have ViaStem, the world's foremost leader in cloning and genetics research. Project Restoration and the soldiers come next. The President recruited corrupt CIA agents, bribed corrupt ViaStem researchers and Kat to assist him in improving his reputation by taking full control of the war by increasing the number of soldiers, as well as quickening the protocol for ViaStem's HESC cloning procedure.

"Project Restoration One was just the President's muse for Project Restoration Two. This is why Calvin couldn't determine how ViaStem had over one thousand subjects in trials. I remember Calvin telling me that in the parking lot at the gym. Warren, I remember the questionable look on his face when he told me, but he continued his conversation. He knew something was wrong."

"Sarah … please go on," Warren says.

"The President was playing both sides of the card. He looks like a hero to the thousands with chronic diseases by accelerating the FDA's approval of the HESC G42 process, but on the dark side he is providing the humans necessary to conduct clinical trials for his ultimate plan, which will make him look like a hero with the strongest military in the world."

Warren is speechless.

"The only humans used in the final clinical trials were volunteers, and there were not nearly enough of them to move this project as quickly as it has moved to launch HESC G42. So our soldiers became the unknowing human subjects for the trials. The government just counted them as killed in action. But then his plan got even sicker, more screwed up. In his sick mind he thought maybe they could eventually clone soldiers so he could look good to the public, look in control. Project Restoration Two. One project funded the next. How fucking twisted is that?" Sarah slurs.

"Enlistments have plummeted recently, but this way he still looks victorious. In his mind, with double or triple the number of soldiers, we can win the war on terrorism. He would be a hero! At least in his own mind. Unfortunately, there had to be a clinical trial to increase the numbers—a control group to complete the pilot project, Project Restoration." Even though Sarah's story is repetitive, choppy, and broken in places, Warren easily grasps the overall theme. "One of the control groups was Stephen's unit." Sarah pauses to swallow her sadness when she says Stephen's name. Clearing her throat again, she continues, "Stephen's men were one of many control groups. They were executed and then cloned and then disposed of to wipe away any traces of evidence ..." Sarah's voice dies from the pain of the souls she found buried.

"Look. All of their initials are here." Sarah points to each one in the mixture of letters and numbers. "Kat most likely received an enormous bribe to use ViaStem's knowledge on cloning procedures. Ya know, Warren, Kat doesn't surprise me at all. Now I know what she was celebrating at lunch that day. Sick bitch," Sarah continues to rant without missing a beat, repeating key issues. "The scientists involved were most likely paid well." Scrolling down the page toward the bottom, Sarah points to a block of letters. "But look, here are her initials. I hope they're her initials. She is going to hell sooner than she plans," Sarah calmly finishes that sentence with vindication in her voice.

Warren sits quietly, absorbing this unconscionable information. After hearing her story and seeing the evidence, he believes Sarah's theory is more than just a theory.

"I couldn't find our initials ... not yet anyway. Warren?" Sarah hesitantly asks.

Jumping up from her position with nearly an inappropriate excitement to add more damning evidence to the intolerable conspiracy, she turns quickly toward him and grabs the encrypted letter. She intensely searches the document until she finds another infectious spore of evidence. "Look. See? KQR." Sarah points to the letters buried in the encryption. "Vice President Kathleen Quinn Roberts. She must have known. She discovered something. Shit. She was the person that balanced that asshole out." Staggering and slurring her words, Sarah blurts out the words, ranting like a drunk. Her withdrawal symptoms are evident yet oscillating.

Sarah is shocked with her discovery, and Warren is just as shocked, but it makes sense.

"The timing makes sense, Warren."

Warren's brain now swirls as he searches for a solution to the discovery of a major conspiracy. "Sarah, we both know the power the President has, but a corrupt President will do anything to protect his reputation. Anything!" Warren begins to pace while Sarah sits back down on the bed and watches him walk back and forth. "We are in grave danger if they know we have this evidence," he warns her. "Do you think anyone saw you? Do you think you left anything— fingerprints, any evidence in Kat's house?"

Sarah lowers her head in shame. In a shallow voice, "Yes, Warren. I believe I did, if they find it. Whenever Kat goes to open that safe, she will know the envelopes are missing, and I'm certain they will look for any hint of who was at the scene, who took the papers."

Warren asks with hesitation, "What do you think you left behind, Sarah?"

Sarah looks into Warren's eyes with pure guilt and rolls her right hand over, showing the blood-crusted puncture wounds on the palm of hand. "I left blood, a single drop of blood temporarily hidden by the shoe rack covering the safe."

Warren rubs his jawline and chin, contemplating their next move. "We have to get out of here. Soon. They will eventually discover the robbery and the missing documents." Warren holds Sarah's arms tightly as she faces him. With brave conviction, he warns her that their lives are nothing to a corrupt government. "What are two more murders to them? We have to escape. We must make a plan. When did you say Kat is moving?"

"In a week. Why?"

"That's our deadline, Sarah."

"But what about Stephen? We can't just leave," Sarah begs, not wanting to believe in Stephen's fate in that cold dark cave in Afghanistan.

Holding Sarah's arms tightly, Warren begins to shout but then drops his voice to a whisper of guilt, knowing he should have told her the truth long ago. "Sarah, Stephen is ... Sarah, Stephen is dead. He is dead!"

Deep inside her heart, she has known the truth but constantly blocked the answer from her mind with hope. She covers her mouth in disbelief. Tears fill her eyes and streak down her face. They desperately cling to her jawline but eventually have to let go and fall to the floor. Now Sarah has to let go. She has to face the truth and let go of Stephen for real, forever, but she is angry with Warren for covering the truth. She forcefully pulls away from him and slaps him across the face.

Warren's eyes are filled with sadness. "I didn't want to hurt you. I didn't find out that his death was final until later, and I just couldn't tell you. You were so very sad and lost. I didn't want … Oh my God, Sarah. Please forgive me. I was going to tell you because I knew you would find out … I'm so sorry. So sorry …"

Sadness and disgust at her only true confidant blatantly lying to her shuts her emotions off with the flick of the truth, like a light switch. Sarah covers her mouth with her hands folded together and her fingers intertwined as she says a silent prayer. She turns and begins walking toward the bathroom to take a much-deserved shower. Turning back to look at a defeated Warren, whose shoulders are slumped forward, she sadly comments, "And this was so much easier … now?"

Sarah disappears into the bathroom to try to wash away the hurt and sadness in her heart. Deep within her heart, she quickly forgives Warren because she knows he hadn't meant to hurt her. *He is the only one I have left.*

She re-enters the bedroom while the water gets hot. Steam seeps out the slightly open door. Looking directly into Warren's blank eyes, she says, "Ironic though, how a single dog tag used to identify a dead soldier also helped identify a major conspiracy. Promise me something, Warren. We need to let the world know about this. Promise me that much."

Warren, speechless, nods in agreement.

The scalding water feels like pins pricking her dry, chapped skin. The pain distracts her momentarily from the truth, which is much more painful. She presses her hands against the tile in front of her, feeling each drop of water hit her face. She weeps. She turns away, wishing she could run from the truth. All she can see in her mind is Stephen. Loops of Stephen's life play through her mind over and over.

Why did all of this happen? I wish we could go back in time, to the way it was before, before all the chaos started, Stephen, Sarah talks to Stephen silently in her mind. Leaning against the hot tile, she slides to the shower floor and holds her knees tightly to her chest, trying to feel safe. She weeps uncontrollably.

Unable to move, Warren sits in shame. He can hear Sarah weeping in agony. His eyes are filled with sadness. They fill with tears, but he holds them tight. He knows he needs to quickly devise a plan to keep Sarah safe, safe from the truth she is now fully aware of. *All of it. She now knows everything now,* Warren thinks to himself, wiping his eyes and clearing his throat. He must find out if they are being watched, if they are in immediate danger. He retrieves the gun from the closet and checks out front but sees nothing unusual. He checks the garage and each door and discovers nothing suspicious.

"Not yet anyway," Warren whispers to himself.

Opening the pocket doors to the dining area Warren discovers the mountain of information Sarah has built and followed over months as she has desperately searched for answers. Answers he held tight. Warren swallows hard but the guilt remains. He scans the pictures, articles, and reports

Sarah stole from his briefcase about findings revealed in Calvin's autopsy report—his vomit and hair.

He reads each sticky note Sarah has stuck on the walls, quietly whispering to himself, "Leading her to nothing until her need for answers led her to conduct her own investigation and the danger she is in now. This is my doing, goddamnit!" He slams down the gun. If he had only told her about Stephen, maybe she would still be safe.

He walks out of the room and seals the vault behind him. After almost tripping over Cooper, he reaches down, picks him up, and carries him outside to the backyard, leaving the French doors ajar behind him. Cooper licks Warren's chin with unconditional kisses. Warren is emotionless and numb from his unintentionally heartless secret. He stands in the bright, warm sun only to feel cold and see darkness. Taking deep drags from his cigarette, he ponders their next move.

They are a true team now. They have no choice. "We must trust one another because there is no one else we can rely on. Her family needs to stay far away from this nightmare for their safety." He prays they will be safe. "I will ensure their safety. Somehow. But for now it is Sarah and I … alone." Warren says with redeeming conviction.

Sarah emerges from her long-awaited shower. She walks slowly to her nightstand and takes two Klonopin that she knows she should have taken long ago. In twenty minutes she will not feel dizzy, clumsy, or mentally cloudy. She will no longer skip thoughts and not be able to recall the next. She will no longer slur her words. Her skin will no longer crawl with a million red ants. Her head will no longer pound in excruciating agony. Her eyes will no longer feel the immense pressure from within. She will no longer hold anger for Warren's lie because she knows they are a true team now.

"We have no choice. We must trust one another because there is no one else we can rely on," she whispers to herself.

Sarah joins Warren on the patio. The feel of the warm sun offers little comfort. She stands next to him in silence for several minutes. They silently watch Cooper play in the grass. Without looking at him, Sarah reaches over and holds Warren's hand in forgiveness. Warren squeezes her hand in hope.

Chapter 20:

The Plan

Sarah's recovery from her manic week in haunting darkness is a renewal of her life. She and Warren anticipate that the single drop of blood she left in Kat's closet will be found by the CIA. If it is discovered and analyzed, they both understand her DNA is a map that will lead the killers to end her life and possibly Warren's also. From the information Kat gave to Sarah on their girls' day out, Sarah knows Kat will be moving from her home in Country Estates within the next week, leaving her and Warren little time.

Without concentrating on the uncontrollable events in her life, Sarah concentrates on enjoying living. Her eyes are bright again with the sparkle of joy and happiness. Her smile frequently alludes to her newfound happiness and stability. Feeling enraptured with energy, she recovers in great strides. In the last few days, Sarah has reined in her use of Klonopin back to her physician's recommended dosage. Sarah no longer has to force herself to get out of bed or be scraped from the ceiling. She is comfortable in her own skin. She feels peaceful. She and Warren enjoy the calm before the storm.

Warren and Sarah are now a cohesive team with identical goals—safety, freedom and the conviction of the President. Now back in San Diego to continue the terrorist investigations, Warren visits Sarah's home regularly to check all the locks on the windows. He performs intricate searches for any listening devices. He thoroughly scouts the perimeter of the house for unusual objects left behind by someone on a stakeout, such as cigarette butts, tread marks left by boot soles, or footprints.

Sarah's once-hidden secret vault overflowing with clues surrounding the conspiracy is now spotlessly neat and clean. No one will ever be aware she knows anything about anything, certainly not a government conspiracy. The room is once again a dining room, not Sarah's obsession to find the truth. She now knows the perilous truth.

Each of Warren's visits to Sarah's home is also the ideal opportunity to discuss, revise, and rehearse their plan of escape. They realize the time will come when they will be forced into seclusion. They will no longer live their current lives as Sarah and Warren. They have no reservations, though; it's just reality. As Sarah often says to Warren, and he joins in simultaneously, "It is what it is."

Sarah's responsibilities to ensure the success of their plan is to tell the world about the indescribable government conspiracy that was designed and executed by the President of the United States, the Commander in Chief who abandoned our U.S. soldiers who risk their lives daily for Americans' freedoms.

She stays busy organizing all evidence, which includes the President's letter to Kat, the encrypted CIA letter filled with initials of death, the packet of arsenic, and Warren's evidence disclosing Calvin's murder. Making numerous copies and dividing any physical evidence into its smallest testable quantities seems like a simple task, but Sarah finds it more difficult than she thought in an effort to maintain her anonymity.

She utilizes several copy stores in different locations to help hide her identity, and she always pays in cash. She researches newspapers with the largest circulations. She reviews her intricate plans for shipping and double packaging the original envelopes to ensure delivery. She has several packages prepared and stored in her garage, hidden in a piece of luggage. However, she always keeps one package in the trunk of her car as her plan B, just in case she cannot reach her house to retrieve the premade packets of evidence. If she needs to print more in an emergency situation, the letters will convincingly demonstrate guilt. She is careful to wear latex gloves when touching all items and only uses self-sealing packaging to prevent leaving any further DNA behind. She longs for this diabolical secret to be everyone's front-page news.

I don't want Stephen, his men, Calvin, and Mr. Stevens to have died in vain. This is Sarah's top priority.

While Sarah works on her part of plan A, which is to stay alive while preparing to alert the world of the conspiracy, Warren concentrates on his part. With the most-trusted, secure contacts he has developed throughout his career, he changes his and Sarah's identities and duplicates new identities into documents of necessity.

They both cash out their 401K programs, annuities, stocks, bonds, life insurance, and savings to gather as much cash as possible before they run. Warren determines their new places of residence and arranges passage to these locations. They will split as a team when it is time to run. Warren believes they will be safer living in different locations, which will be more difficult for the authorities to track. However, he includes several pre-paid phone cards so they can contact one another when they reach their destinations.

Immediately Warren cancels his cell and has Sarah do the same. They switch to pre-paid cell phones for quick disposal. He secures all documents, cash, and plane tickets in separate packages for immediate escapes if necessary. For the time being, Warren has the two packages locked in a safety deposit box at an undisclosed bank. He prays that when the time comes to run, he will have enough time to get the packages from their secured location and disperse them so Sarah and Warren can exit from their current lives. In the safety deposit box, he also has one more package addressed to Sarah's parents with all the same kind of documentation for her entire family. For security reasons, Warren does not disclose any of the details to Sarah. Not until it is time.

Chapter 21:

Temptation

It's an unusually hot day in March for San Diego, where temperatures typically stay around 70 to 75 degrees. Nearly home after their afternoon walk, Sarah and Cooper enjoy the slight breeze. Sarah's nightmare of last week fades in her daily thoughts. Cooper is ecstatic about discovering all the new scents on every twig and leaf, with the goal of leaving his masculine mark on all of them.

"Okay, we're home, bud. Time to wash the car. Let's get some water for you first," Sarah speaks to Cooper as she pets his head softly. Securing him to a chain under a shady tree in the front yard, she sets his water bowl within his reach. He laps up the cool water after his tough job of marking every tree and bush in the neighborhood.

Sarah disappears inside and returns with a bottle of Dawn, a bucket, an oversized sponge, and several towels for drying. "Thank goodness for the cool breeze, huh, Coops?" Sarah remarks as she turns on the hose, releasing too much force and managing to spray cool water all over her cut-off shorts and white tank.

"Wonderful," Sarah says sarcastically to Copper. Cooper backs away to avoid her poor aim. "Don't worry, bud. I won't get you." Not paying attention, she pours too much soap into bucket. "Oh crap." Sarah ends up with suds overflowing from the bucket. "Oh my gosh!" She laughs out loud. "It's okay. I went to college," she jokes.

With a welcomed smile, Sarah turns the hose on her filthy BMW, which was once a beautiful pearl white and is has been temporarily hidden beneath layers of grime. The white has turned to gray from months of neglect. Next she sprays water onto herself to cool her skin. The hot sun quickly absorbs the water on her body. A cool, relaxing breeze feels soothing against her face and body.

Removing a barrette from her jeans, she clips her hair in a messy up-do, leaving stray strands falling in her face. Her face is flushed from the heat, and her skin glistens. She sprays the ground in front of her to cool the hot cement. In between spraying her car, Sarah purposefully sprays herself to keep cool in the heat. "It is really hot out here, Coops."

For such a simple task, Sarah has created a huge mess, leaving more soap and water on her than her car. Laughing and enjoying the moment, she has no worries. She surprises herself by the joy she feels. She smiles and giggles as she continues to wash her car. "No worries, not today," Sarah prays as she directs the conversation to Cooper, who is lying on his back, tummy in the air, ears flopped back with almost a smile on his face. Cooper pays no attention, just twitches deep in a dream. "I am glad to see you have no cares either, my little guy." Cooper barely lifts his head to acknowledge her.

Sarah stands back to soak the roof before rubbing it down with soap. She scrubs the roof and misses a slim line of dirt directly down the center. "Crap," she says.

"Who looks up there anyway? No one will notice," a sultry British accent chimes in from behind her. "You missed the roof," points out her neighbor, Cole Blackman, in a smart-ass tone.

"Well, thank you so very much for informing me. What would I do without that brilliant observation?" Sarah jokingly remarks as she turns to face him with one hand on her hip and a sponge dripping suds down her leg in the other. She smiles cheerfully. "Hello, Cole. How are you? I'm sorry I haven't—"

"Sarah, stop. It's okay," he says in a supportive tone. Changing the subject to a lighter topic, he holds out his hand to introduce himself. "Hello, my name is Cole Blackman; I'm your new neighbor."

Sarah smiles at Cole and goes along with his game to relax the mood. "Well, hello. My name is Sarah Benton. Welcome to the neighborhood." She reaches out and shakes Cole's hand. They both laugh.

"Well, Mrs. Benton, I am fine, but it seems that you are in a bit of trouble," Cole sarcastically refers to Sarah's weakness in car washing.

"Oh no, that's all right, Cole. I am just having a little fun getting myself a bit cleaner than my car," she says and offers a fashion pose, showing off her soaking wet clothing and the suds in her hair, on her face, shirt and shorts, and running down her legs. "I especially dislike the center of the roof. I hate that spot," she jokes.

"Oh my. Allow me," Cole responds in his teasingly charming accent and extends his hand for the sponge. "Come on, give me the sponge." He gestures for her to hand him the sponge. "Come on, Sarah. Give it to me," Cole entices.

Wearing a somewhat devilishly sexy grin, Sarah slyly

whispers, "Absolutely. Sure, Cole." She finds herself tongue-tied, feeling giddy like a teenage girl flirting with her first cute boy and marking the first day of a summer romance. She feels butterflies in her stomach. She doesn't judge it or try to deny it. "Ready, Cole?" Sarah warns him.

She takes the stand of a professional baseball pitcher with the soapy sponge as her baseball, glances left to right as if a player might steal a base, winds up, and whips the sponge at Cole. Suds fly in every direction. She thoroughly enjoys the moment and busts out laughing. There is no response from Cole as he catches the sponge and gets soaked in suds. With Cole not laughing, Sarah becomes a bit more on guard, placing her hands over her mouth to hide her smile, and biting her lips to hide her laughter. Catching herself staring, she realizes she forgot how ruggedly handsome he is and how he exudes such charisma and sex appeal. Their eyes lock intensely. She feels guilty but continues to look at him. Her body fills with excitement and warmth. She smiles her beautiful smile.

"You have the most delightful smile." Cole returns the smile and laughs with her.

Their friendship has survived the past month of Sarah's darkness, but they act as if there was never a break between them. He has placed no pressure on her and made no advancements for anything other than friendship. Their friendship is comfortable, yet today it feels intense. Wonderful yet awkward. They both feel the intensity of their physical attraction. Sarah feels deep inside that she has crossed some fine line of adultery with Stephen. *How can I cheat on him if he is gone? Am I cheating on him?* she thinks to herself.

Cole's eyes are the most intense aqua blue, large and accentuated by thick dark eyelashes. His eyes exude a great love for life and possibly a great love for his new friend. He has strong rugged facial features with a distinguished, sexy cleft in his chin as well as a permanent slight squint. His thick black hair is tussled and shining with sweat from the arduous landscaping he was working on in his backyard before coming over to help. Sarah thinks to herself how tormenting the past several months have been. She is so very grateful to feel happy today.

She continues to study his chiseled face. She cannot resist. His lips are nearly perfect in their slightly crooked smile. His beard is often in need of a shave, and it only accents his handsome face. "Wow, he is really handsome," Sarah whispers to herself, mesmerized. "I hope I didn't say that out loud." Sweat beads cling to his forehead. Smudges of dirt from his landscaping venture seep into deep thought lines between his brows and along his sideburns. "He even looks good dirty," Sarah says to herself.

"What? Did you say something Sarah?" Cole asks.

"Oh, no. No, it's nothing. Just talking to myself," says Sarah, slightly embarrassed.

He lifts his left arm to wipe the sweat from his forehead. Sarah cannot help but observe his strong hands and muscular arms. She fantasizes of Cole holding her tightly. Strangely, she feels safe with him like she used to with Stephen.

Cole stands looking at Sarah. She gently reaches out her right hand, which is covered with soap. She giggles when she has lightly smeared suds across Cole's face. Cole grabs the soapy sponge, grabs Sarah, and then squeezes the sponge over the top of her head. They both laugh as they get doused in suds. She jokingly apologizes as she grabs the hose and relentlessly sprays Cole until he is soaked. They both continue laughing.

"I call a truce," Cole says with his hands in the air. "I

know I needed a bath anyway." "You win. That's enough," Cole surrenders.

"Oh, I am so sorry. I guess the hose just got away from me." Sarah can barely say it without cracking a smile.

Cole slowly approaches her. "It's getting late, so we should probably get this mess cleaned up," he says in a more serious tone.

Sarah feels badly. She wonders if she pushed him too far. Interrupting her next thought, he grabs her around the waist and soaks her with the hose. While he holds Sarah in his arms, they play and flirt.

Cole whispers into Sarah's ear, "Paybacks are a bloody bitch." Sarah breaks his hold and twists to face him, holding onto his arms.

She candidly mocks him. She pushes away from him panting, smiling, and standing vulnerable in her wet tee, cut-offs, and bare feet. Her mussed hair falls slightly over her eyes as her skin glistens in the heat of the sun. She giggles like a child but with the sexiness of a woman. Cole is captivated. He watches her as she continues to frolic. He enjoys her beauty and playfulness. She also enjoys her playfulness after months of feeling like she was drowning in darkness.

Cole knows she has been sad for some time now. A little lightheaded from dancing, she stands straight and braces herself against Cole's arm with one hand. She catches her breath, still smiling at him. He braces her waist and returns a warm, sincere smile. He realizes he has taken their friendship beyond the point of no return. They become still and quiet as though they are in their own world. As they touch one another softly and affectionately, their breathing becomes heavy. Droplets of water stream down their faces, falling like morning dew streaming down a soft flower petal. Not regretting any decisions, they know this is a wonderful moment between them.

Sarah grabs the two towels she threw over her mountain bike in the garage earlier to dry her car. She tosses a towel to Cole. Instead of drying himself, he steps close to Sarah and softly pats her face dry. He then wraps the towel around her shoulders, pulls her close, and whispers, "I have missed you."

Sarah lowers her face into the palm of his hand, keeping her eyes focused on his. "I've missed you too. I just was lost for a while, Cole," she says solemnly. Softly holding the back of his hand with hers, she sensuously kisses his palm . Removing her towel from around her shoulders, she gently dries his face. Seductively she slowly wraps the towel around the back of his neck, pulls him toward her, and kisses him deeply.

"You are an angel, Sarah. Do you know that? I wasn't expecting you to come into my life and have this effect on me," he says. They look into one another's eyes. "Come home with me."

Sarah gathers Cooper and his belongings and secures him in his bed. She fills his "King" bowl with kibbles and refreshes his water. Cole waits by the garage door for Sarah. She punches in the security code as she leaves. He takes her car keys from her, pulls her spotless pearl white BMW—with a stripe of dirt down the center of the roof—into the garage, and shuts the door. He turns the hose off and rolls it neatly against the house.

Once they are inside his home, he places his hands on the sides of her face and gently feels her soft skin. They embrace and become engrossed in a long, romantic kiss that trails to her neck and to her breasts. Their towels fall freely to the floor as they continue to kiss hungrily and undress one another.

Their kisses grow heavier and more intense. Their passion for one another cannot be denied. They feel one another's bodies intimately.

Cole leads Sarah to his bedroom and carefully lays her on white, crisp cotton sheets. Their deep, passionate kissing and exploration of one another's bodies continues as he moves onto her and into her. Their wet bodies become warm and glisten under the moving shadows of the ceiling fan's rotating blades. As they yearn for one another, they are lost in their lovemaking. They lie together as one until dawn awakens them. They look into each other's eyes with kindness and love. They hold one another softly and warmly for a few more precious minutes.

Cole retrieves an extra-large collared, somewhat wrinkled white cotton shirt with the monogram CB on the front pocket from his closet. He helps Sarah into it and buttons all the buttons. The tails of the shirt fall over the tops of her thighs, revealing Sarah's sexy legs.

"Come with me," he says. Leading her to the kitchen by the hand, he offers her a seat at the breakfast bar while he cooks eggs, bacon, toast and makes fresh-squeezed orange juice and some much-needed coffee. Delighted, Sarah smiles warmly at Cole as he treasures this magical, forbidden moment.

Chapter 22:

Butterfly

Like a teenager on cloud nine, Sarah nearly skips home from Cole's house. With her damp cut-offs and Cole's button-down tied in a knot around her waist, she is filled with joy and refuses to wipe the grin from her glowing face. Halfway across the street she catches a glimpse of a black car parked a couple houses down from hers. Sarah avoids direct eye contact with the man leaning against the outside of the Black Crown Vic. She tries to capture as much detail as possible so she can relay the information to Warren. She notices the man is somewhat stocky, with brown hair and a brown mustache. He is wearing black boots, jeans, and a black T-shirt. He pays no attention to Sarah. Sarah has never seen him in her neighborhood and is immediately on high alert.

Quickening her stride, she punches in the alarm on her garage door and locks herself inside her fortress. She then checks to ensure all the doors are bolted. Quickly running through her house, she checks and re-checks all windows, French doors, and sliding doors. She hears a whine and looks down to a lonely puppy longing to go outside and do his business.

"Darn," Sarah whispers to herself. She takes Cooper through her bedroom sliding door to the backyard. "Now hurry, little one. No sniffing around today."

Upon re-entering the bedroom, Sarah locks the door and puts a sawed-off broomstick in the door well for added security. Pacing back and forth, she calms her breathing and tries to reach Warren on her pre-paid cell phone trying. No answer.

"Shit," is the first part of the message she leaves for Warren, along with the news of her suspicious stalker. Sarah tries to convince herself she is overreacting. "He didn't even look at me. He is probably just visiting someone," she tells herself. She is jumpy, knowing the inevitable future that will be coming her way when her DNA is discovered in Kat's house.

She prepares for the worst and hopes for the best, but she still contrives to run. "I hope Warren and I have the opportunity to implement plan A. Otherwise, I at least have plan B for backup."

The first item she pulls out is her Browning 9mm. She checks the two clips; each has a full thirteen rounds. She inserts one of the clips into the butt of the gun. The second is just for extra protection, if necessary. She places the second clip in a side pocket in her purse. Then she racks the slide to chamber a round and thumbs the safety on.

Carrying her new best friend, she quietly walks through her home, scanning each room to make sure she has left no evidence of herself. "Once I am gone, I never existed," Sarah says in a whisper that leaves an eerie feeling in her gut.

She searches each closet. Only the clothes hanging will remain. She cannot take much with her when she runs.

She opens the hallway closet across from the bathroom and remembers downing bottles of warm water in blackness and fear a short time ago. Trying not to relive that week, she continues her search.

"Oh, crap. How could I have forgotten these?" Sarah questions herself, shocked. In the back of the closet, just behind the empty cardboard water carton are the wadded up crusted, blackish gray clothes she had worn to break into Kat's house. She had completely forgotten about them.

"Drug-induced amnesia," she reasons. "It's evidence. I can't believe I forgot about these. I have to get rid of them. But not right now. I will wait until the sun starts to go down."

Sarah begins another plan of escape. All the calmness and joy she has felt over the past week of freedom from the prison she made in her closet, especially her romantic interlude with Cole, is instantly gone. In a flash she is sucked back into her chaotic nightmare.

Sitting in the hallway, petting Cooper, and keeping her 9mm close at her side, she ponders the situation and her best plan of action. Her original plan for today had been to go through old pictures and only take her very favorites, remembering what Warren told her: to travel light and not to leave any documentation behind. "Burn it if you have to," he had said.

She is packed and ready to go, so she sticks with the original plan. During Warren's last visit, he removed four boxes from the attic and placed them in the center of the living room for her to dig through and relive every memory shared by each photo. Dreading this moment, Sarah holds Cooper tightly and stands in front of the mass of memories. She takes a seat and leans against the couch so she has a full view of the front door, garage door, and windows to the backyard. Cooper hops up on the couch and circles a couple times before curling up in a ball and taking one of twenty naps he takes every day. Sarah dumps one box at a time and separates only a few pictures she wants to keep close to her heart.

She walks to the kitchen and removes the drawings from Stevie and Sammy and the *TIME* magazine cover of Stephen. Sitting back in her space, she studies the *TIME* cover. He looks so patriotic in full military dress, strong, brave, and handsome. The intense, lifeless stare from his hazel eyes gives Sarah an uneasy feeling now that she knows about the government's cloning experiment. She places the kids' pictures with the few pictures she wants to keep forever, and after much agony, she chooses to burn the cover photo of her husband.

She opens the flue to the fireplace and piles the rest of the photos, her IDs, birth certificate, and marriage license on the iron rack. On the top she sets the cover photo of Stephen. The picture haunts her; she doesn't really know if it is Stephen or a clone. Lighting a match, she tosses it on the pile and watches Stephen and all her wonderful memories melt into a mound of ash. She doesn't feel cleansed by the experience, only a hollow emptiness. Her heart breaks, but she sheds no tears. She has none left.

She is interrupted by the phone ringing, which causes her heart to skip a beat. She wonders if it is someone wanting to do her harm. Will there only be silence on the other end? The caller ID shows *Blackman*. Knowing it is safe, she excitedly greets Cole with a relieved "hello." The erotic and intimate feelings she felt for the first time with him yesterday flood through her body, making her feel warm and sensual.

Cole's sexy accent returns her greeting, "Well hello, you. I already miss you."

Blushing like a school girl, she says, "I miss you too, Cole. I truly loved yesterday … and breakfast too. I'm still full. By the way, I'm keeping your shirt. It makes me feel sexy." Sarah toys with him.

"You are sexy in it, and it is a gift for you. I want to hold you in my arms right now. Sarah …?"

"Yes, Cole?"

"I realize this may come as a shock and too early for you, but I want you to know I love you."

"Oh … Cole … I …" Sarah stumbles over her words.

"I know you are in a different place, and I would never want you to say something until it comes from your heart, but I can say it from mine. I promise I won't drown you with it."

"You are so sweet and so special to me. You know that, don't you, Cole?"

"Of course I do, Sarah."

Sarah's stomach twists; she knows she will be disappearing soon, but she cannot endanger his life by getting him involved. She bites her lip to hold in the truth.

"Is everything okay over there? There is smoke coming from the stack on your roof."

"I know. It is seventy-five degrees outside, and I am burning a fire. Crazy, huh? Actually, I am burning some old papers because my shredder is broken. Gotta be careful of identity theft, you know." Sarah invents her story as she goes along.

"Okay, love. Just checking. Come by later if you want and we can share a bottle of wine under the moonlight."

"That sounds wonderfully romantic. I have to run some errands, but if isn't too late, I would like that. If not, maybe we can get together tomorrow." Sarah cringes, knowing she may be gone for good by tomorrow. If the man she saw down the street is following her, then she cannot get Cole involved any deeper. She does long to see him though, even if it is just one last time.

Sarah throws on a white T-shirt and a pair of jeans that now hang on her. She tightens her belt and gets moving on her plan. Throwing the crumpled pile of black clothes into a plastic bag, she is ready to go to a nearby 7-11 to dump the evidence. With her gun in her purse, she hustles out the door.

It is now dusk, and she feels confident no one will notice her. Before throwing the evidence away, she goes into the store to purchase a Blueberry-pomegranate Vitamin Water, using it as a excuse to scan the area for unusual suspects or activity. Walking back to her car, she notices cars leaving and others filling the empty spaces. She notices nothing out of the ordinary. Grabbing the bag from her car, she casually walks to the dumpster and tosses it. As she turns back toward her car, she spots the Black Crown Vic in the farthest parking space beside another car. She is certain it is the one she saw earlier in the day. She cannot see anyone near the car.

Quickly jumping into her car, she scans the perimeter and sees the same man she saw earlier in the day standing next to the register. Her heart pounds in her chest. She is certain this is it time. "It's time."

She quickly backs up, taking one last look at the man with brown hair and a brown mustache who is now staring directly at her. Shivers run up her spine. Without hesitation she slams her BMW into first gear, causing a painful grinding noise. She goes for second and squeals away, leaving tire marks as her signature.

"Who the hell is that? This is bad," she says, shifting into third and then fourth gear and dialing Warren on her cell for the second time today. "Come on, Warren. Please pick up. Come on, please. *Shit!*"

She has had no return calls, and she fears he has been discovered and captured … or worse. Sarah tries not to think about that possibility.

She takes several side roads to see if she is being followed. "Nothing," she says aloud.

Driving as quickly as she can to a Long's Drug in Poway, she speeds past a cop and quickly removes her foot from the gas. "Shit!" Sarah cringes, waiting to see if the officer will make a U-turn. Checking her rear view mirror, she begs "Oh, please don't turn around … please." She gets lucky, this time letting out a sigh of relief.

Reaching the parking lot of the store, Sarah brings the car to a screeching halt. She sits back in her seat, her body pumping with adrenaline. Everything is happening so quickly.

"We had this whole thing planned to the T. Shit. *Shit!*" She knows she must go to plan B. Talking to herself aloud, she says, "I need at least five copies of the documents, envelopes, labels, a permanent black marker, clear plastic packing tape, stamps …" Her mind races. "Oh, of course, copies of *San Diego Journal*, *USA Today*, and *The Washington Post*. Is that it? Is that all I need? I think so."

Just to be safe, Sarah scans the parking lot and doesn't see anyone or anything alarming, especially not the unknown man in the Black Crown Vic. "Go."

She opens the driver's door with force and almost jumps from the car, wanting to jump out of her own skin. She grabs her purse and prays she remembers all the items she needs.

Even though she knows her gun is in her bag, she feels for the steel. It makes her feel safe.

Realizing her frantic actions might draw unwanted attention, she relaxes her motions. Slowly closing her car door, she presses the automatic lock on her key remote and then opens the trunk of her car and removes the secret set of papers she had hidden there just in case something like this occurred. Tucking the envelope in her purse, she briskly walks toward the bright lights of the store. She glances from side to side and behind her until she reaches the doors. A short-lived feeling of safety engages her heart and mind.

The automatic doors to the front of the store open, welcoming Sarah. The brightness helps her feel some sense of safety. She quickly scans the aisle headers, grabs a red plastic hand carrier, and darts toward the stationary section, where she grabs five large padded manila envelopes, clear plastic tape, and a black permanent marker. Heading toward the registers, she notices a man with dark hair checking out. She stops in her tracks. She maintains control. She must. To avoid appearing conspicuous, she opens the cooler next to her and selects a bottle of La Crema chardonnay. "Why not my favorite?"

As she places the wine in the carrier, she glances at the register again and sees the man leaving through the automatic doors. She waits for a few minutes before moving quickly to the checkout. As she stands at the counter, she goes unnoticed by the young kid working the register. He's not paying attention to anything but the skateboarding magazine he is enthralled with. Sarah nervously looks around, knowing each second is precious. The store is nearly vacant. There is only one other woman; her three wildly energetic kids race through the aisles, playing tag as she scampers after them, yelling in frustration, "You're all going to get a time-out when we get home. And no ice cream if you don't settle down."

"Excuse me?" Sarah says but gets no response from the young skateboarding fan. "Excuse me, young man?"

The young teen suddenly looks up from his fantasy world, quite embarrassed that he didn't notice her. "Oh, hey. I'm sorry. How are you tonight?"

"I'm fine, thank you, but I need to make some copies. Do you have a copier I can use?"

The young man gestures behind him at the copier with the sign taped on it that reads, *Out of Order*. Sarah's distress is notably obvious to the cashier. Thinking out loud, Sarah sighs. "Oh, what am I going to do now?"

"Excuse me. My manager is out for his dinner break. I can let you use the one in his office, but you have to hurry. He'll be back in a few minutes," the blond California skateboarder offers.

Sarah gratefully nods and follows the young employee into the manager's office. It is unorganized, and the desk is messy, but Sarah spots stamps and hard cardboard first-class shipping envelopes. The young helper offers to make the copies for Sarah, but she explains they are rather personal and asks if he would mind if she makes the copies herself.

"Naw, that's cool. It's right over there. Help yourself. I'll be right out here keeping a watch out for my boss."

"Thank you so very much. You're awesome!"

The skateboarder blushes and saunters away in his baggy plaid shorts and blue uniform smock that clashes with his image. His exit allows Sarah to make her copies in privacy.

She completes her job with a huge sigh of relief. Without thinking, she picks up a cell phone sitting on the messy desk and calls Warren. He immediately answers, and Sarah informs him of the suspicious events of the day. She lets him know she has gone to plan B and is mailing new packages she is currently putting together as they speak. He informs her it is time and she needs to hurry and get home. He will arrange for the delivery of her new identity for her escape.

When she turns to leave the office, she notices a locked suggestion box hanging on the wall. She quickly folds one of the extra two copied letters into fourths and slides it through the opening.

The automatic doors to the store open, and a man in a smock the same color as the skateboarder's walks through, picking his teeth with a toothpick. Sarah quickly ducks down but doesn't leave the office without stealing all the stamps and first-class cardboard envelopes. She hides everything in her large purse.

"I am a liar and a shoplifter now," she whispers to herself.

The young skateboarder nervously looks over his shoulder at Sarah, who is now out of the office, looking at the magazine rack located just beside the door. She flashes a grateful smile and winks at the young man before she grabs the three newspapers she needs to send the envelopes to. When she returns to the register, the young employee checks her out. She turns and says "thank you" and "good-bye" before she disappears through the automatic double doors and into the night.

Adrenaline streams through Sarah's body. She is pleased that her plan B is moving forward without any hitches. Once inside her car, she quickly locks the doors and scans the perimeter of the parking lot again. "Everything looks clear," she says to herself.

Starting her BMW, she pushes it into first and then second gear as she races through the parking lot and off into the night to return home. Sarah spots a couple police cars parked next to each other in a parking lot ahead, the officers likely chatting about their nights. She sees an opportunity to get her plan completed without incident before going home … just in case. Just to be safe. More than anything Sarah wants the President and his co-conspirators severely punished. She wants the world to know everything.

She pulls within the view of the policemen for the sake of safety and begins her tasks, first inserting an earpiece into her ear and pretending to talk on her cell phone, though the end of the wire dangles free. The police officers acknowledge her presence and then return to their conversation. While she carries on a false conversation, she addresses each envelope and fills it with the damning evidence. She places clear tape over the addresses, which are written with black permanent marker. Next she addresses the large white first-class envelopes with the same addresses and encloses the completed envelopes inside the white cardboard.

Self-sealing each envelope, she doubles the protection with the clear packing tape. She also covers the addresses with the tape as well to protect the valuable delivery directions. Balancing each envelope in one hand while continuing to engage in a lively conversation with no one, she sticks more than enough stamps on each envelope. Continuing her conversation with a jovial laugh, she writes the drugstore's address as the return address, which she takes from her receipt. Sarah then carefully folds the extra copy of the President's and CIA's letters and slips them into the side pocket of her purse.

Next, she drives with control from the parking lot, knowing she will pass two post offices on her way home. As she leaves the parking lot, she offers a wave of thanks to the officers.

Up ahead is the first post office. Sarah zips into the drive-through lane and deposits the letters to *San Diego Journal* and *The Washington Post*. Pick-up will be 7:00 a.m. on Monday. She prays the envelopes that will bring down the President of the United States will successfully arrive at their intended locations. Next she zips away to her second drop-off point. At the Ramona post office, she drops her final envelope, addressed to *USA Today,* into the outgoing slot.

As she drives home, Sarah releases a huge sigh of relief. "Oh my gosh. I did it!"

Turning left onto her street, she feels drained of energy yet exhilarated. Passing the home of her friend, Laura, Sarah notices her lights are on. It seems late to Sarah, but when she checks her watch, she is surprised that it is only 9:05 p.m. With a screech, Sarah suddenly stops her car on a dime and puts it into reverse. She pulls into Laura's driveway. Before getting out of her vehicle, Sarah double-checks her purse for the secret papers. *It is safe,* she thinks to herself.

Laura peeks out of her kitchen window, smiling and waving to Sarah. She opens the front door and comes outside to greet her. "Hi, honey. How have you been? What a nice surprise. Come on in," Laura invites Sarah.

"Are you sure it's not too late? I brought our favorite wine, La Crema," Sarah says with a big smile on her face and gently sways the bottle back and forth like a pendulum. She grows nervous once she is outside of her car, fully exposed. "I have a huge favor to ask, Laura," she says.

"Sure, anything. Come on in and let's talk."

"Is it all right if I park my car on the side of your house where it will be out of sight?"

Realizing Sarah's increased level of anxiety, Laura walks over and opens the garage door, letting Sarah fully hide her car. Once inside the house, Laura closes the door behind them and offers Sarah a warm, caring hug. Without Sarah needing to ask, Laura closes all the drapes, locks the front door, and leads Sarah into the living room to visit.

"Sarah, what is going on? Are you okay? You've been acting nervous for weeks," Laura asks in an urgent tone.

"Oh, yes," Sarah says and then pauses for a moment. "No, not really, Laura. Everything is pretty crazy right now." Internally she feels proud for succeeding with plan B, but she is exhausted from the stress of the evening and seeing that strange man in the Crown Vic twice today. She cannot get him out of her mind.

Laura listens from the kitchen as she pours two glasses of wine. "Here you go, sweetie," she says, handing Sarah a glass of relaxation. "I'm so sorry things have been so rough. What can I do to help?"

Before Laura can even get comfortable on the couch, Sarah stands and begins to pace. "Laura, I need a favor."

"Anything, Sarah. What can I do?"

"I need a change. I mean I need to change my looks—drastically!"

"All right, we can do whatever you want," Laura offers, quite aware that Sarah is dealing with something stressful. "Do you want to talk about it?" she asks.

"I can't. Please trust me on this, Laura. I will let you know everything on Monday."

"Of course. You sit and try to calm down and relax, and I will get some magazines to get some ideas," Laura suggests, not prying any deeper.

"That will be great." Sarah takes a few large sips of wine, trying to take the edge off the anxiety of today's events.

The girls sit together, thumbing through several magazines to find a new look for Sarah.

"Here's the one I thought was perfect for you," Laura chimes in. "What do you think about this?"

"I like it." Sarah thinks for a moment, and after only seconds, she says, "Okay. Let's do it."

"I think it would be good if we change your hair color to a creamy milk chocolate. It will be beautiful with your skin tone and green eyes. If you want a different look, I believe that will do it."

"Let's go for it. Oh my God, I can't believe I'm doing this. I guess the wine is doing its job, huh?"

Laura leads Sarah into her home salon. Sarah sits in the grooming chair, and Laura slides a cape over her and comfortably clasps the neck snap. Laura then goes to the back of the room to prepare Sarah's new hair color. She returns with another bottle of wine. She smiles confidently at Sarah and offers her a refill. Sarah offers a faint smile in return and holds out her glass.

Laura applies a lightening solution first to Sarah's hair so her new color will be more vibrant. She excuses herself while Sarah waits an excruciating twenty-five minutes for the egg timer to signal the time to remove the solution. Laura runs back in with a gift wrapped box.

"What's that?" Sarah asks with curiosity.

"I will show you when we are done. It's a gift," Laura remarks with an intriguing look. She then applies the silky chocolate brown color, and they wait another excruciating twenty-five minutes.

Conversation fills the silence.

"Now tell me what's in the box? It's killing me," begs Sarah.

"All right. If you are transforming your look, your wardrobe also needs some transformation. Your clothes are way too big since you've lost so much weight, Sarah. No offense, but those jeans look a bit dorky."

"No offense taken. I appreciate your honesty, Laura. Don't forget, though. I am kind of a dork." Both ladies laugh, tipsy from the wine.

"You'll have to try it on when we're done. I know you'll look fabulous," Laura says with excitement.

The egg timer rings, startling the two. They laugh. The wine has performed its duty; the ladies finally seem relaxed.

After Sarah's hair is washed thoroughly, she sits and stares at herself in the mirror. She glances down at her purse that sits right beside her chair, knowing the powerful evidence inside. She flashes back to the mirror. Gently rubbing under her eyes with both hands, she realizes how tired and gaunt she looks.

So much has happened since Stephen deployed. So much has changed ... forever, Sarah thinks to herself.

Laura turns the chair away from the mirror to complete the styling of Sarah's new look and apply her makeup. Sarah cringes, watching her long locks fall to the floor. Taking another large sip of wine, she puts her trust in Laura's skills as a hairstylist and makeup artist. Minutes slowly tick by.

"Are you ready for the new you?" Laura finally says with a proud grin.

"You bet," Sarah says, smiling back.

"Close your eyes." And with that instruction, Laura swirls the chair around so Sarah can meet the new her. They look into the mirror in silence, admiring her new look. They both smile at the same time.

"Wow, I look completely different!" Sarah exclaims.

"You look so sophisticated. You're beautiful, Sarah." Laura smiles proudly. "Now take this and go change in the bathroom. I want to see you in it." Laura hands the gift box to Sarah.

Sarah comes back to the salon, and they look at the new outfit Laura has put together for her. They laugh and giggle about nothing really.

"It's beautiful, Laura. I can't believe you did this. I just love it." Sarah gives Laura a warm hug.

"Thank you so much ... for everything, Laura."

Both ladies giggle like school girls, clinking their glasses together and cheering Laura's work of art and Sarah's metamorphism into a beautiful butterfly. Sarah and Laura finish the bottle of chardonnay and their evening.

Chapter 23:

Twisted

Sarah pulls into her garage and clicks the automatic remote. The garage door cannot close fast enough. She sits quietly in her BMW, absorbing the day's events. She had begun the day higher than a kite from her romantic tango with Cole and then reverted back to the chaos of the strange man lurking after her and frantically reorganizing the release of the Project Restoration I evidence. Pressing hard against her seat with her arms outstretched, Sarah leans her head backward into the headrest and releases a sigh of victory.

She feels strong and in control of her emotions and actions. "I will not be afraid." She knows she will never see Warren again. The hourglass is empty.

Opening the door, she catches a glimpse of her new look in the rearview mirror, faintly illuminated by the overhead light. Her shoulder-length hair has been transformed into a sophisticated bob. Amazed with the difference in her looks, she smiles and lightly shakes her head, pleased with the outcome of Laura's work.

She punches in the alarm code to enter her home, but it

doesn't engage. Trying it again, she gets frustrated with the possibility of a short or outage with the new system Warren installed two weeks ago. Out of sheer frustration, she punches the door, which moves.

"The door is open. Shit." Her mind begins to race as she decides her next move, but she reins in her thoughts so she can think rationally.

Sarah reaches into her purse and feels for cold steel. Removing the gun from her purse, she also releases its safety. In the past she would run from conflict, but now she is in the midst of conflict and has no other choice than to confront it head on. She has changed so much personally since Stephen's deployment and has been forced to deal with an event most people would never believe it to be true.

Slowly opening the door, she scans the kitchen, TV room, and living room. *Okay, here I go,* Sarah silently encourages herself. Moving stealthily through her home, she seeks the presence of an intruder. Everything looks clear, and nothing seems out of place. Since replacing the locks a few weeks ago, she had been feeling fairly secure in her "fortress," as she had joked to Warren.

Cooper tears around the corner to greet his master. As always, he leaps against her legs, jumping up and down until she picks him up and greets him. Sarah quickly scoops him up, holding him tightly with her left arm, pressing his body against her chest and placing her hand over his muzzle. Cooper begins to struggle against her hand, delivering muffled squeaking. "*Shhh.* Hush, boy," Sarah says in the faintest whisper.

As she moves from room to room, she stops and listens for any unusual noises or sounds. Sarah has mastered the art of shallow breathing so she can listen for someone else's. With all the window locked and doors bolted, she feels it is safe and clicks a small lamp on in her bedroom to offer some low illumination. She doesn't flick on the overhead lights, which would basically shout that she is home, even though she is well aware that the illusive strangers can find her at anytime. She also never turns out all the lights in the house, avoiding complete darkness. Refusing to allow her mind to run wild with imaginative intruders, she always leaves all closet doors and shower curtains open.

She observes Cooper's behaviors as well. He might be small, but he also has a keen sense of possible danger. Even with the few new oddities, his behavior has been normal.

Well aware she will not live like this much longer, she plans to continue the routine until she reaches the safety of her new life.

Feeling somewhat safe, Sarah notices she has only a few more minutes remaining on one of the cell phones Warren provided her. The remaining pre-paid phones are for the trip and emergencies only. Calling Warren, she lets him know she is safely home and spells out the details of the jolting night.

Knowing how close danger is to her, he tells her, "It won't be much longer. Be ready to go, Sarah."

"Warren, I want to call my family one more time. I miss them and may never see them again. I could maybe call them from a payphone—"

"Sarah, listen to me," Warren sternly objects. "Your parent's phone line is most certainly tapped, so you will put them in eminent danger. I know you don't want that. We are dealing with a major conspiracy! They have proven they will not allow anyone to divulge their secrets. They are not screwing around, Sarah. Please be patient. I know it's difficult. You have to trust me when I say I will keep them safe."

"Yes, Warren. I apologize. I got off course. Tonight … it

was just awful." Sarah remarks. "I just want my family safe, Warren. Everyone I love is gone or will be gone soon. Even you."

"Sarah, they will be safe. You will see them again, I promise. And I guarantee we will see one another again … sometime in the future."

"I hope so, Warren. Oh, how I hope and pray for that. How can I ever thank you? How?"

"When you are safe, Sarah, that will be thanks enough." Warren's voice cuts in and out.

"What about your safety?" Sarah questions with great concern.

"Don't worry about me. I can hold my own," Warren responds confidently. "We are almost out of minutes, so listen carefully. Review your exit strategy, what you have packed. Remember to keep it light. Don't take up room with clothes and makeup. Wear something to the airport that is comfortable and in layers. You may be wearing it for a few days. Keep Cooper sedated until you reach your destination, and then you can burn his carrier if you want." He chuckles, knowing how Cooper hates being caged. She catches his humor and also laughs. "Okay, down to a couple minutes."

"Where am I going, Warren?" Sarah asks about her new life.

"I can't tell you. Everything will be in the package set for delivery early tomorrow morning. Be ready to go. Your flight is the first out. The packages you mailed today will arrive Monday to their destinations, so I want you gone! And don't forget to dispose of your weapon where it cannot be found. It's registered to Stephen, so we don't want to leave any traces. Give the pre-made packages to the delivery person. He is on our side. Well, my dear, it is time to say good-bye," Warren warns as their pre-paid minutes tick away.

He hears Sarah begin to cry. "Sarah, it will be okay. Everything will be okay—" The line dies before Warren can relay another word.

Sarah stares at her phone, wanting to hear more of Warren's calm, controlled voice. "Keep it light," she murmurs to herself. "He will take care of me. I know I can trust him with my life." Sarah sits on her bed, not knowing quite what to do with herself. Time seems to drag, but her heart races. She remembers what Warren said: be patient. Sarah gets busy rehearsing, once again, for her escape.

Everything she plans to take is lying on her bed—a light trench coat, a pair of boots, and a small bag of essentials. Sarah grabs the brown paper sack Laura gave her and empties its contents on her bed. A pair of skinny jeans, a deep brown cotton turtleneck, an elegant cream cashmere scarf, and a beautiful brown leather belt with a seawater pearl buckle. Sarah is grateful for the gift.

She whispers to herself, "She knew I was in trouble. Somehow she knew."

Removing Cooper's carrier from the closet, Sarah sets it on the bed. Cooper barks in protest.

"Don't worry, boy. It will only be for a short period of time." Cuddling Cooper for a few minutes offers them both some comfort. Sarah opens the top dresser drawer and removes a silky cream camisole to wear under the turtleneck but that can be worn solo if need be. "I'm not sure where I'm going, so I must be prepared for any climate."

Sarah glances into the mirror in the bathroom and sees a stranger staring back at her. She suddenly stops and becomes motionless. Seconds pass as she stares back at the stranger.

Bravely, she walks in the direction of the stranger with no fear and no gun. She stands motionless for seconds and just stares. Then she stops, leans against the counter, stares at the new woman staring back at her. She prays her new identity and appearance will be enough to disguise her from the enemy that wants her dead.

Undressing from her old favorite baggy jeans, Sarah takes a quick shower, not knowing when her next one will be. Then she slides into her new skinny jeans. They feel strange, so tight against her slim figure. She carefully slips on the cream camisole, followed by the fitted brown cotton turtleneck. The beautiful brown belt fits her slender hips perfectly. Fluffing her hair helps it fall back in place, and her makeup remains untouched. Leaning against her bed, she pulls on a pair of brown leather riding boots, which fit over the tight pant legs. She likes her new look. Sarah prays no one else will.

The reflection in the mirror centers on the illumination of the bedside lamp and the crystal box sitting next to it.

"Stephen's warrior ring …" Sarah sits on the bed next to the table and holds the crystal box. Cooper scurries across the bed and sits beside her, wagging his tail wildly. It's as though he knows it is Stephen's ring.

She removes the top and stares blankly into the box. Her mouth is agape with shock. She places her left hand over her heart in disbelief, still gripping the box in her right hand. Tears fill her eyes, eventually escaping and flowing down her cheeks. "It's gone. No no no! Oh my God, no. Stephen's warrior ring is gone!"

Shaking indignantly, Sarah stands, feeling as if the room is crumbling around her. She screams hysterically to no one but prays the animal that did this hears her anguish, "Who are you? Goddamnit, that was all I had left of him. Don't you get that, you asshole!"

She throws the crystal box across the room, and it shatters against the white brick fireplace. Glass shards splinter everywhere. The tan speckled Berber carpet sparkles, only reflecting Sarah's pain. She falls to her knees and comes unraveled, only temporarily defeated though. Minutes pass, but her time is limited, and she knows she must gain control of her emotions to keep focused. Gathering herself, she stops her tears and takes one last deep breath. Now only anger is displayed across her beautiful face.

"They have taken everything from me. They will not take my life," Sarah vows.

Her fortitude is steadfast. She must be ready to leave as soon as she receives Warren's delivery. Her flight is at 6:15 a.m., so she expects the package to arrive between midnight and 4:00 a.m. Moving to the foyer, Sarah sets her belongings against the wall next to the front door. She places her brown leather satchel next to Cooper's kennel. One tiny pill rests on top of the kennel to sedate Cooper during the blind journey, and another one is hidden in her satchel. Resting the Browning next to the kennel, Sarah waits, watching the second hand on the clock click forward. As she stares at the second hand ticking time away, she is mesmerized, captured by each moment of time slipping by. Each resonates loudly, echoing in her mind. Each hand seems to move in slow motion. The wait is grueling.

"Be patient, Sarah. Be patient."

Pacing in a straight line, Sarah stops to peek through the blinds covering the window beside the front door as she anxiously awaits Warren's valuable delivery. "It's only eleven o'clock. Too early yet," she reprimands herself. Across the street, Sarah notices Cole's bedroom light is on. His shadow appears through his shades.

Knowing she will never see him again makes her yearn for him more than ever. She felt safe in his arms. Her heart overrules her gut, and she slowly opens the front door just a crack to check the perimeter. Her heart beats rapidly.

With a clear view, she sprints to his house, ducking behind a shrub once she reaches his front door. The door is slightly ajar. Sarah finds this a bit unusual but quietly enters Cole's home and slowly walks toward the light at the end of the hallway that leads to Cole's bedroom. She stealthily walks through the foyer, excited to surprise him and see him one last time. As she continues to move toward his bedroom, she passes the empty doorway to the kitchen and waits for someone or something to jump at her. She smiles, knowing she has allowed her imagination to run wild once again.

She continues moving forward toward the back of the house and stops at Cole's office door for a brief moment. The desk lamp is dimly lit, allowing her a slight glimpse into his life. Sarah realizes she really doesn't know what Cole does for a living, only that he works for the British government. *And it is much too boring to talk about,* Sarah remembers Cole saying.

Ready to press forward, Sarah suddenly stops in her tracks when she hears voices echoing from Cole's bedroom. Sarah blushes with embarrassment. It is obvious that Cole and a female companion are in a heated argument as the voices travel down the hallway. Filled with sheer mortification of her untimely visit and with no other place to hide, Sarah ducks into Cole's office. In utter humiliation, she wants to run but is forced to hide from the voices that seem to be moving toward her. Every inch of her wants to run out the front door without being caught in her blundering act. But instead she listens. The agitated voices have quieted. She remains a statue, unable to move. Looking for another way out, she scans the small office. No back door or window. No escape from her discomfort.

Unintentionally, Sarah glances at the papers resting on Cole's desk, which is slightly illuminated by the lamp. She gasps at what she sees. She quickly covers her mouth, hoping she has not revealed her presence. She is frozen. Unable to move, she continues to read the file in front of her. What she reads makes her heart stop. She cannot breathe. The air feels heavy, making it difficult for her lungs to expand. She keeps her left hand tightly over her mouth to muffle any further gasps that express her sheer disbelief at what she has discovered in her lover's home. Her gut wrenches as a wave of nausea sweeps over her.

In plain view are several files clearly marked with the names of Lieutenant Commander Stephen L. Benton, Calvin Giovanni, H.L. Stevens, retired Captain Warren T. McNary, Vice President Kathleen Quinn Roberts, Katarina Giovanni, and Sarah Benton. *We're on the list,* Sarah thinks to herself.

Without realizing it, Sarah has moved over to the desk for a clearer view. Sadness overwhelms her, as does confusion and disbelief. She continues to read.

But, upon hearing a startling noise, Sarah freezes and looks around the room for a place to hide. She hears the voices in another intense argument from down the hall. She remains still. The noise quiets. She is frightened and filled with anger, yet she is purely inquisitive about her findings. She carefully opens Stephen's file first. Shocked by what she reads, Sarah barely hears the ensuing argument from the bedroom only steps away. She quickly thumbs through each file, scanning what information she can absorb. Each file contains a very familiar cover sheet printed on linen paper and stamped with the official insignia of the CIA. All of the files are labeled *Classified* with *Project Restoration I* imprinted in bold lettering. The cover sheet is the same as the one Sarah stole from Kat's safe.

Sarah returns to Stephen's file to read in further detail about Project Restoration I. She scans the file's incriminating data as quickly as she can while biting her lips to keep from shrieking aloud in anger and disbelief. Only speaking in the silence of her mind, she attempts to sort out and comprehend this new discovery. Screaming within, she feels lightheaded as the room seems to spin. She feels uncomfortably hot and faint from the incomprehensible story leaping from the pages.

These pages are filled with the blood of so many people. Stephen, Calvin, Mr. Stevens ... I've got to tell Warren. I've got to get out of here now. But she cannot move beyond the statements in Stephen's file that read, *Clone subject for military surplus program for HESC acceleration.* His medical records are included in the file. The next statements are just as disconcerting to Sarah, *"New dog tags issued. DNA matches incomplete. Cloning project incomplete. Mission incomplete.*

What the hell does that mean? Sarah wonders.

Sarah's mind reverses, taking her back to the dark cave she was trapped in for a week while she unlocked the mystery of the encrypted letter and found all the initials of the people who were murdered or were to be murdered to keep Project Restoration I a secret. Sarah thinks to herself, *I found Stephen's initials, but here I have found mine and Warren's and Kat's, and we're alive. Everything in his file says incomplete. Maybe he got away. He refused to go along with ... Oh my God. Maybe he is alive! But Warren said he is dead.* Startled back to reality by yelling from the hallway, Sarah ducks into a corner to hide, but her thoughts continue to race.

She questions why Cole has these files in his possession. Sarah cannot think quickly enough to wrap her mind around the words she has just read. It is all too outrageous. *Cole must be investigating this catastrophic configuration. That is why he didn't disclose his position in the government.* Sarah scrolls to the bottom of the page, reading the carbon copy line: C.B. Staring at the puzzle in front of her, Sarah feels the blood drain from her face. *Oh, please God, no. C.B.—Cole Blackman. Oh no. Please, not Cole.*

Not Cole Blackman, her companion, her lover. Sarah sees blackness from feeling weak and dizzy, yet neurons are firing anger beyond her weakness. Daggers pierce her heart. She stands, stunned by what is in plain view of the past eight agonizing months of her life.

This can't be happening. It can't get any worse ... Sarah has no tears to shed; she only feels pure anger. Even in the midst of the darkness, her mind won't release the words, *Cloning project incomplete. Mission incomplete.*

Stephen may be missing and not dead, Sarah silently thinks. She continues to read through Calvin's file. Only scanning the first page, she discovers the answer to Kat's elusively frigid behavior regarding Calvin's illness and demise. *Kat is fully involved. She initiated his illness with arsenic poisoning, but the CIA took control of the finality of Calvin's death. They didn't want to draw any attention to Kat. Bastards. Kat murdered Calvin to utilize ViaStem's cloning capabilities. That bitch. Then why is her name on the list?*

Sarah reads on in silence. *ViaStem, under Kat's position as CEO, teamed with the CIA and the President of the United States to use our troops to accelerate the HESC project. But wait*—Sarah reads on. *Project Restoration II: 2014—by cloning to strengthen our troop levels during this war on terrorism … maintain and build confidence in this President. Shit!* Sarah screams within. *Commander in Chief, my ass!* Rage engulfs her.

Sarah glances at Mr. Stevens's file only to read a single statement: *Subject deceased. No involvement.*

How ironic that the President's sinful plan is aided by terrorist acts, Sarah thinks to herself in disgust. Without hesitation she gathers the top copy from each file, tri-folds them, and stashes them in the waist of her jeans. *I can't believe all of this was done to accelerate the HESC project. Why? Or was this done to prepare for Project Restoration II?*

She feels the urgent need to flee, to escape the overwhelming madness she feels at the thought of the American soldiers who gave their lives for their country and their families, their ultimate sacrifices, only to have clones made from their dead bodies

I can't change Project Restoration I, but maybe I can stop the second. How I wish I could get these files to the papers. Maybe I can … there is still some time, Sarah ponders.

She wonders how far the plan has advanced. Agonizing grief consumes her. The room spins out of her control. Finding her equilibrium, she turns to exit the room and exit the house. *I've got to tell Warren.*

The crash of a lamp forces Sarah into the moment. She quickly leans close to the wall beside the study door. Cole and his companion are heading in her direction. Her heart boils with fuming anger, yet she is seized in the fear of the moment. The voices become louder as they grow closer. Their argument ensues.

Sarah recognizes Cole's voice, and the female voice

becomes all too familiar to her. *It's Kat!* Sarah mouths the words. Once again the voices fade as Cole and Kat move back toward the bedroom.

Go! Sarah rushes into the hallway and toward the living room to run out the front door, but she abruptly stops and stands tall when she comes face-to-face with her enemy, Kat, who is standing arrogantly in front of her, aiming a .38 caliber pistol at Sarah's heart. Time stills. The walls close in on Sarah. The air feels hot, thick, and heavy. She focuses on Kat, never breaking eye contact, not even for a second. She stands tall, without fear, without tears; she is only filled with contempt.

Remaining steadfast, Sarah focuses on Kat's novice familiarity with her weapon as she rearranges her hand placement and moves the gun several times to have a better aim at Sarah's heart. Kat's rapid breathing is conspicuous, proving she is a pawn in this deadly game, which is an advantage for Sarah. *She's not set to take the shot. Be ready, Sarah*, Sarah coaches herself silently.

"Always the victim, Sarah," Kat snipes. "Poor little Sarah, so much heartache in your life. I found your little mess in my house, and I'm missing some important items from my safe. Oh, and thanks for the drop of blood. Without it you might have gotten away. But not now. You've been added to the list. You will soon be with Stephen.

"Only with me as CEO could ViaStem be able to be a part of the plan. We needed humans to make the HESC G42 project work. We needed a control group to accelerate the process. And it finally worked. So a few hundred or so were sacrificed. Think of what ViaStem can do now! As soon as soldiers die, we clone them and send them back to battle. It's brilliant!

"Stephen's death and cloning was all the proof we needed to

know Project Restoration One is a success." Kat waves the gun from side to side, lost in her glory. "We had to experiment on someone. We needed one more group, and that just happened to be Stephen's unit. So Sarah, tell me. Did you cry like a baby when you found out Stephen was dead?" Kat continues to dig at Sarah's heart. Sarah grits her teeth in disgust. "It was well worth it for all of this power and money."

Through a clenched jaw and in a throaty venomous voice Sarah engages her, "You bitch. You're on the list too. Did you know that?"

Kat wavers, stunned by Sarah's words.

Sarah remains focused and in control while Kat's arrogance and overzealousness begins to implode. "What's wrong, Kat? Don't like the news?" Sarah removes the papers from her waist and waves them in front of Kat. "Look, Kat. Right here—Katarina Fortunata is next on the list."

"You bitch," Kat fumes. "Give me that."

Sarah quickly folds the papers and tucks them back in the waist of her jeans. "I don't think so." She feels a smile come across her face, which infuriates Kat.

"Get ready to join your husband," Kat says as she realigns her aim, pointing the .38 directly at Sarah's heart.

"Fuck you, bitch," Sarah spews her anger at Kat through gritted teeth and with calculated determination. In that moment, she notices Cole standing in the shadows behind Kat. Kat has no recollection of his presence.

Ricocheting glances from Kat to Cole, Sarah tries to determine who will shoot her first. "My name is also on the list." Sarah locks eyes with Cole as her anger turns to hatred, which is evident through her passionate temper and the veins of rage rising in her neck. "Now you can kill both of us,

Cole. How convenient for you. How could you be involved in something like this?"

"Do you two know each other?" Kat chimes in. "Oh, I get it. You know each other very well, don't you? Maybe poor Sarah isn't so sad. Are you two fuc—"

"Shut the hell up, Kat," demands Cole.

Kat prepares to pull the trigger that will send a bullet straight through Sarah's heart. With the squeeze of a trigger, a life ends. The gunshot explodes in Sarah's ears. The sound is deafening. Everything seems to move laggardly. In a state of shock, Sarah hesitates to open her eyes, not knowing if she's been hit, if she is alive or dead. She thinks to herself, *I can't feel anything.* Opening her eyes, she sees Kat lying in a pool of blood. The squeeze of a trigger ended an evil life.

Sarah shifts her attention to Cole. "Am I next?"

Cole moves forward, "Sarah, please—"

"Don't come near me." With unwavering determination, Sarah longs for some kind of answer. "How could you be involved in something like this? How?"

"Sarah, please listen—"

"You disgust me."

Cole drops the gun to his side and walks toward Sarah. He places the gun on the table within Sarah's reach, allowing her the opportunity to have revenge on him. Sickened by the events, Sarah turns to leave and never looks back, not caring if Cole picks up the gun and shoots her in the back. *At least it would be over.* Sarah's oppression has finally led to her surrender from this nightmare.

"I never meant to hurt you or cause you any pain," Cole tells her. "Falling in love with you was not part of my assignment, but it happened. Sarah, I love you. I know what

I have done, and what I know it is evil, but you don't know the whole story. Stephen—"

Sarah turns to face Cole, not hearing his last words because of the ringing still in her ears. "You seemed so sincere, so caring. And Stephen—this whole time you knew and you …" Sarah lowers her head in despondence. "You made me feel safe when I thought I might never feel safe again." Tears fill Sarah's eyes. "I loved you and trusted you, and now I am forced to feel only hatred for you.

"May God forgive you. Only he can because I'm not sure I have the strength to do so." Sarah takes one step back, turns away, and closes her eyes, waiting to be shot and killed. Waiting to be removed from the list, removed from this life.

"Look at me, Sarah. I work for the British government. I'm investigating this case because we've had reports of NATO soldiers disappearing. I won't make it out of this alive, so I want you to know who I really am."

"I don't care who you are, Cole—"

"I wish I could reverse time, but I cannot. I wish I could have uncovered a sinister plot and done a lot of things differently, but I can't. What I can do is get you out of here alive. You've uncovered a sinister plot that reaches well beyond America's boarders. You are to be executed tomorrow, Sarah, by the CIA. I know McNary has put together a plan for your escape. We know everything, Sarah." Cole loses his breath, drowning in his guilt. "I know McNary will get you out. I know he will Sarah."

Sarah turns slowly back toward Cole in amazement that he knows everything she and Warren have been "secretly" planning. She nearly falls backward, realizing Cole is standing within her reach. Cole firmly holds Sarah's arms as they hanging listlessly by her sides. Fear and overpowering sadness invade her body. She feels turmoil, distracted by her intimate memories of Cole and the guilt that lingers from their affair. Anguish rips at her heart, defeating her ambitions of strength in her world of chaos. The fogginess of the sorrow that consumes her has made her vulnerable once again. Now she is locked in the arms of the man she trusted and loved in the midst of her loneliness and grief.

Sarah cannot look into Cole's eyes of deceit for fear she might lose her spirit. Cole gently takes Sarah's face into his hands, and he raises her face, forcing her to look into his eyes, which are filled with tears of sinful condemnation. She gazes into his once-captivating assurance of love only to succumb to wicked seduction. As she closes her eyes to trap her tears, Cole lovingly kisses her soft lips. Sarah whimpers with love and true pain. She pulls away, her eyes glistening with tears as she gives Cole one last glance. With no more energy or words to waste on him, she turns sharply and walks out of his life for good. In the blackness of night, she leaves forever, never looking back.

"Sarah, wait. You need to know. Stephen …" Cole retreats as Sarah disappears from his life.

A single gunshot echoes from Cole's house as Sarah rushes back to the safety of her fortress. With the resounding gunshot, Sarah flinches, knowing Cole has committed suicide just yards behind her. Her head pounds, and she feels ill. The gravel grinds under her boot soles with each step. Sarah never realized how loud silence can be.

In her front yard, she stops beside the Juniper that reaches toward the stars. A cool sweat overcomes her, and she lurches forward and vomits until she has nothing left in her stomach. Standing slowly, she finds her balance and moves quickly to her front door, barricading herself inside once again. Running to the bathroom, she vomits again.

Weary but not defeated, Sarah's survival instincts kick in, and she pulls herself up. She wets a wash cloth with cool water and pats her face and the back of her neck, not wanting to think about what just occurred.

"I'm alive, and I don't know why."

Sarah quickly brushes her teeth and freshens her face, leaning against the counter in utter dismay. "Mission incomplete ... Stephen might be alive."

Chapter 24:

Hourglass

After waiting faithfully for his owner's return, Cooper nudges at Sarah's leg, sensing her sadness. Sarah gently picks him up, holds him close to her heart, and carries him to the foyer to wait for the package. Physically and psychologically worn out, Sarah leans against the front door and slides down the frame to rest on the cool ceramic tile floor. She cuddles the only loved one left in her life. Time feels stagnant. The wait for the special delivery is truly agonizing. She feels cold and shivers anticipating the fear of the unknown.

"I need to call Warren. I have to warn him," she tells herself. She goes to her car and retrieves her cell phone. Warren told her to cancel it, but she did not, and this time she is glad she didn't listen. His line rings and rings, but there is no answer.

Sarah hears Cole's words that he worked for the British government investigating Project Restoration.

"Was that true or just another lie?"

Sadness and doubt seep back into Sarah's soul. To distract her, Sarah repacks her satchel and takes one Klonopin, as prescribed. After making copies of the newly discovered evidence, she adds them to the packets for the delivery person. She conceals the originals in the pages of the latest Hollywood entertainment magazine stashed in her bag. Then she sets the envelopes by the front door in preparation of the exchange. With no one to talk to and with no ability to alert Warren of the imminent danger, Sarah waits in relentless silence. As she packs her 9mm, she decides where to permanently dispose of it. Sarah reviews her written plan to navigate the quickest route to Lindberg Airport. She tries to convince herself to be the bravest she has ever been because this time it means her life. Time continues to slowly tick away. "This is it. This is really happening."

A deliberate knock at the front door nearly rips Sarah out of her skin. She is dazed from lack of sleep and the horrible events of the evening. It is the package Warren has sent containing her new identity. The package requires no signature, just an exchange for the envelopes containing the damning evidence against the President of the United States. *Those who were murdered in Project Restoration I will not die in vain and Project Restoration II will perish,* Sarah vows.

Once the transfer is complete, Sarah quickly shuts the front door and secures the dead bolt. Ripping open the package, she is anxious to learn her new identity and the location of her new home.

"It's almost over," she says and feels obscure relief and joy. She holds her breath, knowing precious contents are enclosed in the package. Sarah removes several pieces of identification, several pre-paid phone cards, $5,000 in cash, a small brass key, a sealed envelope, and a first-class ticket to her new home. Studying her new driver's license, identification card, shot records, medical records, and passport, she learns her new name—Rebekah M. Angel.

"Rebekah Mary Angel, Rebekah M. Angel," Sarah repeats her new name over and over. "I know I cannot escape this haunting nightmare as Sarah Ryan Benton." She opens the sealed envelope before moving forward in her journey. It is a letter from Warren. Inside the envelope is another smaller sealed envelope. Setting that aside, she reads Warren's letter.

Dear Sarah,

I want to let you know how proud I am of you. You are brave and strong and have accomplished an amazing feat for the American people and the world. You did this, Sarah. You! You have suffered greatly through this ordeal, but I am confident you will be all right and remain strong. You will soon be happy and free again. You will soon be home!

I have arranged your new life to begin in Borris, Ireland. This beautiful, charming town is just south of Dublin. The population is approximately 1000, which I believe will keep you safe. Once you have established residency, the townspeople will sound the alarm to any unwanted strangers who overstay their welcome. Its nickname is the "Sunny South East" of Ireland. It neighbors are the Blackstairs Mountains in the county of Carlow. Other neighboring towns include Kilkenny and Enniscorthy. I have visited this friendly village several times, filling my heart and soul with emotions of happiness, serenity, and security. I know you will be happy there.

Enjoy the unique shops along Main Street and the historical views. Meet Jerry O'Reilly, who owns the only pub on Main Street and give him the brass key. He is holding another $425,000 in cash for you in a safety deposit box. This includes Stephen's death benefit of $200,000 from the government, his life insurance, and cash from your equities. It is much too dangerous traveling with that much cash, no checked bags, and a one-way ticket. None of this is traceable. Don't ask. You can trust Jerry. He will take care of you.

The people are wonderful, and the country is beautiful. Enjoy your new life, Sarah. You deserve to be happy. Do not let fear consume you any longer. You will be safe now.

In the small sealed envelope is a piece of Stephen I want you to have. A military confidant sent them to me, and I want you to have them. They are crucial evidence, so do not wear them openly.

I will be in touch soon.

With much love,

Warren

P.S. Your new name—Rebekah—means "beautiful" in Hebrew, and Angel, well, you just are.

Sarah sits silently, reading the letter to herself while tears of love stream down her cheeks and a warm smile shines on her lovely face. "I love you, Warren. Thank you."

Staring at the small envelope, Sarah finally breaks the seal and removes Stephen's original dog tags. She folds the chain gently in her left hand and strokes the two tags with her right. All the information is correct. The dog tags are in near perfect condition. Kissing them softly, she speaks the words, "Someday we will be together again, and then we will be home."

Sarah gently holds Cooper in her arms as she has him swallow the tiny pill to send him into a slumber. Then she places him in the carrier. "Good night, sweet boy."

She looks at the clock, which signals 3:40 a.m. She knows she must go. After wrapping the cashmere scarf around her neck, she buttons the tan belted trench and tucks the scarf under the collar. She slips on thin matching leather gloves and takes one last glance in the mirror. Grabbing the remaining items, she hustles to the garage, packs Cooper's carrier in the back seat, and tucks her scantly belongings in the passenger's seat. She takes one last walk through her home, the home she and Stephen planned to have their family grow in, the home she and Stephen planned to grow old together in. Memories loop through Sarah's mind as she travels from room to room before exiting her life as Sarah Ryan Benton.

Sarah steadily backs out of her driveway and closes the garage door behind her. Keeping her lights off, she begins what seems like the longest drive down her quiet street in the remaining darkness of night. She takes one last sentimental look at her home before putting her car into drive. Out the passenger's side window, she spots Rudy standing at the fence, watching her. He begins nodding his head up and down as he always does. Rio is lying down comfortably, snoozing. Sarah smiles. As she passes Cole's house, she places her hand on the side window. She shudders, knowing two people she loved at one time in her life lie dead inside.

"I will try to forgive …" Sarah sadly shakes her head. Tears well up in her eyes, but she holds her emotions deep inside.

She continues to calmly drive from her neighborhood, looking forward yet continuously looking back. Passing Sammy and Stevie's home on the right, Sarah cannot help but smile slightly. Scanning everything around her, she has learned to always be conscious of her surroundings. As she passes Laura's house on the left, Sarah smiles again. "Thank you for being my friend, and thank you for my new look." Once out of the neighborhood, her frantic drive to the airport begins. In preparation, Sarah bravely states, "Here we go, Cooper."

With dawn around the corner, Sarah has no time to waste. Taking a right onto Arena and driving a short distance to San Vicente Boulevard, she takes another right. Shifting her BMW into second and then third gear, she turns left through the blinking yellow light onto Wildcat Canyon Road. With that, Sarah begins the end of her journey. Immediately shifting into fourth and then fifth gear, she gains speed. There are no streetlights to help her navigate the treacherous, meandering roads, forcing Sarah to be on high alert and intently focused on the pathway to her final destination. She drives at reckless speeds, but she has no choice; she has very little time to dispose of her gun and reach the airport in time to catch her flight. However, she is confident her BMW can handle the deviations of the road because she has made several practice runs. If the road remains clear, she can get to the airport in twenty-three minutes driving at speeds of 70 miles per hour.

Unfortunately, coyotes and cows can be dangerous and deadly obstacles. "So far, so good," Sarah reassures herself.

Spotting faint headlights far behind her, she shudders as the car quickly gains on her. She finds herself concentrating on the car speeding toward her more than what is in front of her, causing her to almost hit a coyote that wanders into the road. Swerving sharply, Sarah just misses the animal and regains control of her car, still maintaining her view of the headlights quickly approaching her. The car is now closing in on her bumper. Sarah's grip on the steering wheel tightens, causing the blood to leave her hands. Every muscle in her back contracts tightly, causing an ache so deep she can feel it in her bones. The car trails her for a mile or two and then suddenly jerks left, crossing the double yellow lines and recklessly swerving around her. Matching her speed of 75 miles per hour, the car drives side by side with her BMW, spreading fear through Sarah like a lightning bolt. Glancing at the suspicious car, Sarah sees nothing but pitch black tinted windows. In a matter of seconds, the driver of the car punches the gas, speeds forward, and disappears around the next bend. With a great relief, Sarah sighs loudly. "Thank you, God."

She reaches Freeway 67, which leads her to San Diego Freeway 25 to 5. Her speeds continue in excess of 75 miles per hour. She is surprised by amount of traffic. Driving wildly, she frantically fills every space between cars, oblivious to the honks and rude gestures.

"Sorry, sir. Trust me, this is necessary," Sarah apologizes aloud to the man she just about kisses fenders with. Up ahead she sees the large green sign on the overpass with the arrow exiting right to the airport. Recklessly, she forces her merge through traffic and takes the exit.

The airport is in sight. Locating long-term parking by

the arrow pointing to the right, Sarah instead exits to the left and heads toward Harbor Island, which runs parallel to the airport. She parks along the road adjacent to the harbor, which overlooks the stunning San Diego skyline and the blue Coronado Bridge, which reaches over the bay to Coronado Island to the past home of Stephen's SEAL team and the Berkeley ferryboat, where she and Stephen were married. Sarah grabs the 9mm and the extra clip from her bag, tucks it in her waistband, and quickly exits her car. The sun peeks over the horizon, shimmering on the still water.

As she walks over to the edge of the water, a car speeds past, loudly honking at her while several drunk college students yell obscenities at her. "Jerks," she remarks as she observes the stunningly serene view.

A police officer slows to ask her, "Is everything okay, miss?"

"Oh yes, officer. I'm just enjoying the view one last time before my flight. I'm sure going to miss your city. It is so beautiful … so special," Sarah says sentimentally.

The officer agrees and continues on his route.

Sarah then removes the 9mm from her waistband and takes the clip from the gun. Digging into the front pocket of her jeans, she grasps the second empty clip and the bullets. She throws the gun as far as she can into the Bay, followed by its accessories. She does the same with the handful of bullets and hears them plop individually into the water in small rhythmic splashes. She digs in the other pocket of her jeans, removes Stephen's charred tag, and tosses it into the bay. Only then does she continue her journey to Lindberg Airport to catch the flight of her life.

Once she reaches Lindberg, Sarah chooses long-term parking, section A, row 3. Sitting for a moment, she holds her old cell phone tightly in her hand, wanting to call Warren one last time. He will be angry that she never cancelled her policy, but she doesn't care at this point. She just wants to say good-bye.

"I know I'm already being followed according to Cole, so what does it matter?" Taking a deep breath, she dials Warren's number. It rings once, twice, and then an answer. There is silence on the other line.

"Hello … Warren? Warren, are you there? It's Sarah. Please answer me. Please, Warren," Sarah pleads.

"I'm here." Warren sounds despondent.

"I just needed to say good-bye—" Sarah attempts to speak but is cut-off by Warren.

"Just go. Now. *Go!*" his voice rises sternly with each warning. Then Sarah hears the sound of a gun firing at close range explode through the receiver. Then silence.

Sarah grips the phone in fear.

"Hello, Sarah," returns a strange voice.

Sarah loses her breath as it feels as though her lungs have imploded. She quickly shuts her phone and is frozen with fear. "Oh my God, Warren. They killed Warren!" Sarah screams. Shaking uncontrollably, she pounds on the steering wheel, screaming to the heavens. "No no no! Not Warren! Please stop this nightmare!" Sarah bows her head, leaning it on the steering wheel, not knowing what to do.

"He said my name. They will find me. I need to get out of here now!"

Flinging the car door open, she jumps from her seat and runs around the rear of the car, where she retrieves Cooper, slams the door, and then grabs her bag from the passenger's side. She takes a quick glance through the car and slams the door behind her. She begins her sprint to the airport, leaving the driver's side door open with the keys still in the ignition, hoping it will be stolen by a criminal fleeing to Mexico, ultimately eliminating one more piece of evidence of her life. She tosses her cell phone ahead of her and crushes it with the heel of her boot as she continues her race to the terminal.

Finally reaching the terminal, she encounters the next challenge of what seems to be an endless journey—the security check point. The review of her ticket and passport are successful. She knows the routine: boots off, place them in a heavy plastic gray bin along with the single Ziploc baggie of her liquids of 3 ounces or less. In a second bin Sarah places her belt and trench coat. Her jewelry, Klonopin, and Stephen's dog tags are placed in a separate round container. She prays the security guard will not scrutinize the evidence. Walking through the security archway in her new socks, she hears "Code Orange" splashed across the loud speakers, warning passengers and visitors to be on alert for unusual activities. All the while she prays she will not have her bag searched by the TSA employees. She will be stuck forever if the evidence in her bag is discovered. She successfully gets through the archway and waits at the end of the beltway that carries her boots, personal items, coat, and satchel toward her. The first thing Sarah does is slip Stephen's dog tags over her neck and tuck them under her top. They rest against her heart.

She quickly slips on her wedding band and watch and tucks her Klonopin safely in her satchel. Pulling on her boots, she feels her heart racing, threatening to explode from her chest. She puts her trench on, buttons it, and tightens the belt around her slim waist. Placing the liquids back into her large satchel, she waits for Cooper's carrier. After the terrorist attacks last year, the guards analyze his carrier thoroughly by sending it through the body scan. Time seems to reverse. Sarah feels hot, and beads of sweat form on her forehead.

Please don't blow this, Sarah, she talks silently to herself. *Come on ... come on!* Sarah yells at the guards from within.

"Miss." The guard signals Sarah to come over to Cooper's carrier. Sarah's anxiety peaks, and she wishes she could pop a couple Klonopin now.

"Yes, sir?" Sarah acknowledges the security officer and walks to his location.

"Is your dog okay?"

"Oh, yes. Cooper is just taking a nice long nap for his trip. He gets a little nauseous when he travels."

"Well, he is out cold." The guard smiles and hands the carrier to Sarah.

"Thank you, and have a nice day." Sarah says in her calmest voice. "I've gotta run. Thanks again."

Sarah hurries as quickly as she can through the terminal, running on the moving walkways. "Excuse me. On the left. Excuse me, please," Sarah warns passengers on the right who are sightseeing. "Oh my God, that was frightening," Sarah says to sleeping beauty. At the end of each moving walkway, Sarah takes baby steps, timing her perfect exit onto stationary flooring.

"Not too much farther to the safe zone, Cooper. Hang on, bud."

Chapter 25:

The Fugitive

Sarah runs as fast as she can through what seems an endless terminal in San Diego's Lindberg Airport, slowing only to dodge new passenger arrivals. She slows to give Cooper a rest from the jostling, but only for a moment. Looking inside his kennel, Sarah finds him fast asleep from the sedative she gave him earlier. She picks up her pace, anticipating her arrival to her "safe zone," Gate 61, the last gate of Terminal C.

Sarah gasps in frustration from her tiring haul when she finally reaches the passenger holding area for Sky America's International Flight 1905 to Ireland. Scanning the terminal and the holding area for suspicious-looking characters, she studies faces, clothing, and carry-on items to help ensure her safety, which has become second nature to her. A little girl dressed in bright fuchsia is the only person that stands out in the crowd. Sarah releases a sigh of relief. Though Sarah knows she cannot be complacent until she is on the plane. She considers herself a target until Flight 1905 lifts off from the tarmac.

Taking a seat away from the other passengers but in clear

view of her surrounding environment, Sarah rests Cooper's kennel at her feet. Feeling her nerves calm, time begins to slow as well, and Sarah's anxiety level begins to subside. Images of Warren being shot stream through her mind. The deafening blast that traveled through the wireless connection still left her ears ringing.

I can't believe he is dead. Oh my God. My dearest Warren … *Poor Warren,* Sarah thinks to herself over and over, stunned by its reality.

She knows there will always be doubts and unanswered questions around this horrible mess, but she must forge on. There are so many pieces to this enormous puzzle that might never fit, and she must be strong to prevent them from haunting her as she begins her new life as Rebekah M. Angel. She can no longer live in the past. *Warren told me not to quit, no matter what, even if something happened to him. I promised him I would never quit,* Sarah says silently to herself.

Trying to distract herself, she checks on Cooper, who is still sleeping soundly. Now that they are stationary, he has moved into his favorite position of lying on his back with his tummy in the air, ears flopped back, and what appears to be a smile on his little furry face. Sarah smiles at her little guy, wondering if he thinks he's flying somewhere fun in his dreams as one of his hind leg twitches.

Unable to stay away from her thoughts, she reviews the events of the past several months over in her mind, again and again. She prays the persistence of these thoughts will dissipate once she is away from the danger and in her new life and home.

How could this have happened? she wonders. *How can people be so damned evil, so unbelievably cruel? How many others died besides those so close to me? Kat said the total body count of the war would be lower, but they needed soldiers for their experiment to accelerate the HESC procedure in Project Restoration I. It is absolutely unconceivable to think that President Cannon was going to begin Project Restoration II to actually clone our soldiers killed in action. Is that what those hundreds of extra letters and numbers in the encrypted letter from the CIA were? Do all those figures lead to a young soldier?*

Sarah begins losing control of her thoughts as they swirl in her mind. "So many gone … and for what? So the political polls look good, strong in the face of the infinite war on terrorism?" Sarah says nearly in an audible tone with pure disgust. She catches herself and quiets herself.

Sarah chooses to stand, too nervous to sit after pondering the many questions she has asked herself a thousand times during this endless maze. With a quivering chin, she presses her lips tightly together to hold in her emotions. Her eyes pool with tears as she thinks of her family. *I didn't say goodbye. I didn't return all those calls from my mom. I pray Warren was able to help them.* Sarah loses energy, as do her thoughts. Her head pounds with anger and sadness at the so many unanswered questions that linger.

She clutches her large brown satchel tightly, keeping her life belongings close to her. Cooper and the items in her bag are all she has left from this life.

Sarah uses the ladies room once more before they announce the boarding call for her flight. She keeps Cooper and her bag close to her. Scanning the ladies room, she finds it empty. She uses the handicapped stall at the far end of the rest room to allow room for Cooper's kennel and her satchel.

After washing her hands, she freshens up. In the mirror, Sarah stares back at a woman she doesn't even recognize. Turning to her left, she faces the full-length mirror. Slowly tucking in her shirt, she breaks into a long-awaited smile. She has tried her best to disguise herself with much appreciated help from Laura.

"I pray it is good enough. So far so good," she says. Standing in front of the mirror, she just stares at Rebekah M. Angel.

Shaking her head from left to right, Sarah watches as each strand of her shiny chocolate brown hair falls perfectly back in its place. She smiles. Moving closer to the mirror, she notices the strained capillaries running in all directions in her eyes from pure exhaustion. *Ouch!* Sarah smiles, noticing some sparkle of her love for life returning.

She wears little jewelry other than her Omega sterling silver watch and her diamond stud earrings that Stephen gave her for their first wedding anniversary. She always wears them. And of course, her Celtic wedding band with matching diamond eternity bands. They are a part of him that is always with her. Especially since his wedding ring was stolen. She feels grateful for Warren's mystery friend in the military who dared to give Stephen's real dog tags to her, which she has tucked under her top. She gently places her hand over her heart and feels his tags and the correct engraved letters and numbers identifying him.

But no Stephen. Sarah holds her sadness in silence.

The eternity she dreamed she would spend with Stephen is forever gone. Sarah's beliefs that they will be together again are strong, even if they are only together in heaven. Her faith offers her comfort through this madness. She is filled with despair and sadness but has learned not to show it unless in private. She wanted to keep Stephen's charred dog tag but it would have drawn too much attention going through security.

It told the truth.

One last look and then off to her new life.

I feel different. I guess the plan worked if I feel different.

Sarah gives a faint smile, knowing her new life as Rebekah M. Angel is to begin in less than an hour. Excitement rather than fear sweeps through her.

She carries only one bag—the large brown leather satchel that contains only the essentials. The contents are slight, holding a first-class ticket to her final destination, her wallet, her new identification forms, cash, and a several pre-paid phone cards. The powerful evidentiary letters stolen from Cole's house and Kat's safe are hidden in a *People* magazine. Not needing much makeup, Sarah packed one Blistex, one tube of lipstick, blush, and one baggie of 3 ounce liquids. Most importantly, though, is a four-by-six-inch Bible given to her by her mother, Catherine, on her wedding day as something "old." It is very sentimental. The back cover is made of white leather, and the front cover is the most beautiful mother of pearl with the insignia, *Holy Bible.* Inside the front cover is a small black-and-white photo of her parents on their wedding day. A second, more recent photo of her mom is placed directly behind the antiqued picture. A third photo of Stephen and Sarah on their wedding day is also tucked behind the antiqued picture.

Sarah softly touches the picture before moving to a photo of Warren and Stephen that is also tucked safely in the Bible. She then removes the two drawings from Sammy and Stevie of Cooper and the "hero" she had tucked in a side pocket. All of these pieces of her life are the loveliest memorabilia that Sarah treasures. If only she had Stephen's wedding ring. That would make everything perfect. She holds her treasures tightly. Its contents are all she owns.

The airline attendant calls for the boarding of Flight

1905. First-class passengers are called to board. Sarah quickly gathers her belongings, picks up Cooper's carrier, and takes one last look at her past. "This is it, Cooper. This is really it!" she said.

Everything seems to move in slow motion and every sound seems to echo in a three-second delay as Sarah scans the other passengers as she walks to the checkpoint. She says a fond prayer to God to keep her family safe. She has no other family to worry about now, just stuff. Sarah's life passes in front of her, and she begins to quiver. Her body feels hot, and her head feels dizzy. Her chin quivers, and tears well in her eyes.

Stop! Sarah demands of herself in silence. Taking a deep breath, she pulls herself together.

Her Ray-Ban aviator sunglasses are perched atop her head for a quick cover if any tears escape. It seems like it takes an eternity to finally reach the attendant, who smiles and asks Sarah for her ticket. The flight attendant scans the ticket after verifying it through a scanner. She politely hands the ticket stub back to Sarah and says, "Thank you, Ms. Angel. Thank you for flying with us today, and have a nice flight to your final destination."

"Thank you, Ms. Angel," Sarah repeats under her breath as she advances down the Jetway—Rebekah M. Angel beginning the walk down the Jetway to her new life. During her long journey to the entrance of the plane, Sarah flashes a full, confident smile. *I did it. I made it.* Sarah had fought back and won. She is not weak but filled with integrity and strength. She is proud.

As Rebekah M. Angel enters the Boeing 747, she slips her sunglasses over her eyes to cover any tears that might unexpectedly come and is greeted by two attendants, one female and one male. She responds with a soft "hello" and a slight smile. Her smile grows, as do her emotions. Her confidant and bodyguard, Warren T. McNary, had done a superb job helping Sarah become a new person to escape, but Warren T. McNary is gone. According to Warren, the name Rebekah M. Angel is perfectly fitting. The light of Stephen's life, Calvin's life, and Warren's life has faded, as well as the life of Sarah Ryan Benton.

Chapter 26:

Fly Away Home

Rebekah walks slowly through the first-class cabin, looking up at the seat assignments and then looking down at her ticket. Her hands are trembling. She locates row 3, seat A—the window seat. Before sitting down, she scans the area around her. She doesn't see anyone acting suspicious.

Rebekah is exhausted from always looking back and wondering who might be there. Her large satchel barely fits under the seat next to Cooper's kennel. He is calm and quiet, lost in dreamland. She once again scans the row behind her and across the aisle and finds only empty seats. Rebekah somberly watches passengers walk by to locate their seats. She notices chaotic moms and dads trying to control their tired, restless children; a sleeping baby propped on a mom's shoulder, so sweet and peaceful; couples, young and old, excited about going on vacation or returning home. A young teen listens intently to his iPod, stating his independence with the streak of blue in his jet black hair and the piercings in his cheeks, eyebrows, and lips. A young girl is weeping as she leaves her long-distance boyfriend. Newlyweds gaze into one another's eyes, holding hands, kissing, and giggling. Business travelers take one last look at the messages on their Blackberries or make that one last closing deal via their cell phone before the airline attendants request all electronic devices be turned off for takeoff. Rebekah smiles warmly at the visions of all these unique individuals, of normalcy.

Ironically, a sweet little girl sits in the seat next to her, and Rebekah knows she is one in eight million. Rebekah's attention is fully captured by this tiny, frail girl who is obviously a progeria child. The disease affects one in eight million. The girl is tiny but proud and exudes much confidence. Stuffing her bright pink *Dora the Explorer* backpack under the seat in front of her, the girl climbs up onto the large leather seat in row 3, seat B, with her knee resting on the seat and her hands gripped on the armrests to pull herself up. She wants no assistance. Once up, she swivels around and plops her bottom onto the center of the soft chair. She smiles brightly, swinging her little legs up and down. She is proud of herself and is joyous about life.

Her mother, sitting directly across from her, prompts her to buckle up, and the girl quickly follows directions. Her tiny legs swing excitedly as she waits for the gigantic plane to take off. Rebekah cannot take her eyes off this precious child who obviously is enjoying every moment of her journey. Rebekah's eyes hide behind her tinted lenses, but she cannot hide her caring smile. The little girl wears an all-pink *Dora the Explorer* ensemble with a bright pink ball cap with white capital letters spelling *ABBY*.

Abby turns to Rebekah and says in a sweet, nasally voice, "Hi, I'm Abby, Abigail if I'm in trouble." Her features reveals classic progeria traits with a smaller nose and mouth, large eyes and head, no eyelashes or eyebrows, and roadmaps of veins peeking through her paper-thin skin.

"Well hello, Abby. I'm Sa—Rebekah, if I'm in trouble or not."

The little girl giggles, and Rebekah joins in.

Rebekah continues the precious conversation with a warm, bright smile. "Are you going home or leaving on vacation?" she asks Abby.

Rebekah catches a hint of an Irish accent when little Abby responds, "Going home to Dublin, Ireland. We were visiting my doctors here." She doesn't offer any further information into her condition, nor does Rebekah ask.

Rebekah silently estimates Abby is about seven or eight years old, which in the life of a progeria patient, is equivalent to seventy or eighty years old. Out of nowhere, Abby blurts, "I'm eight today."

Rebekah cheerfully responds, "Well, happy birthday. I hope you have a really fun day today."

"Yep. It's a great birthday. My doctors said I'm doing great, and I haven't had any more heart attacks. I'm on a new treatment." Abby excitedly claps her tiny hands with only her palms and her little fingers stretched out like a fan.

Rebekah is stunned by the casual comment by her little neighbor but not surprised. The two chat a bit more before Abby begins to yawn. She then pulls her downy pink *Dora the Explorer* blanket over her tiny frame and closes her eyes. Rebekah glances at Abby's mother, who is reading a medical report from the "Journal of the American Medical Association" (JAMA) about a breakthrough procedure, HESC G42.

Goose bumps sweep over Rebekah's body with such happiness and gratefulness that Harold and Ruth Stevens's dream came true for their son David. *Kat did not destroy it.*

Thank you, God. Sarah remembers Mrs. Stevens sharing the news that the company would not be controlled by Kat when she visited her in the Hospice center.

Abby is an angel with a message for Rebekah, reassuring her that H.L. Stevens's vision is alive. Rebekah feels so very fortunate to be sitting next to a miracle. *Little Miss Abigail ... who did everything perfect today.*

Rebekah relaxes into the comfort of her first-class, over-sized, soft leather lounge chair. The distinct rich scent of leather wraps around her and comforts her like a blanket. It is a beautiful day with bright blue skies and wispy clouds. A single ray of sunshine beaming through the oval window illuminates Rebekah's face. The sun feels warm, and she finally feels safe. One tear streams from under her sunglasses and makes its way down her cheek. She quickly catches it with a soft tissue. She feels confident that her disguise has been successful, and soon she will be in the air away from this nightmare.

Rebekah is groggy from her treacherous journey and catches herself nodding off. She barely hears the announcement from the pilot that the plane will be backing away from the Jetway in preparation for takeoff. Falling into a light slumber, Rebekah plays Sarah's entire life in her dreams. She and Stephen are together with her family and Warren at their wedding. It is so vivid that she feels as if she can reach out and touch them. Many memories of her and Stephen loop through her mind, playing over and over. Good memories. Happy memories.

Without notice, in an instant, darkness invades her mind—Stephen's murder, his charred dog tag, Calvin's death, H.L. Stevens's death, the terrorist attacks on America, Cole's death by his own hand, Kat's death, Project Restoration, the hundreds of unclaimed initials (or soldiers) on the encrypted CIA letter. Suddenly Rebekah is startled back to reality and covered in a cool sweat. Shivering, she prays she will escape these horrifying thoughts once the sadistic plot is foiled and revealed to the entire world tomorrow morning. How she longs for the comfort of rebuilding her life in her new home in Ireland. How she wishes she knew the truth about Stephen.

What if he is alive and finds his way home to an empty house?

She pats her face with the tissue gripped in her hand to absorb the cool sweat. Sadness begins to creep up on her, but she knows in her heart and her gut that the only option for her is to move forward in life. *It is the only way to be free from all the chaos and death*, she thinks to herself.

Her faith that the evidence she and Warren discovered will reveal to the world the diabolical Project Restoration I, meant to accelerate the HESC G42 procedure and make headway for Project Restoration II.

Many have been murdered for this cloning project, and many will be hurt to learn of this conspiracy, but the world must know, Rebekah says silently, stricken with grief.

She begins to relax once again in her supple leather seat but fights to stay awake until the plane lifts off from the tarmac and reaches its flying altitude. She checks on Cooper, who is fast asleep. She smiles to have him with her. She looks at the peacefully sleeping Abby, and a warm smile greets her once anxiety-stricken soul. As she settles back in her seat, she relaxes a bit more and perches her sunglasses atop her head. Her hands unclench from her armrests, allowing blood to return to her fingers, erasing the white striations on her skin.

She feels her chest over her heart, where Stephen's dog

tags rest. Her body releases the tension that burns so deeply in every muscle. *It is time for peace and new opportunities.* Feeling the warmth of the sun on her face, Rebekah allows her eyes to fully close. It feels so soothing and so wonderfully peaceful. As the plane reaches its flying altitude, Rebekah's body becomes listless. She relaxes into her own quiet world, where it feels good and she feels safe.

Soon after the 747 reaches its flying altitude of 47,000 feet, Rebekah believes she is caught in a dark dream playing tricks on her.

From behind, a large, rugged hand grips her left shoulder. Suddenly on guard once again, Rebekah shivers with fear. Frozen, she tries to fight the fear. She tries to move, to get away, but she cannot escape the grip of her panic. She wants to scream for help, but she has lost her voice. *This can't be happening. Oh dear God, please tell me what to do. Please help me.* It feels as though her heart has stopped, and the pain in her chest is unbearable. She feels lightheaded and nauseous. She screams within, *I don't know what to do!* She is consumed by fear, and tears flow down her cheeks. Wiping them away doesn't help wipe the fear away.

She is fully awake and alert and realizes it is not another nightmare. Trying desperately to make some kind of decision, she quivers with each breath she takes. Tears well in her eyes, but she closes them tightly, fearing what might happen next. She cannot run. There is no place to go. She has no plan. She is held hostage in time, and it seems endless.

Slowly sliding her right hand across her body, Rebekah touches the stranger's hand. His grip loosens but remains firm. Rebekah feels a ring on the large hand. The shape is familiar. The ring is an oval shape. What she feels astounds her. *It can't be. I don't believe it. It's a cruel joke. They have found me, the ones who stole Stephen's wedding ring. Oh my God, please help me survive this.* As she keeps her eyes tightly shut, tears stream from the edges of her eyes and down her face.

With no other choice, she dares to open her eyes and once again discover she is not caught in another horrifying nightmare. Her eyes are not filled with sadness any longer but sparkle as a warm smile illuminates her beautiful face. *Oh dear God, it can't be …"*

Her emerald eyes sparkle with life. She feels the hand intimately and then traces the Celtic knots etched into the face of the oval ring. For the first time in almost a year, Sarah cries tears of joy.

Only the love of her life has these strong, rugged hands and wears a traditional Celtic warrior ring. From the seat behind her, she listens as he whispers in her ear, "As long as we are together, we are home."

Sarah warmly kisses his hand, rests her face against it, and breathes his wonderful scent that only she recognizes. Sarah is home.

CPSIA information can be obtained at www.ICGtesting.com
226608LV00001B/8/P